"You have nothing to fear, Meg,"

Clay muttered. "Not from me—not anymore. Just go back to sleep." He got to his feet and strode into the inky night without a backward glance.

Tears pooling in her eyes, Meg felt so ashamed. For a while she had responded to his intimate touch, even initiated it, and up until Clay loomed over her and she felt the evidence of his desire, she had forgotten her fears. Then, abruptly, the man towering above her hadn't been Clay, but a memory.

The tears spilled from her eyes as she wondered if she'd hurt him. Her fists and legs had shot out so ferociously and so unexpectedly, yet he hadn't fought back or tried to protect himself. He'd even take the blame, when he'd done nothing but make her feel beautiful and desirable.

He had mistakenly assumed she didn't want him, but she wouldn't have the courage to admit the truth—a truth that would drive him away as effectively as had her attack.

Dear Reader,

Once again, we've rounded up a month of top-notch reading for you—just right for the hot weather! Heather Graham Pozzessere, a *New York Times* bestselling author, has penned our American Hero title, *Between Roc and a Hard Place*. This is the story of a not-quite-divorced couple who meet up again in a very... unique way. And once they do, boy! The sparks really start flying then—and you'll want to be there to catch all the action.

The rest of the month is pretty special, too. Marie Ferrarella returns with the second title in her series called "Those Sinclairs!" *Heroes Great and Small* is a fitting follow-up to last month's *Holding Out for a Hero*. And later in the year look for brother Nik's story in *Christmas Every Day*. Dallas Schulze makes a welcome return appearance in the line with *Secondhand Husband*, a tale of love growing—as I guess it always does—in strange and mysterious ways. Finish off your reading with Barbara Faith's *Cloud Man* (this hero makes an absolutely unforgettable entrance), Desire author Cathryn Clare's *Chasing Destiny* and new author Debbie Bryce's *Edge of Darkness*. As always, it's a lineup of books so good you'll want to read every one.

And in coming months, look for more great romantic reading here at Intimate Moments, with books by favorite authors like Naomi Horton, Justine Davis, Emilie Richards, Marilyn Pappano and Doreen Roberts, to name only a few. Join us!

Yours,

Leslie Wainger
Senior Editor and Editorial Coordinator

EDGE OF DARKNESS

Debbie Bryce

Silhouette®
INTIMATE™ MOMENTS®
Published by Silhouette Books New York
America's Publisher of Contemporary Romance

SILHOUETTE BOOKS
300 East 42nd St., New York, N.Y. 10017

EDGE OF DARKNESS

Copyright © 1993 by Debra Sue Lang

ISBN: 0-373-07504-9

First Silhouette Books printing June 1993

DEBBIE BRYCE

has loved books since early childhood. Her favorite stories are those in which good triumphs over evil, love conquers all, and everyone lives happily ever after, which is why she enjoys reading and writing romance novels. Her other interests include golf, swimming and a Yorkshire terrier named Duffy.

To Mom and Dad, with love and thanks.

Prologue

"I have to do something, Dave. I haven't heard from Ted in almost three weeks. He always calls at least once a week, more often if he can."

"Usually, but not always," the voice at the other end of the telephone line remarked. "I remember when he was in Afghanistan. You didn't hear from him for over a month."

"That was different," she protested. "He was still very upset about losing Cathy."

"So were you. So were those two little boys." Dave Thornton's deep voice remained calm and controlled. "But he took off on some ridiculous assignment, put his life on the line and left you to take care of the twins, something you're still doing, I guess."

Meg Andrews gripped the phone tighter. "I thought you were his friend," she mumbled. Anxiety squeezed her heart. Dave was about the only hope she had of getting her brother home safely.

"I am his friend. That's why I think he ought to stay closer to home to take pictures. That's what he was doing before Cathy died and it's what he should be doing now, what he would be doing if you didn't make it so darn convenient for him to take off." After an uncomfortable silence, he cleared his throat. "Look, Meg, I'm sorry. What you do is none of my business. Neither is what Ted does. I just don't like him going to places like Costa del Palma. I warned him not to go, told him it was very unstable down there and no place for Americans, but he refused to listen, or maybe he really enjoys being on the front lines."

"Isn't that sort of like the pot calling the kettle black?" she asked softly.

Deep laughter reverberated over the line. "I don't exactly know what Ted told you, but I'm not much more than a pencil-pushing bureaucrat now."

"I thought you might know of someone down there who could help find Ted—"

"Communication between here and there is nearly nonexistent. Their government is in shambles. Most of the leaders from the democratic government are dead or in prison. The current ruling faction is an uneasy alliance of fascists and drug lords. There's a small resistance composed of students, some journalists and a handful of survivors from President Castillo's administration. We support them, of course, but it's a very sensitive situation. And a dangerous one. Our government warned Americans over a month ago that they should leave. The embassy has only a skeleton staff, and since the bombing, they rarely venture from the compound. They won't be sympathetic to a citizen who ignored the warning, especially not a journalist."

"Then you can't help." Meg's throat tightened.

"Not officially," he replied carefully. "If I could get away for a couple of weeks, I'd go down myself. I know a few people from the Castillo government who would probably be willing to help. I can't take a chance on calling them from the office, though. It would put them in jeopardy if anyone found out they'd been contacted by a federal agent."

"I understand." Defeat crashed over Meg like a tidal wave.

"You're really sure he's in trouble and not off in the hills somewhere?"

"I'm very sure," she murmured. "The twins' birthday was three days ago. No card, no call, no package...that isn't like my brother. He might be away too much but he loves the boys, adores them. He's never forgotten their birthday." She swallowed back the rising lump of apprehension. "Besides, I told you that his friend's newspaper was bombed... Eduardo died in the bombing but Ted wasn't there."

"The person who called you might have been involved in some cruel hoax. I know the newspaper was bombed, but no mention of Ted has been made in any of the reports."

"I know. That's why the State Department refuses to help. They say I have no proof that Ted was taken prisoner." Frustration underlay every word.

"You don't, Meg. Not really. An anonymous call saying Ted and someone else from the paper were led away by soldiers isn't proof of anything."

"But I know he's in trouble. If he wasn't, he would call or send some sort of message."

"I can't disagree with that, but you and I know him. I wish I could help you myself, but I have to leave for London. It's something I can't get out of," he told her. "But I may know someone who might be willing to help... if he's free. Stay close to your phone and keep your fingers crossed. I'll get back to you as soon as I can."

Chapter 1

Sweat trickled down Meg's back to soak the waistband of her linen skirt. Her cotton sweater and panty hose clung to her damp flesh. The cool ocean breeze wafting over the balcony of her hotel room was absent in the narrow alley. So was the lush, tropical beauty and reassuring bustle of the tourist district. While her apprehension grew, she had somehow maintained an outward composure, mostly for Ted's twins who, having lost their mother, were alarmed by their father's unusually prolonged absence.

When Dave had phoned to tell Meg where to locate help, her relief had been short-lived. To contact Clay Terhune, the mercenary Dave recommended, Meg was forced to leave the familiar security of her Ohio home to go to Puerto Rico. On the long flight from Cleveland to San Juan, her tentative serenity faltered and doubt, ever present, started to fill in the cracks and crannies of her weakened confidence. As always, when she varied from reassuring routine, apprehension nearly crippled her. Only by sheer force of will had she managed to leave the sanctuary of her hotel room and go in search of Terhune.

Although her legs trembled as she passed through the alley and went farther and farther from her luxurious hotel, Meg fought back the rising tide of terror. As she entered an area rife with blight and decay, the effort to control her emotions grew more and more challenging.

When the cantina that Dave had told her about came into view, Meg stopped in the middle of the deserted street. She hadn't expected anything fancy, not in this neighborhood, but she hadn't expected anything quite so unappealing, either.

With a mixture of disgust and hope, she studied the battered sign, hanging by a single bolt. Cantina American. At least, the owner probably spoke English, she decided, but the idea did nothing to quell her anxiety.

If Ted's life didn't depend on finding—and hiring— Terhune, she would have taken off as quickly as her high heels would allow. The sort of man who frequented a place like Cantina American was hardly the sort she cared to meet, but then any man who sold himself to the highest bidder had to be lacking in morals, values, principles. A hard shudder racked her body. A soldier of fortune had no alliances, no sense of duty or, most likely, any of right or wrong.

With determined effort, she recalled Dave's assurance that Terhune was reliable and trustworthy, even if somewhat unorthodox in his methods and manner. He had also told her that the Cantina American was the most likely place to find Terhune. But, a small inner voice asked, what if he wasn't inside? What if, instead of Terhune, Meg found a crowd of drunken men? Years had passed since she'd felt confident enough to walk alone into any sort of bar, let alone one as clearly disreputable as the one before her.

Meg sucked in a deep breath. Rarely did the old demons torment her, but when they did, they were as fearsome and forceful as ever. In the sparkling sunlight, ice formed in her veins and goose bumps broke out on her flesh. Panic clawed at her tenuous confidence, but Meg struggled to retain control and, finally, felt stable enough to open the door.

As she slipped inside the dim cantina, the odor of stale smoke and cheap whiskey assaulted her nostrils. A fresh quiver of anxiety played along her spine. If the exterior was unappealing, the interior was appalling. Dirty and dingy, the place reeked of sweat and decay. Tables and chairs were strewn about the small room, as if a brawl had just taken place. Behind the bar was a streaked, chipped mirror and in front of it were several stools. Only one stood on its legs and no two matched. Meg wrinkled her nose in disgust.

The only redeeming quality of the place was that it was empty, or nearly so, and not jammed with leering males as she had feared.

Meg hitched the shoulder strap of her purse more firmly over her arm, then advanced to the far end of the bar where a white-haired man methodically washed glasses.

"Excuse me, sir," she murmured. Meg laid one hand on the counter but quickly snatched it away as a thin film of goo coated her fingertips. Her mouth twisted with disgust.

Watery, faded eyes of an indeterminate color narrowed on her. "Don't open till five."

The voice was unmistakably American and clearly perturbed. Meg scanned the room again. One booth was occupied, although its inhabitant looked to be asleep, or possibly unconscious. Quickly, she glanced back at the man who went on with his task as if she'd never spoken. Meg cleared her throat. "I don't want a drink. Only some information."

"Best ask at one of the hotels." He continued his work without sparing her another glance.

Meg frowned. "They don't have the sort of information I'm looking for." If only her brother had stayed home, or at least in the States, she thought for what must have been the millionth time.

"And what makes you think I do?" the man asked as he went about stacking the glassware.

A resigned sigh left her lips. "A friend of mine spoke with someone here, at this bar, a few days ago," she murmured. "That person, the owner, told my friend that a man by the name of Clay Terhune comes here nearly every day."

The old man pivoted to face her. "You the one with the brother in Costa del Palma?" he asked in a soft voice at odds with his earlier curtness.

Meg swallowed hard over the lump in her throat. Despite his original antipathy, the man suddenly seemed sympathetic. "Yes," she replied. "My name is Meg Andrews. My brother, Ted, is a free-lance photographer. He was on assignment in Costa del Palma, but I haven't heard from him in weeks...." Her voice trailed off.

"And you're hoping Clay can find him," he said in a hushed voice.

"Yes, yes, I am," she mumbled. "I'm hoping Mr. Terhune can find him and bring him home."

"If anyone can do it, it's Clay, but most likely your friend already told you that or you wouldn't be here."

She nodded in agreement. "Have you seen Mr. Terhune recently? Dave, my friend, wasn't able to reach him. I assume Dave had spoken to you."

"Sure have seen him," he said with a smile that lit up his lined face. "He came in about an hour ago." He jerked his head toward the corner booth. "I told him about your friend Dave calling, that someone was coming to talk to him about a rescue but not that it'd be a lady." He glanced back at the booth and his grin faded. "This is the first vacation he's taken in a long time, too long. He's only been here a few days and he hasn't got much rest. His place was damaged in a storm and he's had to spend a lot of time getting it repaired. He's tired, Miss Andrews, bone-tired and, when he gets that way..." He shrugged.

Meg caught her lower lip between her teeth. "Then maybe he won't want to help me."

"Oh, I wouldn't give up just yet. When I told Clay that Dave Thornton had called, he said he'd make sure he was here every afternoon and he has been. Every day since your friend called, Clay's come in before I open and stayed until almost closing time."

Meg gave the man a tentative smile. "Thanks, I needed a little reassurance."

He smiled back. "No matter how he seems, Clay's a good man. Don't let his, er, his way put you off. He's not one to be overly friendly with strangers." He paused a moment before going on in a low whisper. "He's not very trusting of anyone he doesn't know well, especially women."

Meg's gaze widened with dismay and confusion. "He doesn't like women?"

"I didn't say he didn't like women. He just doesn't trust them much, but you don't need to worry. Even if Clay doesn't trust other people, you can trust him. He may not be real friendly but he's a good man. Honest and reliable."

"He doesn't have to like me. Or even trust me. All he has to do is find my brother and bring him home."

The old man opened his mouth, then snapped it shut. "I got to get some beer," he muttered before disappearing behind a battered door.

After a steadying breath, Meg turned on her heel and wove her way through the multitude of tables crowding the floor. As she drew closer to the last booth, her anxiety resurfaced. Surely the hulk lounging in the corner wasn't the man who Dave had termed strictly disciplined or who the bartender called reliable. From the look of him, Clay Terhune spent more time holding a bottle than a gun. Closer inspection provided no relief.

Wisps of dark hair tumbled over his frayed collar. Even darker stubble covered his jaw. When his broad shoulders straightened, Meg stopped a few inches from the table. In the dimness, the color of his eyes wasn't clear, but she felt them bore into her like a laser. Meg nervously cleared her throat and gripped her purse more tightly.

"The man at the bar told me you're Clay Terhune," she began in a small, quivering voice that sounded more like a child's than a grown woman's.

"And if I am?" His deep baritone rolled over Meg like a ream of pure silk.

At least he didn't sound intoxicated, Meg decided with a profound sense of relief. "I—I have some business I'd like to discuss with you."

His pulse accelerated. Ever since Hank had told him about Dave's call and the impending arrival of a friend, Clay had been on edge. The peaceful rest, well deserved and desperately needed, was spoiled by anxious anticipation. Despite the hard physical labor involved in getting his cottage back in shape, sleep had been elusive. Although he had tried to contact Thornton several times, Clay was told he was unavailable. That fact, combined with the appearance of the woman before him, did nothing to reassure Clay, who figured Dave was sending another federal agent. He shifted restlessly on the hard bench.

What if someone other than Dave had called? What if this woman wasn't a friend of Dave's? Until he reached Thornton, Clay had to rely on his instinct, which he didn't trust where women were concerned. Once he had let instinct and emotion rule his reaction to a woman who needed his professional services, and it had nearly killed him. With grim determination, he activated his defenses. He couldn't afford to make the same mistake again.

His insolent gaze raked her from head to toe. The beige skirt and sweater, while shapeless and bland, were expensive. So was the watch on her right wrist. A scowl appeared on his face. A spoiled, rich girl just like Annette, he decided. Her face was as colorless as her attire. A pair of blue, or maybe green, eyes gazed steadily at him. Her hair, an indeterminate shade of brown and scraped back into a bun, did nothing to enhance her looks.

Rich and spoiled, yes, but not vain, he concluded. Although his senses had shifted to full alert from the moment she walked into the bar, Clay continued to relax in the corner of the booth as if perfectly at ease.

"I can't imagine what sort of business we might discuss," he drawled as he gave her another lazy inspection. "You aren't exactly the type of woman I usually have business with."

Hot color surged into her pale cheeks. His intense survey and crude insinuation had her trembling so badly that she could barely stand. The urge to slap Terhune surged through her. If she didn't need his help so desperately, she would have taken pleasure in seeing the imprint of her hand on his hard face. Although his blatant masculinity and insolent manner shook the roots of her confidence, Meg sensed this man, no matter what his occupation, wouldn't harm her. Something in his manner indicated he wasn't as implacable as he seemed.

Meg lifted her chin a fraction. "It's my understanding that you accept certain special jobs, difficult jobs."

"And how did you happen to come by that bit of information?" His gaze drifted to the bar. "Not from old Hank, I hope. He's a cagey old guy, always looking for a way to make a few extra bucks, but a little free and easy with the truth. And prone to exaggerate, if it suits his purpose." When he glanced back at Meg, a cynical smile twisted his mouth.

Meg, tired and anxious, allowed impatience to erode restraint. "What difference does it make how I heard about you? It's true that you're a hired gun, isn't it?" Fatigue and worry sharpened her tongue. "I have a job for you, and I'm willing to pay quite well for your services."

The cynical smile widened into a feral grin that revealed even, white teeth. "Are you now? I don't come cheap, honey, not cheap at all."

Meg bit back a nasty retort. The man obviously had no manners or breeding, but then anyone who sold himself could hardly be expected to be polite, she supposed. "I'm willing to pay whatever is necessary," she replied in a cold, clipped tone. "As long as you're successful."

Clay shifted. The look of utter disdain on the woman's face irritated him far more than it should have. Her contemptuous disapproval brought back agonizing memories. "Like I said, I don't come cheap."

Meg stared at his faded and frayed shirt before glancing to the floor where his dirty sneakers poked out from beneath the table. "I'm sure the sum I can pay would be most attractive." When she looked back at his face, her expression was devoid of emotion.

Clay's irritation mushroomed into embarrassment. Although his attire was old and worn, he had far better, more expensive clothing in his closet. Still, he recalled all too well a time when his clothes, only a step from the ragbag, were a source of amusement to his classmates.

He glanced at the floor. Next to his dirty and shabby sneakers her eelskin pumps winked up at him as if in mockery. Clay fought down the painful recollections and tried to focus on the present. Seldom did people's opinions concern him. As a rule, he didn't compare himself to others or wonder what they thought of him. That this woman made him worry about his appearance left Clay with a hard knot of cold fury twisting his guts.

"You haven't explained where you heard about me, or how you learned where I was. I'm not listed in the yellow pages," he muttered.

Meg sighed. His penetrating perusal made her feel ill at ease and uncertain. "Dave Thornton told me I might be able to hire you. He also told me where to find you." She glanced at the vacant seat opposite him. While grimy, it offered a place to rest. Considering the way her legs continued to tremble, sitting down seemed wise. She scrunched her burning toes inside her shoes. Wearing high heels, although they gave her added height, hadn't been prudent as her aching feet reminded her.

"Do you mind if I sit down?" she asked in a stilted murmur.

He shrugged. "Suit yourself."

As she settled on the bench, she studied his unyielding and heavily shadowed face. Nothing about him offered reassurance. He was rude, surly and unkempt, hardly the sort of man to inspire trust, especially in a woman as suspicious as Meg. Whatever trace of humanity she saw earlier had vanished. Mentioning money hadn't helped her cause, nor had Dave's name. Perhaps a more direct approach would work.

"I do hope you'll be able to help me, Mr. Terhune. I've tried every means possible, the State Department, Justice...I don't know where else to turn."

His nostrils flared with a sharp intake of breath. She didn't have to tell him that he was a last resort. Clay knew all too well that no woman like this one would seek him out unless it was an emergency. From the tip of her head to the toes of her shoes, she exuded money and privilege and arrogance. The touch-me-not air about her only increased his aversion. His instinct was to tell her that he was on vacation and unavailable, but he couldn't. Not until he had some idea of why Thornton had sent her.

"I assume you've come quite a distance to find me."

She nodded. "From Ohio."

"You could've called the cantina from Ohio and left your phone number."

"But you might not have called me back," she mumbled. Calling from home had been her original plan, but Dave had vetoed it, suggesting that she'd be more likely to secure Clay's assistance if she spoke to him in person.

"Maybe so, but you might have wasted a trip instead of just a phone call," he pointed out. "I don't even know why you're here, why Thornton sent you."

Meg licked her dry lips. "Dave said you'd be able to locate my brother," she replied in a barely audible voice. "He's missing. The government says they can't help, that I have no proof he's being held against his will, that he's being held at all.'' Her words came out in a breathless rush.

"Slow down, lady. Where is your brother and why do you think he's been kidnaped?''

"He's in Costa del Palma. I think he's being held by those narcoterrorists who took over the government.''

"What in hell was he doing down there? It's no place for Americans.'' Not law-abiding ones, he thought as a dart of apprehension pierced him. Costa del Palma, once a model of democracy, was rife with corruption. As an FBI agent, Dave Thornton knew that better than most people, so why had he sent this woman?

"My brother is a free-lance photographer. He went down about six weeks ago. An old friend of his from college owned a newspaper in the capital. My brother called on a regular basis until about a month ago. The last time he called was the day before our embassy was bombed. After that, he didn't call and I couldn't get any information from the State Department. I tried to contact the newspaper office but it was bombed, too.'' She pressed her lips together to still their trembling before she continued. "His friend was killed and the paper has stopped publication.''

Clay's expression didn't alter. "What about others at the paper? Did you try to contact any of them?''

"Of course I did. I tried to call every person he ever mentioned but most of them are on the run and some are missing, like my brother.''

"There's been nothing on the news about an American journalist disappearing, and according to you, the government isn't particularly convinced that your brother is in danger.''

Angry color formed two splotches on her cheeks. "I know he's in danger because I know my brother. If he was free, he'd call. Besides, one of the people I managed to contact said someone at the paper, someone who's gone into hiding, saw my brother and another man being taken away by men in uniform shortly before the bombing.''

Clay's fingers tightened on the beer bottle. He had been in Costa del Palma in recent months and knew how unstable it was. No one with sense would return voluntarily.

He shrugged. "So, one person, someone you don't know, says your brother was taken by soldiers. How do you know he wasn't released later? How do you know he isn't taking a little vacation, having a little fun in the sun?"

She shook her head. "He wouldn't disappear without a word. He's a mature man, very responsible. Something is very wrong. If he was okay he would call or write or wire. Somehow, he'd get in touch with us. No matter where he's been or what's happened, he's never forgotten his sons' birthday, Mr. Terhune. He loves his boys and their sixth birthday was two weeks ago."

"It seems reasonable that a man would keep in touch with his family," he agreed, even though he'd never had a family to contact. "But it doesn't seem particularly reasonable for a married man to go to an unstable place like Costa del Palma, even for an old friend."

"My sister-in-law died several years ago."

"Even worse," Clay muttered.

Privately, Meg agreed, but loving her brother as she did, she remained loyally silent. "He's a very well-known photojournalist. He didn't think there'd be any particular problem or that he'd be gone long, only a couple of weeks. He went because his friend hoped he could bring back some evidence of the extent of the corruption and suffering down there."

"A regular paragon of virtue," Clay mumbled with unconcealed contempt.

Meg's eyes narrowed. "He's a man of principle, Mr. Terhune. Something you obviously know nothing about."

Fury burned through Clay, but when he spoke, his tone was laced with ice. "If I was, you wouldn't be asking for my help."

Cautious hope crept into Meg's heart. "Then you'll help me. I'm willing to pay whatever you ask." Beneath the scarred table she pressed her damp palms together.

The chill in his tone spread to his gaze. Over the years, he had taken far more punishing assaults but few stung as much as her continuing assumption that money could make him do anything.

"I don't have to take this job, lady. I've got a cottage on the beach that I've worked my tail off to put back in condition. I've got plenty of money, and for the first time in a couple of years, I've got time to enjoy both."

For a moment, confused by his hostility, she faltered. "I—I—I can't imagine that money doesn't interest you at all. Not considering your line of work."

Clay opened his mouth to contradict her, then shut it. "For the time being, I've got enough to live quite well."

"But a little more would be welcome. I can pay a lot if you're successful. If you're as good as Dave says, this won't take very long. Then you can come back here and have your vacation."

"Maybe I don't want to wait to take my vacation. Maybe I'd rather relax on the beach than risk my neck hunting for some guy who should've had sense enough to go home to his kids weeks ago, or to stay there in the first place." While his expression remained hard and remote, unexpected envy twisted his guts. If he'd had her brother's advantages— A steel door, honed by a lifetime of use, snapped into place before the thought completely formed. Wishing and dreaming were luxuries reserved for people weaker than Clay Terhune.

Panic gripped Meg at his words. "Dave said he was sure you'd help me." Her voice quavered with anxiety. "He said you were the only one who had any real chance of succeeding. The only one he'd trust." Hot tears prickled her eyes but she blinked them away. She couldn't afford to let this man, this soldier of fortune, realize how truly frightened and desperate she was.

The sudden softening of her features, along with the trembling in her voice, made Clay narrow his gaze. Doubt and suspicion prickled along his nerve ends. "You say Thornton sent you, but I've got only your word on it. I haven't talked to him in months. How do I know you're telling the truth?" Deceit was part of his work, part of his world and the ability to ferret it out often meant the difference between success and failure, between life and death. Because this woman was so different from most people he met, Clay found his senses clouded.

Her shimmering gaze met his. "He called here and left a message for you." Despite her best efforts, a tremor rippled through her. Despair mingled with desperation but she persisted. "The bartender told me he gave you Dave's message."

Clay's jaw tightened as he fought the urge to comfort her. Meg Andrews's concern for her brother seemed real enough. The anxiety in her tone and posture sent a surge of protectiveness over him. Intense as it was unusual, the sensation alarmed him. He tore his gaze from hers. Looking into her eyes weakened him in a way he didn't care to examine. "Someone identifying himself as Dave Thornton called here, but Hank doesn't know Thornton. He wouldn't recognize his voice, so anyone could've called and used the name to get me here."

"But it wasn't just anyone. It was Dave. And he was talking about me coming here to meet you." Fresh anxiety roughened her voice. She hadn't figured on having trouble convincing this man that she was on the level.

"That doesn't mean the caller was Dave, and just because you say your brother disappeared in Costa del Palma doesn't make it true."

"But you must have heard about the paper being bombed," she said quickly.

"Sure, but that doesn't mean it had anything to do with your brother, if you actually have one." Clay forced himself to remain calm and composed while he studied her. She appeared to be honest, but as he had learned, appearances were quite often deceiving.

Surprise rounded her eyes. "I don't understand, Mr. Terhune. If I didn't have a brother in trouble in Costa del Palma, I wouldn't be here."

Clay stared at Meg Andrews as if trying to determine whether she was real or a mirage. Maybe she was as naive as she claimed. He'd like to believe there were still people in the world who were, but his experience had taught him differently. In a voice he might have used with a small child, he said, "I've made more than one enemy in this world, Miss Andrews. It strikes me as a distinct possibility that one of them might try to lure me into a trap."

A puzzled frown crinkled her forehead. The possibility had never occurred to her, nor did she understand why he held it. "I, uh, I suppose in your line of work you do make enemies," she mumbled, "but if someone wanted to trap you, do you honestly think they'd send someone like me?" She knew, because she looked in the mirror daily, that she wasn't beautiful and, without makeup, a flattering hairstyle and fashionable clothes, she wasn't even attractive. Not that she sought male attention. She didn't, and hadn't for a long time.

To that, Clay made no reply. Although not a gentleman, he wasn't cruel. And she was right. She wasn't the type to lure a man into anything. He cleared his throat. "Well, maybe you can tell me how to contact Thornton. His office says he's away, although they weren't inclined to say where, or when he'll be back. If you know him so well, you must know how to get in touch with him."

Meg licked her dry lips. Although she didn't actually know Dave Thornton at all, she kept that information to herself. "He's in England on some business. He can't be reached right now."

"How convenient," Clay mumbled. "So I suppose that's why he isn't here with you."

Meg cleared her throat. "He wanted to come but he couldn't," she mumbled.

"That still doesn't explain why he sent you to me. There are other people available."

"I told you, he was sure you'd help. He said you were the one he'd want coming after him if he was in Ted Andrews's place."

Clay's lower jaw dropped. "Your brother is Ted Andrews?" Shock and dismay roughened his voice.

"Yes," Meg murmured. "Didn't I say so before?" Confused, she hurried on. "I guess you've seen his work?" Was this man, this mercenary, interested in photography? Was that why Dave was sure he'd help? Because he was a fan of her brother's? Although the possibility seemed remote, she went on, "He's not famous really, unless you know photography, but he has won some awards."

"Right," Clay muttered. He hoped he didn't look as foolish as he felt. Knowing who her brother was, Clay understood Thornton's reasoning. His gaze searched her face. Evidently the FBI agent hadn't shared the reason for his confidence with her, which was just as well. Having her know everything might be an unwelcome complication, but he needed to discover the extent of her knowledge. "So is Thornton a particular friend of yours, or of your brother's?"

Hot color stained Meg's cheeks and she was glad for the bar's dimness cloaking it. "Both," she mumbled, furthering his obvious misconception. "I met him through Ted. They were in Vietnam together."

Meg watched as his face once again hardened into an implacable mask and was reminded of a jungle predator, vigilant and watchful, on guard against some vaguely sensed threat.

"I see," Clay muttered. "But that doesn't explain why Thornton sent you to me."

"I already told you why. He said you take various jobs and that you'd worked together a few times, that you're very good at what you do, one of the best.'' She paused for a moment before continuing. ''He also said he'd like to talk you into working for him on a permanent basis.'' She swallowed convulsively. ''And he was very sure you'd help me, if you were free.''

Clay ignored her comment about working for the bureau and concentrated on her final words. ''He was, huh?'' Thornton knew Clay well, maybe too well. He also knew Clay was free for the first time in ages. And he knew that no matter how badly Clay needed a break, he wouldn't, couldn't, refuse this mission. A resigned sigh escaped him.

Meg sensed Clay wavering. Hope and fear propelled her. ''Will you help me, Mr. Terhune? If you don't...well, I don't know how I'll ever find Ted. I don't know anyone in Costa del Palma, or even how to hire anyone else to help...'' Her mouth trembled. ''I can't even get in touch with Dave.''

The entreaty in her tone chipped away at the last of his resolve. As much as he wanted to refuse, he couldn't. And taking the job shouldn't involve anything beyond getting Ted Andrews out of jail. It shouldn't involve his emotions at all.

Clay tamped down the urge to soothe this woman's worries and concentrated on the task ahead.

''I know some people in Costa del Palma, people who would probably help. First, I have to know if he has actually been arrested, then find out exactly where he's being held.'' Clay's nostrils flared with a sharp intake of breath. He didn't doubt that Ted Andrews was a captive, and he greatly feared he knew exactly where the man was being detained. Cold dread formed a hard knot in his gut, but none of his qualms showed in his expression. ''Once I know that, I can get some help in Costa del Palma.... Of course, there'll be a price to pay.'' He knew she would assume he meant money but that didn't bother him. A wry smile wrenched his mouth. It wouldn't do for this woman to realize that it was conscience, not greed, motivating him.

As relief swept through her, Meg closed her eyes against the sudden onslaught of tears. "Of course," she readily agreed.

"Getting information won't be easy, Miss Andrews. Neither will getting him out." Quite the contrary, he knew, but he saw no point in upsetting her more. Although the bar's minimal lighting masked her face, the purple smudges ringing her eyes were clear, as was the worry and concern for a brother she evidently loved a great deal.

"As long as Ted gets home safely, I don't care about anything else, Mr. Terhune."

Something akin to jealousy tugged at Clay's heart and, for a moment, he sat in stunned silence. Was he actually envious of Ted Andrews? he wondered, jealous that the man had someone in the world who cared about his safety, something Clay had never had and never missed.

He had long ago accepted that if he failed to return from a job, there would be no one to miss him, no one to mourn for him. He had accepted the fact because it simplified his strange life. Now he wondered how it would be to have someone to worry about him, someone to care. Pure, potent regret replaced envy before he marshaled his defenses. He didn't want or need complications that forming attachments led to. No, Clay decided, he was the lucky one, lucky because he could go wherever he wanted, do whatever he desired and never worry about those left behind.

"I'll do my best to get him out," he murmured.

For the first time, Meg heard real emotion in Terhune's deep voice, and she stared in amazement. "Thank you," she replied. "I know you will."

"I'll make some calls right away," Clay said, eager to escape the strange feelings this woman had provoked, eager to once again be in complete control. "Perhaps we could meet later, discuss what I find out."

Meg pressed her hands together. She didn't want to return to the cantina after dark. By then, the place would undoubtedly be filled with people, many of them male. As much as she wanted to find her brother, the idea of returning to this place sent shivers down her spine. "Well, I, that is..."

Her hesitance cut through Clay like a hot knife in butter. "I just thought you'd want to know what I find out." He didn't need to be told she wanted to escape his company as soon as possible. Her distaste had been evident from the first moment.

"I do," she said quickly. "I just...I don't know San Juan very well..." Her voice trailed off. How could she explain her reluctance to come back to the bar without sounding ridiculous?

"There's no need for you to wander around," he told her. "I can meet you in the lobby of your hotel, or the lounge, if you prefer."

"The lounge is fine," Meg replied, and told him where she was staying. Relief relaxed her mouth into a genuine smile. As she rose, she extended her hand. "Thank you, Mr. Terhune."

For a moment, Clay glanced at her slim hand. Her nails, neatly manicured and of moderate length, were bare of polish. Her fingers, long and tapering, were unadorned. Briefly he wondered if he hadn't been hasty in his judgment of this woman. Then, he saw again the costly watch circling her wrist and bitter memories assailed him. He forced his attention back to the nearly empty bottle. "Your check will be thanks enough," he mumbled as he lifted the container to his lips.

Chilled by the blatant rejection, she stepped away. "You'll get your money as soon as Ted is safe."

"That's the usual procedure." His gaze didn't return to her.

"Then I'll see you later. You can call the desk and leave a message as to the time," she said before stalking out.

Clay watched her retreating figure with a sense of foreboding. Just his luck, he thought with dismay. The first vacation he'd taken in years and Thornton had to spoil it. If anyone other than Ted Andrews had disappeared, Clay could have refused to help and not felt a moment's remorse. After all, when private citizens ignored repeated warnings and went to unstable, hostile countries, they ought to accept the consequences.

A humorless smile twisted his mouth. Few people who knew him would believe Clay would ever become embroiled in a job as foolish and futile as this one. The chances of extracting a political prisoner from Costa del Palma were next to nil. The chances of dying in the attempt, or worse, were tremendous.

Clay fingered the cool bottle. Risking his life was part of his work, but few who knew him would believe he'd court danger for a friend. Of course, other then Hank, Dave and Carlotta no one knew he had any friends.

Over the years, Clay had carefully cultivated a reputation for being cold, calculating, even callous. Such a reputation kept most people at a distance, which was exactly where Clay wanted them.

In his experience, most people proved unreliable and shallow at best, and often cruel and traitorous. Maintaining distance was one sure way not to be disappointed.

Clay expected little from others, even when he put himself in danger for them. In his work, he often put his life on the line for others, but in all his forty-two years only two people had ever risked their lives for him. Ted Andrews was one of them.

Chapter 2

Meg glanced at her watch. Nearly eight o'clock and no sign of Terhune. The message he'd left with the desk told her to meet him in the hotel's cocktail lounge at 7:30 and she'd been there on time.

With a sigh, she took another sip of the soft drink, but the icy liquid did nothing to soothe her knotted stomach. She couldn't shake the fear that he might not show up.

While reviewing her options, she scanned the room. When Terhune strode toward her, a relieved smile lifted the corners of her mouth and she forgot his earlier chilliness.

As Clay sank into the chair opposite her and caught sight of her expression, unfamiliar warmth spread through him. Although her hair and clothes were as plain as before and her face remained devoid of makeup, the genuine smile made her look almost pretty. He felt an answering grin start to form, then forced his mouth into a grim line. Getting friendly with this woman wasn't part of the job, he told himself as he turned toward the bar and signaled the waitress.

Meg's happiness faltered, then faded as she watched Clay flirt outrageously with the leggy blonde before ordering a beer. The leering perusal he gave the woman's retreating figure reminded her of all the reasons she needed to maintain her cold disdain.

While Clay studied the blonde, Meg studied him. The light in the lounge, though minimal, provided more illumination than that in the cantina, and she was able to identify his eyes as golden and his hair as dark brown shot with strands of copper and amber. When he shifted to face her, Meg quickly looked away before she noticed the spark of male interest remaining in his gaze as it settled on her. When the waitress returned promptly with his drink, Clay murmured something provocative, but his attention remained on Meg. As soon as the woman left, he opened his mouth to speak, but Meg interrupted.

"I've been waiting for you," she said in a hard, flat tone that resulted more from his flirting with the other woman than from his tardiness.

The ice in her gaze chilled him. "I was making phone calls, calls concerning your brother." He looked down at the beer, a grimace etching his face. He'd spent every moment since leaving Hank's place working, gathering information and making plans. Exhaustion tore at him, as did dread. From what he had learned, Ted Andrews was in trouble, big trouble. If Clay had hope of getting him out, he had to move quickly.

"What did you find out?" All pretense of anger fled as her primary concern took priority.

Clay gulped down a slug of beer. "He's being detained, just as you thought."

"But you can rescue him, can't you?" Fear and desperation showed on her face.

"I think so," Clay replied, despite the doubts hammering in his head. She didn't need to know what political prisons in Costa del Palma were like, how hard it was to penetrate one or what would happen to both Ted and Clay if the attempt failed. He brushed aside the very real concerns ahead. "I spoke with some people who are willing to help. I trust them and they have their own reasons for hating the current regime. They're well trained and well armed. I think we have a reasonable chance of succeeding, Miss Andrews, but I can't guarantee anything."

A frown shadowed her face. Was he trying to back out? she wondered. Anxiety prompted her next words. "I won't pay you if you don't succeed, Mr. Terhune. You won't—"

Clay's cold, clipped voice cut her off. "I'm not worried about that. If I don't get him out, chances are that I won't be coming out, either."

Meg's fingers tightened on the edge of the table. For the first time, she realized the enormity of the task she'd asked to be performed and her heart turned over. "I didn't think," she mumbled, "I hadn't considered..."

"That's rather obvious," he muttered. He was nothing more than a tool to her, something to be used and discarded. That's what he'd been all the years of his adult life, and wanting to be something more to this woman wasn't worth considering.

Warm color seeped into her face. "I'm sorry. Dave didn't say...and I didn't know, or maybe I just didn't want to think about how bad the situation really was."

"There's no need to be sorry." Her concern surprised him, but he didn't want it, couldn't have it. "I've been in worse situations. It's part of my job and I get paid quite well for what I do."

His words reminded her that he wasn't going after her brother out of the goodness of his heart but because she'd promised to pay him. "I know you said I could pay you later, but, well, do you need an advance or anything?"

"It isn't necessary," he said, though that was his normal procedure. "You, or your brother, can reimburse me later. I've got supplies and made my arrangements already. I plan to leave in the morning, so I won't be seeing you again." Which was to the good, he knew. Something about Ted

Andrews's sister made Clay think about things he had long ago deemed foolish.

He scanned her face and wondered why she, of all women, provoked such a response. If she tried, she'd probably be pretty, but she quite clearly made no effort to that end. A sudden suspicion entered his head. Maybe Dave had suggested she look as bland as possible while he wasn't around to keep other men at bay.

But, more to the point, even if she was beautiful, her attitude toward Clay was far from friendly. Not that he blamed her. Not really. They were from different worlds and they both knew it.

"I won't be able to call you from Costa del Palma, of course," he continued, eager to end their meeting and get home where he could steal a few hours of sleep. "I plan to go back to Venezuela, to the place I'm leaving the plane, and I will call, will have your brother call, from there. It'll be a few days, maybe a week or more. I can't say for sure." Nor could he say that a stranger would call if the rescue attempt failed.

Meg's gaze moved to the flickering candle. Anxiety threatened to immobilize her, as it so often had. She swallowed convulsively, trying to hold back the fear, trying to regain the determination that had propelled her to San Juan.

"In another ten days or so this will all be behind you. Your brother will be safe and you'll be at home with him and your nephews."

His reference to the boys was the catalyst Meg needed. Her promise to them, to bring their father home, rang in her ears. In an effort to present a more resolute demeanor, she lifted her chin.

"Evidently you misunderstood me, Mr. Terhune. I won't be waiting here. I'll be going with you. I can make it, Mr. Terhune." Meg sucked in a deep breath. Something inside, something deeper than haunting anxiety, more profound than the promise she'd made the twins, urged her on. For far too long, terror had held her hostage. Before leaving

Ohio, she had made a vow not only to the boys but to herself, as well. She had promised not to let anxiety keep her from doing everything in her power to free Ted. To do so, she didn't allow herself to think about the danger or difficulties ahead. Meg, pleased that her voice sounded sure and strong, smiled confidently.

From Clay's point of view, her gesture made it appear that she was staring down her nose at him in an imperious manner that was reflected in her smirk. Even worse, her words sounded like a command. Disbelief, shock and finally anger chased each other across his face. "No way, lady. This job will be difficult enough without having a spoiled brat in tow. This isn't some cheap thrill. It's life and death, quite possibly mine."

Although she blanched at his all-too-true assertion, Meg's commitment remained strong. An image of her nephews' faces formed in her head. Her smile disappeared but the light of battle remained in her eyes. "I have to go, Mr. Terhune. I promised two little boys that I'd bring their father home to them, and nothing you say will keep me from seeing that promise made good." Wasn't that why she had taken a leave of absence from the library?

Determination was something Clay understood and respected, yet he resisted. "I have to fly into Venezuela tomorrow, then drive several hours before making the last leg of the journey on foot through rough and varied terrain. As for the actual rescue, I wouldn't even consider taking any woman. It's too dangerous."

"I don't have to go that far," she said quickly. "I just want to be as close as possible." She licked her dry lips. "What if you have to make other travel arrangements and can't come back to Puerto Rico? Then I'd be staying here for no reason."

"You could go home," Clay suggested, even though he knew she wouldn't give up so easily.

Meg sighed. "Do you have friends in Venezuela?" she asked.

"One friend," he replied with reluctance.

"And you know people in Costa del Palma, too."

"Yes," he agreed. Confusion crinkled his forehead. He greatly feared she was about to make a suggestion he had no real defense for.

Meg didn't disappoint him. "Then I could go along and stay with your friend in Venezuela, or go on to Costa del Palma and stay with the people you know there. I wouldn't slow you down, Mr. Terhune. I know how important time is."

The sincerity in her tone chipped at Clay's resolve. He gulped down a bit more beer while he tried to figure a way to dissuade her.

Meg, sensing his vacillation, pressed her advantage. "If you won't take me with you, I'll go to Costa del Palma on my own."

Anger flashed like golden lightning in his gaze. "You told me this afternoon that you didn't know what you'd do if I didn't help you."

Meg bowed her head. "I still don't now how I'd rescue Ted but I could get to Costa del Palma. You know I could." Her head came up and determination burned like blue fire in her eyes. "I need to be there, Mr. Terhune. I need to keep my promise to my nephews."

Clay understood promises, admired resolve, but he didn't want, or need, this woman's presence. Something about her bothered him in a fundamental way. "This isn't a picnic or a party."

Meg swallowed hard. "I won't be a bother," she promised.

She would and he knew it, but she'd be a bigger bother if she went on her own and got in trouble.

"I could leave without telling you," he muttered.

"You could, but I would follow." Meg straightened her shoulders as if preparing to meet a mighty foe. "I will get there somehow."

Clay scowled. "That would be extremely foolish. Americans aren't welcome. The embassy is nearly empty. You'd be in danger." Tremendous danger, he knew. Enough to make his protective urges flow thick and wild. He couldn't let her go alone and he knew it. He just wasn't ready for her to know it yet.

The familiar terror hammered at Meg, but she forced it back, wielding the only weapon she possessed: her word, the one she'd given the boys—the one she'd given herself.

"I'd still have to go," she murmured.

Empathy and dismay tangled inside Clay. Although he sensed he was making an error, perhaps a critical one, he posed a rhetorical question. "Are you always so stubborn?"

A tremulous smile lifted Meg's lips. "Only when absolutely necessary." He need never know the extent of her fear, or the fortitude it took to accompany a strange man into a strange land. But her fear had nothing to do with Clay Terhune. She sensed she'd be in less danger with him than with most men. He was, quite clearly, a man whose livelihood and life depended on exercising firm control. Besides, he didn't like her, let alone find her attractive. Their time together might be difficult but only because they both wanted distance.

Clay shoved back his chair and stood up. After tossing some money on the table, he glanced back at her. "I doubt if you'll be smiling tomorrow night," he muttered. "Be ready and outside at eight. If you're not, I'll leave without you." Then, without a backward glance, he strode from the room.

As Meg watched his departure, her smile disappeared. Although she had won, she felt far from triumphant. Instead, she wondered if she'd made the worst mistake of her life. No, she amended. Certainly not the worst.

Meg, her single suitcase at her feet, stood on the sidewalk in front of the hotel and again wondered if she was wrong. Maybe she ought to wait in San Juan, the weak part of her suggested.

As she was reconsidering her decision, a dirty battered truck rumbled up to the curb.

"Good morning," Meg murmured when Clay jumped out of the vehicle and came around to grab her bag.

"Let's get going," he muttered without sparing her a glance. After he'd spent a nearly sleepless night, his fatigue became exhaustion that destroyed his minimal patience. Over and over, he had reviewed the task ahead and chastised himself for not figuring a way to keep Ted Andrews's sister safe in San Juan. The protective instincts she inspired were trouble and he knew it. She was trouble, distracting trouble he didn't need.

Despite her drab appearance and sometimes snooty manner, she had awakened a sense of responsibility long dormant. Ensuring her safety had somehow become as important as rescuing her brother, yet Clay knew, for his own self-preservation, he dared not let his cool control waver. Women like Meg Andrews would use any trace of power over a man to destroy him.

As soon as she climbed into the passenger seat beside him, Clay engaged the gear and started off. Although he felt Meg's glare on him, he kept his attention on the road. He didn't want her along and she might as well realize it.

The first few moments Meg was too busy fastening her safety belt and struggling to stay seated to speak. When she finally felt that she wasn't in imminent danger of being tossed from the vehicle she turned toward Clay. Fury, vile and vivid, burned in her gaze. "I said good-morning to you, Mr. Terhune."

"I heard you," he muttered. The imperious and judgmental tone in her voice sparked the ashes of his banked resentment.

Her gaze scanned his chiseled profile. Sunglasses guarded his eyes, but his ruggedly handsome features were clearly visible in the bright light of day. Ambivalent emotions, anxiety and appreciation, buffeted Meg. Recalling that the best defense was a good offense, she tore her gaze away and went on the attack.

"Common courtesy dictates a response."

Clay clenched his teeth until a muscle jumped in his jaw. "I don't waste my time reading up on etiquette," he ground out.

"I'm quite sure you don't, Mr. Terhune, but most civilized people use good manners as a sign of respect for others."

The reproach in her voice scraped a raw nerve. "People like you. People like Dave Thornton."

The mention of Dave's name drove her attention back to Clay's face. Seeing his rigid jaw, she paused. The previous day, she had allowed him to believe that she knew Dave better than she did, had even furthered the possible misconception that she and Dave were involved. Perpetrating a lie went against Meg's basic character, but since Clay Terhune would never know the truth, it seemed like another useful barrier.

She cleared her throat. "Dave is a gentleman. He's always very polite."

The river of undiluted jealousy pulsing through Clay came as an unwelcome and unfamiliar intrusion, one he denied even to himself.

Dave Thornton was perfect for Ted Andrews's sister. Almost perfect, Clay amended. If the man had any sense, he would have rearranged his damn schedule and accompanied her.

Anger at Thornton evolved into self-disgust. He wasn't Dave Thornton and never would be. "I hope your perfect gentleman understands when you tell him that you spent several days, and nights, with another man."

Crimson flamed in Meg's cheeks. "Dave trusts me," she murmured. He did, of course. Not that he'd care what she did. "And he trusts you, too. After all, he recommended you."

"Right," Clay mumbled. Thornton, like most people, probably thought Clay was some sort of automaton. Hell, that's what he wanted them to think, he thought. His entire adult life had been an exercise in self-denial. Well, almost his entire adult life, he considered, as memory flashed like a neon sign in his head. His fingers tightened on the steering wheel. "Well, Thornton doesn't need to worry and neither do you. This is purely business."

Meg didn't need to be reminded he had no interest in her. That had been clear from their initial meeting. His reassurance, for she recognized it as that, should have been welcome. Why it wasn't, Meg didn't care to examine.

Instead, she let her head fall back against the seat and stared out the side window. As they continued toward the airfield, the pair maintained an uneasy silence.

If the truck was alarmingly shabby, the Cessna was incredibly sleek. A thrill of anticipation raced through Meg as the plane soared into the air. Clay's proficiency impressed her, although she refrained from saying so.

His hands, long fingered and deeply tanned, rested on the controls with confidence. His preoccupation gave her an opportunity to resume the study she had started in the hotel bar.

He hadn't bothered to shave but the damp hair he'd met her with at the hotel indicated a recent shower and his clothing, while well worn, was spotless. The khaki shirt clung to his broad shoulders and wide chest before disappearing into the waistband of his faded fatigues. As unexpected and unusual as it was, Meg found herself mesmerized by his rugged masculinity, and her reaction to it. Without doubt, he was one of the most attractive men she had ever met. With a shave, haircut and some decent clothes, he would be devastating.

Suddenly, the amber eyes were looking straight into hers and embarrassment drove out admiration. Meg blushed to the roots of her hair and quickly looked away.

"I know how to fly, Miss Andrews. You needn't keep watch over me every second," he muttered before returning his concentration to the instrument panel. Her intense scrutiny unnerved him. The woman had already made it clear she considered him a boor. Did she think she had to watch over him as if he were some errant schoolboy?

"I—I was just..." Meg's voice trailed off as she wondered how to explain her attention without revealing her attraction. She lifted her chin a fraction, formed what she hoped was a cool, dismissive expression and offered part of the truth. "I've always been interested in flying, but I've never been in a cockpit before. I was interested in how things work." She shifted so she again faced forward. "Sorry if it bothered you," she finished in a tone that clearly said she wasn't sorry in the least. For a brief time last night, Meg had actually thought she could grow to like Clay Terhune, despite his occupation. Now the distance she knew they both wanted had become a chasm, and she had no intention of trying to breach it.

Clay took a quick glance at her averted profile and stiff shoulders. He started to apologize, then stopped before a single word escaped. Why bother? She wouldn't appreciate the gesture. She'd figure it was insincere, as insincere as her own.

When he spoke, he ignored her hollow excuse. "You'd be better off resting. It's not a very long flight but you might as well take it easy while you've got the chance." Besides, he knew he couldn't concentrate with those sea blue eyes of hers on him. He could look down at the Gulf of Mexico if he needed to see that particular mixture of blues and greens.

He sucked in a deep breath to clear his head but found his nostrils filled with a delicate floral scent. Sparks of awareness skyrocketed through him and his fingers tightened on the throttle. He had been alone too long and too long without a woman. That had to be the reason his body was responding so eagerly to someone as haughty and aloof as this woman. He exhaled sharply. He couldn't, wouldn't, let her see this vulnerability.

Bitter memories burned his brain like acid. Once he had trusted such a woman, but never again. "When you get home, have your brother or Thornton buy you some flying lessons," he muttered in a voice laced with contempt. "Right now, get some rest. You'll need it later."

Meg gritted her teeth against the angry retort rising in her throat. At the same time, embarrassed color again invaded her cheeks. None of her family or friends knew about her interest in flying. Why had she been stupid enough to mention it to someone as insensitive as Clay Terhune, a man she barely knew, a man whose occupation appalled her. Had she taken leave of her senses?

Unwilling to examine her motivations too carefully, she shut her eyes. If he wanted to be alone, so be it.

Meg jerked awake as soon as the wheels hit the runway. She looked immediately at Clay, who was busy guiding the plane down the bumpy tarmac. Some of the tension left over from her troubled dreams dissipated. The images of Ted and Clay, both imprisoned and threatened with death, slowly faded as she glanced out at the landscape.

"Where are we?" she asked in confusion. Her gaze swept over the towering mountains before resting on Clay.

"At my friend's place. I'll leave the plane here. It'll be safe." He brought the Cessna to a halt, then killed the engine. "This is as close as we can get to Costa del Palma. Carlotta, my friend, has a Rover we can borrow to drive a bit closer to the border." He glanced at Meg before looking out the window. "You could stay here, you know. You'd be safe and comfortable."

Meg swallowed convulsively. "That's just the problem," she mumbled, almost to herself. "I've been safe and comfortable for far too long."

A puzzled frown knitted his brow. "The trip is difficult."

"So you said. And, as I said, I am going to Costa del Palma, one way or another."

Clay disentangled his big body from the cockpit, grabbed his bag and exited the plane. His jerky motions telegraphed his anger, but Meg wouldn't let herself be dissuaded. Not now.

As she jumped down from the plane, Clay caught her around the waist and swung her out of the craft. The feel of his large, strong hands on her sent hot waves of awareness washing through her. Even though her feet hit the ground, Clay didn't release her. For long, silent seconds, she stayed in his grasp, relishing the wild warmth heating her blood. Then, abruptly, his hands dropped to his sides as if burned, and he spun away.

Embarrassed by the flush of desire staining his cheeks, Clay couldn't face Meg. He was worse than an adolescent boy, he thought with disgust. The most casual contact, even with the barrier of her shirt and sweater, had his breath coming in short gasps and sweat beading his brow. "Let's get up to the house," he said in a voice gruffer than he intended.

Meg scurried to keep up with his long, rapid strides. By the time they reached a winding trail, she was breathless. "How much farther?" she asked in a harsh murmur.

Clay turned to face her. Anger at himself froze his features into an icy mask. "You need to rest already, Miss Andrews?" he asked in a voice laced with contempt.

Meg forgot her anxiety, forgot her doubt, forgot everything except her need to prove herself a whole person. As the light of battle lit her gaze, she squared her shoulders. "My name is Meg," she told him.

"You didn't answer my question," he muttered.

The lingering disgust in his attitude stiffened her spine as well as her resolve. Not Clay Terhune, or anyone or anything else, was going to stop her now. "I'm not tired," she informed him in a cool tone, "just stiff from sitting so long."

"Then there's no point in wasting time," he said as he turned and continued down the path. "Besides, walking will loosen you up."

Meg's only response was to trail behind him. When they emerged from the dense foliage, a massive villa loomed ahead. Meg stopped in her tracks as new waves of apprehension washed over her.

"That's your friend's house?" she asked.

Clay stopped but didn't turn back to her. "Yes, it is. I imagine Carlotta's waiting inside," he murmured before going on.

As they grew closer, the house became more impressive. The stucco-and-tile structure rambled across the rolling terrain in undisguised grandeur. A profusion of potted plants dotted the myriad balconies overlooking the front courtyard. At the end of the curving path was a wrought-iron gate. There Clay paused to ring the massive bell suspended from a fancy grille.

As they waited for a response, Meg shifted from one foot to the another. Only moments earlier she had been firm in her resolve to unflinchingly face whatever came. Now alarm grasped her heart in its unrelenting grip. How could Clay's friend afford to live in such splendor? she wondered. How did someone accumulate the wealth necessary to construct such an estate and why choose so remote an area? One answer circled through Meg's mind like a hungry hawk. The woman, or perhaps her husband, was a drug dealer or a gunrunner. They were close enough to Costa del Palma to make a fortune in either endeavor, she realized with a sinking sensation.

Meg wiped her damp palms on her trousers. A man like Clay Terhune could easily have friends involved in such activities. After all, his job was illegal as well as immoral. He sold his services not to help people in danger but to make money.

A shiver rippled through Meg, one she knew didn't result from the cool, crisp mountain air. Clay didn't always work for law-abiding citizens; in fact, the opposite was most likely the case.

Trepidation slipped into the cracks and crevices of Meg's newfound determination. What had she gotten into?

When an elderly man opened the gate, she relaxed a bit. He looked harmless. While he and Clay conversèd in what she assumed was Spanish, Meg watched Clay's hard expression soften.

The older man smiled down at Meg, then waved her inside.

"Go ahead," Clay murmured. "He'll take you to Carlotta while I get the rest of the gear and secure the plane."

A protest rose in her throat, but Meg swallowed it back. "Fine," she mumbled as she stepped inside the flower-filled courtyard.

Clay watched for a moment, looking as if he wanted to say more, then turned on his heel and strode back down the path and out of sight.

Entering the house, Meg found the interior as impressive as the outside. Although she couldn't help but admire the gleaming tile floor, antique furniture and well-chosen accessories, such obvious wealth made her uncomfortable and uncertain. Since she hadn't understood a word that passed between the gentleman and Clay, she didn't know if her presence was a surprise, or if Clay's friend expected her.

She was about to try communicating with her guide when he stopped at a set of carved doors and rapped. After a feminine voice responded, in Spanish as well, he threw open the doors.

"Come in, my dear."

The slightly accented voice, Meg saw, came from a tiny but exquisitely lovely woman of advanced years. Her hostess, a smile on her lined face, looked like a kindly grandmother, hardly what Meg had anticipated. To cover her shock, she bowed her head as she advanced toward the twin sofas flanking a stone fireplace. When the woman patted a place beside her, Meg reluctantly perched on the edge of the seat.

"You must be Miss Andrews," the woman said softly.

Warmth and welcome shone in the woman's ebony eyes and, despite her doubts, Meg found her lips curving into an answering smile. "Yes, I am," she murmured. "I wasn't sure you knew I'd be with Mr. Terhune." The truth was, Meg wasn't sure of much at all. Only her word of honor to her nephews and herself kept her going, that and knowing if she didn't do everything in her power to rescue her brother, she'd never be able to live with herself.

"Clay called last night to tell me."

Meg wanted to ask what else Clay had told her but good manners, and discretion, forbade it. "I see," she murmured.

Further discussion was halted by the reappearance of the elderly gentleman who, after placing a well-laden tray on the massive coffee table, again disappeared.

Meg was enjoying the light repast and her hostess's pleasant small talk when Clay joined them. The woman's face lit up when she caught sight of Clay and Clay's expression stunned Meg. The look on his face could only be described as pure joy. In the seconds she stared at him, Meg wished to have him direct that same emotion toward her. As the thought surfaced, she immediately turned away as if that would somehow destroy the wish. With effort, she fixed her attention on her food while the pair greeted each other.

Their words, in Spanish, were lost on Meg but their mutual affection was not. When Clay knelt before Carlotta to take her frail hands in his strong, lean ones, Meg couldn't deny the jealousy that seized her, nor could she ignore her stupidity. Envying an elderly woman the attentions of a mercenary was insane, but logic did a poor job of routing need.

When she felt the other woman's kindly gaze on her, Meg forced a smile.

"Clay says the two of you must leave as soon as possible."

Meg's attention shot to Clay. She wasn't surprised to note that his face had once again hardened. She wasn't surprised but, damning herself for weakness, she was disappointed. "Time is important," Meg mumbled as she bowed her head.

"I understand that," Carlotta said. "And I hope you are successful."

Clay got to his feet. "I need to pack the Rover."

Carlotta's ebony gaze skimmed over him. "You need to eat something. You are much too thin. And tired, as well. It would be better, for both of you, if you waited until morning."

He shook his head. "We can't, but I promise that on the way back I'll stay for a day or so." One big hand gently brushed her slim shoulder.

"But you will eat before you leave."

His hard mouth softened. "Yes, I will eat," he agreed before striding out of the room.

Meg stared after him in stunned silence. The man of the past few minutes seemed like a stranger. She realized her confusion must have been written on her face when Carlotta turned to her.

"Try not to let Clay bother you."

"He doesn't bother me," she protested. "I know he doesn't like me, but that really doesn't matter. I don't care if he ignores me."

The older woman sighed. "It is Clay's way. He is . . . reserved with all women."

The woman's observation reminded Meg of what the bartender in the cantina had said. Curiosity and confusion formed her reply. "He's nice to you. More than nice."

Carlotta smiled. "But I am like a mother to him."

Another memory took the stage in Meg's mind. "I don't think that cocktail waitress last night was like a mother to him," she muttered.

A peal of laughter filled the room. "He flirted with her?"

"You could say that," Meg replied.

"Then perhaps, it was to make you jealous."

Meg shook her head. "I don't think so. He's not interested in me. He as much as said so." Not that she wanted him to be. Hadn't she perpetrated the misconception that she was involved with Dave Thornton to keep a safe distance?

"How interesting."

"Not really. I don't much care. All I really care about is getting my brother out of Costa del Palma. That's the only reason I'd spend any time with Clay Terhune."

"Then you do not find Clay attractive?"

Honesty, Meg knew, was not always the best policy. "I find him rude and uncouth."

"He can be rather rude," Carlotta admitted, "but he can also be thoughtful and considerate. Clay is a very complicated man, a man who does not trust easily, especially where a woman is involved."

"I'm not involved in any way except as his employer," Meg corrected. She laid her plate on the table. "I know Clay is a friend of yours..."

"Because I know there is more to him than he allows most people to see. I know you have not seen that part of him. I know you do not trust him, but you can. Clay will not harm you. He will see that you are safe, and, if it is within his power, he will see your brother safe, as well."

"I trust him to do his job," Meg murmured, but she couldn't explain why she lacked trust in men. Not even to this kindly woman who seemed to understand, to sense so much.

"He will do the best he can for you," Carlotta murmured. "And I hope, when you come back, you will realize that."

Confusion clouded Meg's gaze. "I don't understand what you mean."

"Not now, perhaps, but maybe soon. Just give him a chance, dear. He so desperately needs one."

Meg was still pondering her hostess's words when Clay returned.

The next hour was a flurry of activity during which Clay ate and Meg changed clothes and went through her suitcase for the bare essentials she would need. As they got ready to leave, Carlotta's fervent wishes for a safe and successful journey made a lump form in Meg's throat. Briefly, she considered backing out and staying with the older woman in her pleasant villa. Even if the place had been purchased with dirty money, it represented serenity and security, neither of which she'd enjoy in Clay's company. In the end, determination won, and with Carlotta's good wishes ringing in her ears, Meg left the peace of the house to join Clay beside the Rover.

His slow survey made her blood pound in her temples. The cotton sweater, camp shirt and khaki trousers revealed her figure more than her usual attire, something she wasn't sure she liked until she saw a flash of appreciation light Clay's normally cold eyes. The same sort of appreciation he had afforded the cocktail waitress and not the pure joy he'd shown Carlotta. Suddenly, Meg felt both deflated and uneasy. Dave, Hank and Carlotta had said Clay was trustworthy, but what did they know of real terror or repression? Less than nothing, she was sure.

Clay jerked his gaze to her feet as soon as he realized she had noted his attention. "I hope you can walk in those shoes," he muttered as he tossed the pack he had given her into the rear compartment where other gear already rested. He hoped she didn't notice the catch in his voice the way she had been aware of his perusal. The sight of her clad in form-fitting attire made him imagine things that were neither wise nor appropriate. Unaccustomed to any loss of control, he inwardly chastised himself. If she sensed any weakness, she would undoubtedly, in typical feminine style, use it to her advantage.

His jaw tightened. Seeing her seated with Carlotta, the one woman in the world he trusted, had agitated him beyond all reason. In some way he couldn't fathom, he had feared leaving the pair alone, which was why he insisted on leaving immediately.

Meg glanced at her sneakers. "I've hiked in them plenty of times. They're a lot more comfortable than those boots you wanted me to borrow from Carlotta," she said, referring to the footwear the older woman, at Clay's behest, had offered.

Clay grimaced. "This is going to be slightly more than a hike. I told you, we have to cover some very rough terrain. Boots are better support." Her stubbornness grated on his nerves.

"I put them in the pack," she admitted, "but I still don't want to wear them."

Somewhat mollified, Clay nodded. "You'll change your mind after we get started."

Irritated by his smug expression, Meg said nothing, but she silently vowed not to let Clay Terhune intimidate her, or at least not to let him realize it if he did.

Two hours later, the oppressive silence wore Meg down. Unable to bear another second of it, she took a reassuring breath and glanced at Clay's stern profile.

"Where are we headed?" she asked in a pleasant, conversational tone.

He shot her a puzzled frown before his customary mask fell back into place. "To Costa del Palma."

Meg gritted her teeth against an angry retort. The man really was insufferable, but since they were forced into each other's company, she figured they ought to reach some sort of truce, even an uneasy one.

"I meant, where do you plan to leave the car?"

For a moment, Clay considered telling her that she didn't need any details, then relented. If she could make a pretense at civility, so could he. "To a place near the border. The route we take from there will let us cross into Costa del Palma unnoticed."

"Near the coast?" she asked.

His gaze shot back to her. "What makes you ask that?"

"We're headed northwest," she replied.

His dark eyebrows lifted a fraction. "You must have a pretty good sense of direction," he commented as his attention returned to the rutted road.

"I have an excellent sense of direction." Since she was looking out the side window, she failed to detect his tentative smile. "So you plan to cross in a remote area," she murmured.

"Most of Costa del Palma is remote," he muttered. A dour expression blanketed his handsome face. "There are some decent roads in this end of the country, but few, and we have to stay away from them, anyhow. Even though the area is remote and not under government control, we could run into military patrols."

A lump of apprehension formed in her throat. "You're sure you know how to get where we're going without following the roads?"

"I'm sure," he ground out. "I've been in and out of Costa del Palma before." Clay stopped abruptly. Normally a man of few and carefully chosen words, he seldom discussed his past assignments. To do so wasn't wise.

Relief spread through Meg as she turned back toward him. While his face was partially obscured by his growing beard, his sculpted lips, set in a flat line, were visible. Remembering how those lips had lifted into a smile at the sight of Carlotta, Meg felt the sting of envy once again. How she wished she might, just once, see him smile at her. Unbidden, another wish entered her mind. The wish to feel those smooth, carved lips against her own. Would they be coaxing or demanding? she wondered. Would his whiskers tickle?

As the Rover careened around a bend in the road, Meg grabbed the roll bar for support. At the same time, she realized how foolish she was being and tore her gaze from Clay before he noticed her intense scrutiny. Wishing for kisses from a stranger, a mercenary, was dangerous. The altitude must have cut the oxygen getting to her brain, she decided as she fought to return her thoughts to safer turf.

While the vehicle rumbled downhill, wind whipped tendrils of hair loose from her neat bun, but repairing the damage proved impossible. Meg was too busy hanging on to do or think about anything else. When the Rover slowed to a more sedate pace, she had forgotten her errant wishes and shot Clay a killing glare.

"Your driving skills could use a little work, Mr. Terhune," she muttered.

His icy glance skimmed over her before returning to the road. "I never said the trip would be easy, Miss Andrews."

Fresh anger simmered inside Meg. Rude, insolent beast, she thought to herself. Although she knew he was trying to be difficult, Meg had no intention of allowing him to have the upper hand. After all, she was his boss. He needed to remember that simple fact.

"What are your plans for rescuing my brother?" she asked in the same commanding tone she had used at their first meeting.

"I'll get him out. That's all you really need to know."

The simmering anger bubbled until, like steam in a pressure cooker, it threatened to blow the lid off Meg's control. "That's not good enough, Mr. Terhune. I want to know how you plan to rescue my brother."

Clay's shoulders stiffened, but his gaze remained on the road. "I'll tell you what you need to know when I think you need to know it." His chilly tone had dropped several degrees.

The building anger billowed into fury. "I'm paying you, Mr. Terhune." If his voice was cold, hers flamed red hot. "That makes me your boss. And since I'm also accompanying you, I think now is a good time to outline your plans."

His amber gaze filled with contempt. His first impression of her had been correct. She really was a selfish, bossy snob. Why he'd ever felt one moment's concern for her was beyond him. This woman didn't need protection, certainly not his. If he had a particle of sense, he'd have left her in San Juan. If she'd somehow gotten to Costa del Palma on her own, she wouldn't have been his problem, which, unfortunately, she now was.

"You don't own me, lady. I could turn this rig around and go back to Carlotta right now."

The chill of fear doused her fury. "But you won't," she said with far more confidence than she felt.

Clay's jaw tightened. The hell of it was, she was right. He couldn't turn back. "No, I'm not going back, but I'm not putting up with your high-handed ways, either. I'm doing a job for you, but that doesn't make you my boss and you'd be smart to remember that."

His warning reverberated inside Meg. Baiting wasn't smart. For a moment, she closed her eyes. Maintaining distance while trapped together wasn't easy. Neither was being domineering and disdainful. If only she could just be herself, she thought. The problem was, more and more, Meg thought she needed to make some changes in her life. Wasn't that why she had insisted on accompanying Clay Terhune? Wasn't that why she had gone to Puerto Rico? For years, she had been existing, not living. If she didn't make some changes soon, when would she? Thirty-three was too young to live in such a constrained life.

When Meg said nothing more, Clay looked back at her and was surprised to see her eyes shut. The same protective streak he had just berated himself for feeling earlier resurfaced with a vengeance. With color in her cheeks and her hair escaping in tendrils from its confinement, she appeared tired and vulnerable and, worst of all, attractive. Of the three, fatigue seemed the best place to concentrate his attention. Then, her lashes opened and she was looking straight at him. Hastily, Clay glanced away. "Now's a good time to rest. We don't have much farther to go, then we'll be walking."

"I'm not tired," Meg replied. "I was just thinking."

The underlying anxiety in her tone made Clay lower his guard. "I really do have a valid plan."

A flash of guilt sparked in Meg since she hadn't been thinking about Ted's plight. Immediately, she sat up straighter. "I'm sure you do," she murmured. There must be some middle ground between friction and friendship, Meg thought. "I'd just like to know a little about it."

Since she had every right and reason to be curious, Clay didn't argue further. Telling her some of the details didn't mean he wasn't still in control. "I told you I knew some people who will help. They live in a village in the hills. The entire town resisted the drug lords and is working to overthrow them. It was the hometown of Castillo, the former president, and many of those who live there now were government officials or military officers under the democratic regime. It's an outpost of sorts, a refuge. I know some of them very well. They've rescued others from the prison."

Uncertainty knotted Meg's stomach. Exactly how did Clay know these men? From what he said they were good people who wanted to reestablish democracy in their country. "Did you work for them, or something?" Meg asked with a trace of skepticism.

Her suspicion reactivated Clay's defenses. His ebony lashes pulled together until his eyes resembled slits. "You sound surprised. It isn't only dictators and drug dealers who hire mercenaries, you know. Sometimes decent people come to me, too." His angry gaze raked her. "After all, you did."

Crimson formed two spots high on her cheeks. "I didn't mean—"

Clay's voice, as sharp as a saber and just as cutting, slashed through hers. "You meant, why would decent men help a dirty mercenary, didn't you?" Icy rage spurred him on. "Maybe because they are decent. And, even though they trust me as much as I do them, you don't have to worry. They aren't as coarse and common as I am."

Meg bit back a nasty retort as she saw not only anger but anguish darken his golden eyes. When she spoke, her voice was soft. "If they're anything like Carlotta, I know I'll like them." She kept her attention on Clay's carved profile. "The two of you seem very close."

Tension tightened his jaw. "I've known her a long time, but I seldom see her," he mumbled.

"She regards you like family, like a son," Meg observed.

A small muscle near his cheek twitched violently. "She's a lonely old lady," he murmured. "She lost her husband and sons in a dirty little war that most people in the States never knew existed. Because I got her last son home to her before he died, she welcomes me into her home, in spite of my background."

Empathy squeezed Meg's heart, empathy for both Carlotta and Clay. "How awful to lose her whole family."

"She's survived," he responded in a terse tone that would have warned anyone else off. He didn't want to discuss Carlotta for fear of revealing more of himself.

"She's done more than survive," Meg stated, ignoring his implicit warning. "Survival alone can't destroy bitterness or restore trust and hope."

Something in Meg's voice made Clay turn back to her. Although her features were composed, torment burned in her gaze, torment that resulted from more than fear for her brother. The urge to offer protection and comfort hit him like a bullet, tearing into his heart with devastating destruction. At the same time, he wondered what someone like her would know about survival, or bitterness and despair. He couldn't began to guess. All he knew for sure was that her torment reached deep into his soul, reached beyond the indifference, beyond the apathy, beyond the cynicism and went directly to the core of understanding and compassion that hadn't died but only hibernated.

Knowing emotion meant weakness, Clay hastened to shore up his battered battlements. He jerked his attention back to the dusty road. "You ought to be resting instead of talking so much."

Meg blinked in surprise, but since she knew prodding him further was likely to widen the breach between them, she murmured her agreement. Weary and confused, she closed her eyes and feigned sleep.

When Clay heard her breathing grow deep and even, some of his residual tension abated. He wasn't accustomed to company, especially not a woman's, but he found Meg a pleasant companion. In fact, he found her far more than pleasant. He found her intriguing in a way that wasn't sensible or wise. He found her intriguing in a way that might spell danger, not to his life or mission, but to his heart and soul.

Chapter 3

After struggling into her backpack, Meg turned to Clay who was draping a large canteen around his neck. Dismay filled her as she saw the rest of his burden. While her pack was small, his extended from his neck to well beyond his lean waist and was twice as big in circumference as he was. A machete was suspended from it. Slung over one broad shoulder was a rifle. Strapped to his muscular thigh, a revolver. How could he stand under so much weight, let alone walk? His warnings about the rugged terrain resurfaced and a low groan escaped her.

Seeing Meg's uneasy expression but misinterpreting its cause, Clay scowled. "The rifle is a necessity. So is the sidearm. If I thought you could shoot, I'd have brought a weapon for you, too," he muttered, "even though you might use it on me."

Filled with dismay, Meg scarcely heard his words. "Are you sure you can carry all that? Maybe I could take something?"

The concern in her voice caught him off guard, and for a moment, he stared at her as if she were some sort of apparition. Worry darkened her eyes to the color of a stormy sea. Worry for him, he realized with astonishment. Her interest couldn't be personal, he reasoned, not when she so obviously mistrusted and disliked him. Nonetheless, it warmed him. Confused by her solicitude, and his reaction, Clay busied himself securing the car.

"I'll be fine," he mumbled. "We'd best get moving."

Rebuffed at his distant tone, Meg gave the vehicle a last look of longing. "Will it be safe here?" Since her honest concern had met with another brusque rejoinder, she felt silly and more useless than ever. Why try to be civil? Why worry about him? For all she cared, he could carry the Rover to Costa del Palma if he chose. If he fell flat on his face, she would merely step over his muscular body and proceed without him. The image brought a smile to her face, and Meg had to bite her lip to keep from laughing out loud.

Clay turned just in time to catch the grin. A grimace twisted his mouth as a surge of anger and resentment welled up inside him. Her concern was merely a sham. Was he really so starved for attention that he was willing to accept any crumb her highness tossed at him?

"The car is the least of our worries," he snapped. "Let's get going." Without a backward glance, he marched down the dusty road.

Meg sighed and started after him. With every step, she vowed to be as little trouble as possible and to treat Clay Terhune as coldly as he treated her.

As Meg preceded Clay up the narrow, twisting path, he found concentrating on his rescue plans increasingly difficult. The mousy, unattractive creature he had met in Hank's cantina had slowly disappeared. Even before leaving Carlotta's villa, Clay had glimpsed hints that her shapeless garb and plain hairstyle hid an attractive woman. Those hints had whetted his appetite, but the continuing view of her pinched waist and rounded bottom had him breathless and sweating, and not only from the taxing terrain.

As Meg climbed steadily upward, her hips danced provocatively before his eyes. The trim trousers hugged her in a way Clay couldn't help but admire. Unrelenting desire, surprising in its potency, tore at him. Years had passed since he'd experienced such profound need. Years since he'd found out, the hard way, not to let any woman, no matter how sweetly alluring, tempt him. Ignoring his needs had honed his self-control until it was instinctive, stronger than the instincts most people considered basic. For Clay, denial, not need, had become second nature. Logic, not longing, ruled him.

Bitter experience had taught him how unwise relaxing his guard with a woman could be. After nursing both a broken heart and a battered body; a young Clay had gathered his defenses around him again, reassembling them with the brick and mortar of anguish and pain. A loner since boyhood, he had retreated further into himself, maintaining strict control over every aspect of his life. By doing so, he had built a reputation as being remote and ruthless, one that served him well in his work, even if it crippled any chance for a normal emotional life. Only Hank knew he wasn't really ruthless. Only Carlotta knew he wasn't really remote. Now he was in danger of revealing far too much of himself to Meg Andrews.

Her occasional and unanticipated concern and interest undermined his attempts at indifference, rattled his core of cynicism. It wasn't just that she was prettier and more desirable than he had first figured. She was nicer. Much nicer. As much as he wanted to touch her, Clay wanted to talk to her, as well. He wanted to know about her life, her hopes and dreams.

A grimace curved his mouth. Was he losing his mind? Over the years, Clay had grown accustomed to being alone and seldom felt lonely. Only rarely did his childhood dreams haunt him. On those rare and isolated occasions, the man he was relentlessly routed the boy's fantasies because the adult Clay knew what the child Clay had not. Love and home and family weren't meant for someone like him. Those luxuries were reserved for people like Meg Andrews.

He forced his attention to the nape of her willowy neck. In the bright sunlight, copper and gold streaked her auburn hair, making it look anything but mousy. His fingers itched to brush the loose lock clinging to her damp flesh, but he tightened them on the straps of his pack instead. His weakness where she was concerned burned his throat like bitter acid. Hadn't he learned his lesson with Annette? Where was his restraint? He had never needed a woman, and he sure as hell couldn't afford to need this one.

Clay struggled to gather his thoughts, to concentrate on the task ahead. Even the slightest loss of concentration could prove hazardous, possibly lethal.

While Clay engaged in an internal battle, Meg spent every ounce of her energy on putting one foot in front of the other. Despite cool temperatures and deepening shadows, a thin film of perspiration glazed her skin. It seemed an eternity since they had left the dirt road to climb higher into the mountains. Meg felt as if she had been walking for days, not hours. Only pride kept her protesting body in motion. Clay Terhune would never hear a word of complaint from her, not even if it was her last one.

By late afternoon, every joint and muscle in her body screamed for rest, but there was no break. Clay moved inexorably ahead. When he stepped in front of Meg to take the lead, she had been grateful, since her weary body had started to lurch along in an uncoordinated and ungainly manner. While she kept telling herself Clay's opinion didn't matter, a shred of self-esteem made her want to hide her fatigue. She had promised she wouldn't slow him down, and she planned to keep her promise.

Once they left the mountains for a densely covered path, relief flooded Meg as they proceeded at a slower pace. Despite the thick vegetation he hacked from their path, Clay continued with only a momentary stop to discard his shirt.

Stripped to the waist, his bronze skin gleaming with sweat, he chopped at the vines and foliage with seeming ease. Although the broad pack hid much of his back, Meg admired what was visible. He really was a beautiful man. Tall and tanned, lithe and lean, he exuded a potent masculinity that both fascinated and frightened her. If his manners were better and his vocation more suitable, Clay Terhune would have been a real ladykiller, she decided. He certainly had all the physical attributes to make a woman's mouth water. Even a woman like Meg who never ogled any man.

As she kept her gaze on him, Meg found the contraction and relaxation of his biceps fascinating until discomfort eroded attraction.

As cool mountain air gave way to heat and humidity, her energy lagged. Insects buzzed around her continuously, but she lacked the strength to swat them away.

A dozen times, she opened her mouth to ask if they could rest, only to quickly snap it shut. Her promise kept her silent. If she asked for some concession, Clay Terhune would only too gladly remind her she should have stayed home. Recalling his rudeness, Meg felt more in control. Although the man was undeniably attractive in a purely masculine manner, he was insolent and insensitive.

Since they had left the Rover, his only conversation had been commands, barked like a drillmaster. His cold detachment and autocratic manner contradicted his physical appeal. He only had to open his mouth to remind her what he really was, she decided as she tramped behind him.

Frustrated and fatigued, and blaming both on Clay, Meg silently called him every nasty name she knew, and after eight years as a high school librarian, she knew a great many.

Despite his superb condition, Clay's arms ached with every swing of the machete. Exhaustion invaded every cell as he fought to continue. Since Dave's call, he hadn't gotten a decent night's rest, and worn and weary before returning to Puerto Rico, he was on the edge of collapse. Adrenaline and nerves were all that kept him going. That and the fact that Ted Andrews was in grave danger.

Sweat ran down his back, soaking the pack and his trousers. The heavy pack lay against his sore back like wet cement, its straps cutting into his damp flesh like ribbons of steel.

He wondered how his companion was faring but didn't waste energy checking. Long ago, hours maybe, he had said to let him know when she needed a break. So far, she hadn't, and he hadn't stopped because he didn't want her to realize how close to the edge he was. Showing weakness was something Clay avoided at all cost. Not under any circumstances, not to any person and certainly not to Meg Andrews, who had already, without the slightest effort, made inroads into his elaborate defenses, would he reveal his weariness.

He sucked in a deep breath and kept moving.

The rumbling of his belly forced Clay's attention to his watch. Less than three hours of daylight remained. Briefly, he debated whether to stop for supper or push on until darkness. Meg hadn't uttered even a single word of complaint, but she must have been as tired and hungry as he was, he decided.

When a small clearing appeared in the distance, he made his decision.

Meg fell into a graceless heap as soon as Clay stopped and announced supper. As her overworked muscles twitched, she wondered if she'd be able to get up again, but at the moment, she didn't care.

Without a glance in Meg's direction, Clay extracted a canteen from his pack and removed the other from his neck. After retrieving a bit of dried fruit, he handed her both food and water.

She started in surprise at the offering but accepted it. "Thank you," she murmured, gulping down the liquid and gnawing on the dehydrated apricots.

Clay studied her crimson face with a sinking sensation. They should have stopped much earlier. She should have insisted they stop, he decided. That she was overheated and exhausted was obvious. Didn't she have a particle of sense? "I'll fix some sandwiches," he told her in a voice as hard and flat as slate. "You better rest for a while. We've got a couple more hours of daylight, and I plan to take advantage of them."

The annoyance in his tone reached Meg, but the effort to respond proved too great. Instead, she shifted to her side, closed her eyes and was immediately asleep.

The abrupt dismissal stung, and Clay went about the task of preparing their meal with a heavy heart. Repeatedly, his glance returned to her huddled form. How had he ever thought her unappealing? With her glossy hair streaming from the tight bun and her face flushed with color, she seemed far too alluring for his peace of mind. Even her clothes, although rumpled and stained, suited her far better than the expensive but unflattering garb she had sported in San Juan—clothing that hid her womanly curves and a hairstyle that detracted from her natural beauty.

Why, he wondered, would any woman purposefully make herself unattractive? It didn't make sense, and yet he was sure that had been her aim. And she had succeeded until Mother Nature stripped away her disguise. But why the need for camouflage? Again, he wondered if the idea had been Dave Thornton's.

Remembering the FBI agent and his evident involvement with Meg Andrews provoked dismay. Clay's job was to rescue Ted, not get involved with his sister. If she wanted to look plain and drab, that was her business.

He turned his attention to the task at hand. When the sandwiches were ready, he glanced back at Meg, who remained sound asleep.

Despite his resolve to stay detached and distant, remorse quivered through Clay. In his work, he had to be hard, sometimes brutal, but he hadn't meant to make her suffer. He had driven his own body past its limits but had ignored her.

His only excuse was his need to conceal the effect she had on him, to show that her aloof manner didn't bother him because her opinion didn't matter. In his heart, he had expected, even wanted, her to ask for some concession, to grouse and complain. Then he could have reminded her of his prophesy that she would slow him down.

The childishness of his wishes weren't lost on Clay. He knew their source and understood them. A woman like Meg Andrews wouldn't spend five minutes in his company unless she was using him. Her cool indifference and snobbery reactivated insecurities born in childhood and intensified by Annette's betrayal. Meg's intimation that she was his boss had added insult to what he perceived as injury. Since then, he had determined to show her exactly who was in charge.

His efforts hadn't worked. Meg Andrews hadn't argued or whined. She had simply marched along in silence, never asking for any concession, which was something Clay understood.

Since leaving his small hometown, since running from the father who didn't want him, Clay had sworn never to let anyone make him feel inferior again. He had vowed to be independent, emotionally and physically. Until Annette, and after her, he had followed those strictures. He carefully avoided relationships. With the exceptions of Hank and Carlotta, he had no friends, or even close acquaintances. And, except for Ted and Dave, Clay had never relied on another human being or put himself in the debt of others.

Clay clearly understood his need to deny weakness, but he didn't understand Meg's. Her stubborn insistence that she go to Costa del Palma had irritated him. If she was the spoiled, pampered snob he believed, she should have jumped at the chance to spend a few days sunning and partying in San Juan. If she was a spoiled, pampered snob, she should have asked him to stop hours ago and begged and wheedled until he did. That she hadn't puzzled and troubled him. Meg Andrews grew more and more mysterious.

Again, he glanced at his watch, then reluctantly shook her awake. "We'll be moving out in fifteen minutes," he muttered before handing her a sandwich and striding away.

"Rude clod," she muttered in a drowsy voice. "Insensitive brute . . . overbearing, obnoxious beast," she said between bites. None of her observations explained why her dreams had been filled with a tall, lean stranger with dark hair and eyes of gold.

Only the thud of boot against ground disturbed the uneasy silence. Before leaving the clearing, Clay had wordlessly extracted the boots and handed them to Meg. Accepting them annoyed her; it was about the same as admitting she'd been wrong, but she put them on her weary feet without comment.

Although the sun was sinking, the heat seemed unmerciful. Meg tried to picture her neat cottage overlooking Lake Erie but the vision of cool, fresh water didn't help. It only made her more miserable and much thirstier.

Her leg muscles twitched in protest as she followed Clay up yet another rise. Under the small backpack, her narrow shoulders slumped. There wasn't a single place in her body that didn't ache or burn or throb.

How Clay maintained such a brutal pace, she couldn't fathom, especially since he toted most of their supplies on his broad back. Besides, she thought, his arms should have been exhausted from chopping through the dense foliage clogging their pace.

He simply wasn't human, Meg thought before she recalled Hank's comment that Clay badly needed a vacation. On the heels of that memory came an image of Clay's heavily shadowed and red-rimmed eyes when he had handed her the sandwich. Remorse started to squeeze her heart before she routed it.

Men like Clay Terhune didn't deserve sympathy. After all, he'd taken this job to make money, not out of any concern for humanity or a wish to be helpful. Still, Meg took comfort in knowing the man wasn't as invincible as he tried to appear.

She reached for her canteen and found it empty. Dismay and envy seized her as she saw a similar vessel bouncing enticingly against Clay's hip. She wished he would offer her some but knew how unlikely that was. As unlikely as her asking for it.

Her attention moved to his lean flanks and muscular legs. With each fluid stride, his muscles worked effortlessly. No matter how callous or rude, the man truly was a magnificent specimen, one no woman could ignore despite her experiences or fears. Superbly formed and in peak condition, Clay was as sleek and supple as a jungle cat and probably, Meg decided, just as lethal. He certainly wasn't the sort of a man to make a woman, especially one like Meg, comfortable or complacent.

He was too intensely male, too patently virile. Strength emanated from him like a physical aura. That aura seemed to reach out to Meg, to entice her soul despite the protest of her mind.

As the aura around Clay became a dense, swirling fog, Meg's steps faltered and she tripped over a small rock, plowing into Clay.

Unprepared for the impact, he dropped the machete and staggered forward a few feet before regaining his balance. Swearing under his breath, he spun around and grabbed Meg's arm.

Embarrassed and confused, she ducked her spinning head. "Sorry," she mumbled in a voice that seemed to come from far away. "I guess I wasn't watching where I was going."

"I guess not," he shot back.

Damp strands of hair clung to her neck while grime streaked her face and sweat-soaked clothes. The color in her face had heightened to an unnatural flush while, beneath her pack, her shoulders slumped. Her earlier fatigue had rapidly evolved into dangerous exhaustion. "Haven't you been drinking water?" he said in a voice laced with rage at himself. Despite his need to maintain professional distance, Clay knew Meg Andrews was his responsibility.

A ragged sigh escaped him. His hard-won and firmly held control hadn't yet crumbled, but it definitely suffered cracks. Into those tiny fissures seeped rivulets of need and desire that Clay, despite his ongoing effort, couldn't seem to stem. When he spoke again, his voice, in agitation, rose a fraction. "You can't afford to get dehydrated or overheated. If you pass out, what am I supposed to do? Carry you the rest of the way?" Guilt and fatigue sharpened his tone.

Clay's words drifted to Meg through a thick fog of incoherence. She heard his voice, sharp as a razor, but didn't comprehend the words. The weakness in her legs seemed to rise through her body like floodwater against a straining dam. Although Meg fought the rising tide, it continued unabated. She opened her mouth but no sound emerged.

As soon as Clay saw the unnatural color drain from her face, he reached out with his free hand, but he was too late. Before his stunned gaze, Meg crumpled to the ground.

Clay shrugged out of his pack, tossed the gun over his shoulder and dropped to his knees. "Meg...Meg...can you hear me?" In his agitation, Clay didn't notice that for the first time, he had called her by her given name.

His big hands gently clasped her slim shoulders. The cinnamon lashes resting against her ashen cheeks didn't even flutter in response.

"Meg...can you hear me?" His voice was gruff, demanding...frightened.

But Meg, lost in the fog, made no reply.

* * *

Meg awoke slowly. As consciousness returned to her, a vague wariness ensued. Something was wrong, but she couldn't recall exactly what. As she squinted into the darkness, a thousand hammers banging inside her skull made focusing on her surroundings impossible.

"Finally awake, I see." Relief underscored each word. For what seemed like an eternity but had only been a couple of hours, Clay had stood vigil over Meg, wondering and worrying. As he knelt beside her, his callused fingertips gently pushed back her lids and he stared into each eye.

"What are you doing?" Meg managed to choke out of her arid throat. She twisted her head to resist him but the hammers increased their pounding to double-time.

He settled back on his haunches. "You passed out, probably from heat exhaustion." He hoped nothing worse ailed her. As he laid one palm against the soft silk of her cheek, he again scanned her face. The initial grayness had given way to mere pallor but her gaze remained cloudy. Anxiety knotted his insides. "How do you feel?" he asked in a whisper.

The rough hand grazing her skin was surprisingly gentle, his soft voice unexpectedly concerned. A curtain of fatigue and uncertainty floated around Meg. She closed her eyes as responding proved too great an effort.

"Meg, don't go back to sleep yet." His tone became urgent. "C'mon, sweetheart. Open those big eyes for me."

His softly spoken endearment permeated her befuddled mind. Was that really Clay Terhune talking to her, or was it a dream? With effort, she lifted her weighted lids and stared into his tiger eyes. Seeing the apprehension in them made her more baffled.

Where was the gruff stranger who made no secret of his contempt? What had happened to the hardened mercenary who cared for nothing beyond money?

"I'm so groggy," she mumbled, as if to explain her doubts. Meg looked past Clay, unable to face his intense gaze, unprepared to interpret the uncustomary warmth glowing in it. "Where are we?"

"In a cave," he replied, withdrawing his hand and settling back on his haunches. "I brought you here after you fainted." Guilt again gripped him as he gestured around the stone cavern. "It's the best I could do, better than the tent, I thought." Certainty that Meg Andrews never made do with such primitive conditions put regret and dismay into his words. Even if he hadn't pushed her too hard, they would've camped out tonight, used the tents he had carried. Many nights Clay had found less comfort, but he knew Meg Andrews couldn't say the same.

"It's fine," she mumbled, then shifted to sit up until a wave of dizzying pain forced her back. When Clay replaced his comforting hand on her brow and brushed back the loose curls there, his touch permeated the swirl of anguish threatening to again carry her off. Meg let her lids drift shut while she enjoyed the reassuring brush of his fingers. Surprising, she thought, how such a strong, capable hand could bring such solace. In the dim cave, with Clay beside her, Meg forgot her fears.

"You took a bad tumble. On the top of the heat exhaustion, I imagine it's taken a toll," he murmured. "Maybe a couple of aspirin would help."

"Yes," she agreed, as she licked her parched lips. "And water, please."

"Of course."

Within moments, he was carefully lifting her head and slipping two small pills between her lips. When a cup was pressed to her mouth, Meg swallowed gratefully. After she had her fill, Clay eased her back into the makeshift bed.

"You're still very warm," he murmured. "I should probably rinse you off again."

Since her flesh flamed with cloying heat, his suggestion sounded like heaven. Still lost in hazy semiconsciousness, Meg didn't take in the complete implication of his statement.

While Clay dampened a cloth, her eyes remained shut but flew open as he started to pull back the covers. Her fingers clutched at the edge of the blanket.

Clay paused, surprised at her reaction and stung by the consternation in her expression. "I've already seen everything, Miss Andrews. You were burning up. I had to rinse you off to keep your temperature from getting dangerously high." He gritted his teeth. "I'm sorry if it embarrasses you, but there's no one else here to do it." Even to his own ears, he sounded as defensive as a kid caught with his hand in the cookie jar. He could only be grateful Meg shuttered her eyes before embarrassed color stained his cheeks.

"Heat exhaustion can be very serious," he said in a cool, clipped tone that masked his inner turmoil. "If your fever escalates, I've got no way to get a doctor or medicine." Clay saw Meg bite her lower lip as if anticipating some horrendous torment, and the chill of rejection stung him. "I know I'm not the person you'd choose to do this if it could be avoided, but it is necessary, and unfortunately for both of us, I'm the only one around."

The ice in his tone froze Meg's explanation on her lips, not that she knew how to explain her trepidation without uncovering very private demons. An innate sense of modesty combined with ugly experience made her hypersensitive about revealing her body. But she couldn't explain any of that to Clay Terhune, not the rugged warrior or the concerned caregiver.

When she looked at him again, she didn't know which man sat beside her, but she knew neither would do her any harm. "Okay," she mumbled as she released her hold on the covers and shut her eyes. For some reason she didn't care to examine, she knew Clay was as trustworthy as Carlotta had claimed.

Carefully and judiciously, Clay eased back the blankets. A muscle worked in his jaw as her lush body was exposed to view. Earlier, when she had lain unconscious, he had felt the quickening in his loins and been relieved she couldn't see the desire scorching his cheeks or feel the tremors of need shaking his hands. Only a heathen would lust for an insensible woman. And, though Clay was no saint, he wasn't completely lost to propriety, either.

A quick glance at her face reassured him. As long as her eyes stayed shut, he might mask the longing still haunting him.

With gentle, efficient strokes, he rinsed her from head to toe. By the time he finished, hot claws of desire tore at him, and so did self-reproach. How could he want her when she so clearly saw him as beneath her? Only grim necessity had forced her to accede to his ministrations, ministrations that appalled her but made him hard with need.

A lengthy period of celibacy might have made many men react so strongly but, for Clay, denial had been a way of life. But that fact didn't explain his current condition. If Meg opened her eyes, there was no way he could hide his reaction. Before temptation overrode common sense, he tucked the covers around her and turned away.

To Meg, Clay's manner seemed efficient and undemanding, but that didn't stop unfamiliar warmth from stealing through her. Although she hadn't completely relaxed, she hadn't found the experience as arduous as she had feared. Quite the opposite, she decided as she opened her eyes in time to see Clay, a strained expression on his handsome face, glance over his shoulder at her. Before she assessed his attitude, he again averted his face.

"Thank you," she whispered in a small, tremulous voice.

"No problem," he muttered. After discarding the damp cloth, he moved into the deep shadows to cloak his lingering arousal.

Shivers, more from his withdrawal than from cold, rippled through her.

"Are you cold?" Clay asked. "Do you want another blanket?"

"Not really."

Ensconced in the fluffy sleeping bag, Meg looked very vulnerable and impossibly innocent. The feeling of pure male protectiveness swamped Clay. This time, however, he didn't succeed in vanquishing it. Instead, the rogue emotion took charge before he could muster his defenses.

At the same time, an alien neediness invaded his unprotected flank and Clay found himself mesmerized by Meg.

Earlier, when he had settled her in the cave, Clay released her tight bun to free a mass of shoulder-length waves. In the flickering light of the fire, her auburn tresses gleamed like polished copper. Looking at her hair now, he remembered how it had slithered between his rough fingers like the finest silk, felt as sensuous as her satin skin beneath his hands. The banked coals of yearning warming his belly flared to flame at the sight of her.

He sighed raggedly. Harboring such renegade feelings could easily spell disaster but neither danger nor dismay proved an effective barrier. His own lectures on control didn't help, either. For the first time in years, emotions long denied were surfacing with a vengeance, and Clay felt powerless in the face of the onslaught.

Giving Meg the careful study he could never have managed with her sea-blue gaze on him, Clay wondered what about this particular woman moved him. As pretty as she was, despite her masquerade, he had seen more beautiful women. No, he decided, it wasn't her looks or her charm.

A humorless smile jerked at his mouth. Meg Andrews hadn't used charm on him. Nor had she used friendliness. Up until a short time ago, he hadn't figured her to be anything but a pampered snob. Yet, even while he had maintained a brutal pace, she hadn't murmured a word of complaint. Not about the pace, the heat, the humidity, the insects or his ill humor. She hadn't whined or pouted when he ignored her. Nor did she seem to blame him for her illness.

When most women, most men, would have complained bitterly and insisted on stopping, she kept going. Only falling in a dead faint had stopped her. Maybe he had been wrong about her. Maybe both her appearance and manner were affectations, he thought. Maybe she was more like her brother than he'd originally figured, which only added to his dilemma. Dismissing a drab, bossy snob was easy. Dismissing a tender yet gutsy beauty was not.

Clay let his head fall back against the wall as uncertainty and weariness filled him. He tried to remind himself that by this time tomorrow, they'd be at Juan's house where the presence of others would surely mute her growing appeal— but his heart and soul were unconvinced. The woman sleeping so peacefully only a few feet away was completely different from the one he had met in Hank's cantina.

Clay blinked in surprise. Had he met her only a day earlier? It seemed as if he'd known her forever, as if she'd been a part of his life since its beginning.

Because their acquaintance was so brief, he tried to explain away his rapidly growing attraction by chalking it up to stress and impending danger. When a man and woman were thrown together as he and Meg were, getting chemistry confused with deeper emotion was all too common. Clay knew firsthand how easy it was to mistake infatuation for love, and how dangerous.

He closed his eyes in an effort to shut out the sight of her, but the sound of her deep, rhythmic breathing seemed to echo in the dim cavern. Reverberating need and residual desire kept his weary body and troubled mind from enjoying the healing balm of sleep for a long time.

Chapter 4

Hours later, incoherent mumbling had Clay on his feet and at Meg's side. As she thrashed in the tangle of bedding, she cried out.

His hands gently grasped her arms as he murmured, "Meg, wake up. You're having a bad dream."

Her eyes flew open in alarm, and she looked up at him, uncertainty darkening her gaze.

"You must have been dreaming." He kept his tone soft and soothing. Automatically, as if by habit, his hand went to stroke her brow.

"Yes," she agreed. Although, as always, the dream was hazy. It was familiar, too familiar. Her heart raced with a terror expanding inside her like a balloon, threatening to drive the air from her lungs, threatening to deflate her hard-won confidence. She focused her attention on Clay's tender expression, using it as an anchor, a touchstone. Although she barely knew him, Meg trusted Clay.

Clay recognized her panic and hurried to reassure her. "I'm not surprised you had a bad dream. Lots of people do when they're sick or hurt."

A shuddering sigh left her. Since she couldn't tell him the real source of her demons, she nodded in agreement. "You're probably right." Her tongue darted out to moisten her dry lips.

"Would you like a drink of water?" he asked. "Maybe a couple more aspirin?"

"Yes, thank you."

Clay retrieved the canteen and held it to her lips while slipping his free hand behind her head for support. Meg started to sit up but winced in pain that not only drove her back but supplanted her fear.

"The aspirin will help," he assured her as he tucked the blankets around her.

"Thank you," Meg murmured. "I'm sorry to be so much trouble. I know I'm slowing you down, just like you said I would." The admission tasted like bitter gall but Meg knew she had been wrong. She wasn't a help. She was a hindrance, one that might hamper Clay's efforts and put both him and Ted in greater jeopardy.

Fresh remorse tore at his soul. "We had to stop for the night, anyhow. If we have to stay here tomorrow, another day won't make that much difference."

In the flickering firelight, the shadows beneath her turquoise eyes appeared almost black. Suddenly Clay felt like a monster for misjudging her, pushing her. He was the one who was sorry.

Meg saw tension tighten his face and closed her eyes against the sudden sting of tears. Pain, fatigue and despair sapped her spirit. One lone tear trickled out before disappearing in her hair. She pressed her lids together more tightly but another escaped, and another, until a steady stream ensued.

Clay's self-loathing increased with each droplet, and he swore under his breath.

"I'm sorry," Meg repeated. "I hardly ever cry. I don't know what's wrong with me." Hastily, she swiped at the moisture.

With a sigh of surrender, Clay drew her into the shelter of his embrace, soothing her with unintelligible murmurings and brushing the dampness from her face. "I know what's wrong with you," he muttered. "You're hurt, exhausted, thousands of miles from home, alone with a selfish bastard who hasn't given a moment's thought to your comfort. You've got every right to cry, Meg. Every right in the world."

She twisted so she could see his face. The remorse there, and in his deep voice, stunned her. Perhaps he was a man without a country, but he wasn't without compassion. Even as she settled back into the reassuring warmth of his arms, doubt danced on the fringes of her mind. Logic told her not to trust a man like Clay Terhune, but her soul shouted surrender. With him and him alone, her anxieties and apprehension melted away.

Perhaps she was wrong to take comfort from him. Perhaps she was wrong to trust a virtual stranger, but she didn't want to think so. In his arms, she didn't want to think at all.

"It's okay, Meg. Everything will be okay," he whispered as he stroked her silken hair. Clay knew he spoke the words as much for himself as for her.

"I really am sorry," she said in a firmer voice. "I honestly thought I could keep up. I take the boys on lots of hikes."

"Boys?" he asked in confusion.

"Yes, my nephews. My brother's sons. They're twins. Josh and Jake."

He'd forgotten Ted Andrews's kids. Hell, he'd forgotten Ted. With Meg's soft body cushioning his hard one, he forgot everything but her. He cleared his throat. "Where are they now?"

"With their grandparents," she replied. "With Cathy's parents. They live in Florida."

"Cathy?" As lost as he felt, Clay was certain Meg had never mentioned this Cathy.

A tremulous breath left her. "Cathy was Ted's wife and my best friend. She got leukemia several years ago." Meg swallowed hard before continuing in a hoarse whisper that barely masked old pain. "That's when I went to live with them, or at least in the guest cottage. My parents left their property to both of us, but since my brother had a family, I thought he should have the house and I could use the cottage weekends and summers. Then Cathy got sick and, well, she needed help with the kids."

Her reference to a guest house reminded Clay of the gulf between them, of the fact that they came from two different worlds. Worlds so far apart that they might as well be from different planets. "So you came back to help her."

"Yes, and when . . . when she died, I stayed on to help Ted."

"So you take care of your brother's responsibilities while he wanders the globe." Bitterness, the offspring of frustration, laced his tone. What Meg Andrews did was none of his business, but because she did it in a place totally unavailable to him, fury seized him.

Meg bristled at the open disapproval. Since Ted's protracted absences gave her an excuse not to return to the city, Meg had never minded. "He isn't gone that much," she murmured.

"What about his kids? Isn't it hard on them being without their mother and father?"

"They're used to me," Meg replied. "We get along very well."

"They're lucky, then," he whispered. Envy replaced anger. "Some kids don't have anybody."

Meg shifted so she could see his face better, but his carefully schooled features revealed nothing. "Did you . . . lose your parents?"

Clay's jaw tightened. "You could say that."

Sensing an indirect approach might elicit more information, Meg said, "My parents were killed in a car accident a couple of months after I graduated from college. I still miss them terribly. We were very close, but I was lucky to have my brother and Cathy."

"Yes, you were lucky," Clay agreed.

Meg sighed. "You don't have brothers or sisters?"

"I've got no one," he muttered.

"Your parents are gone?"

Clay sucked in a long breath. "My mother died when I was little. I don't really remember her." Both his expression and tone remained guarded. His childhood was something Clay preferred to forget.

"That must have been difficult for both you and your dad. Raising a child alone is a difficult job," she said with sympathy.

"Right. It's a job some people don't want."

Tension invaded his lean body. Meg felt it immediately, and although she knew Clay wouldn't welcome prying, she pressed ahead.

"You and your dad weren't close?"

"No."

The single-word reply should have stopped her. If not that, common sense might have intervened. After all, she wasn't a fool. She knew she was playing with fire and likely to burn them both if she wasn't careful.

"You must have been lonely," she whispered.

Clay gritted his teeth to keep from saying he still was, he just hadn't had sense enough to realize it until she came into his life. His childhood, a hellish nightmare, was something he never discussed. Shame and pain and yearning for things he couldn't have were the only memories of his father's house. "I survived," he mumbled.

"Did you have other relatives in town?"

"None that would recognize us." He released her and moved away, though only a few feet. "My father was the town drunk. He wasn't sober any longer than strictly necessary, and he owed everyone in the county, I guess. Anyhow, that's how it seemed. My mother's folks lived nearby, but they never had anything to do with us and I couldn't blame them." Clay paused. The uncharacteristic confession appalled him but when he saw nothing but understanding on Meg's sweet face, he relaxed. "I had a few guys I ran with. You couldn't really call them friends. They weren't very nice guys, but then I wasn't very nice, either." His mouth twitched. "But I guess that hardly surprises you. I've been a real bastard, but you haven't uttered a word of complaint."

In an effort to ease the building tension, Meg grinned. "It's a good thing you don't read minds. I've thought some not very nice things." Her mouth flattened. "And I haven't been exactly friendly." She paused a moment before admitting the truth. "I'm usually not so stubborn or bossy, though I'm sure some of my former students would disagree."

"Students?" Surprise underscored the query.

"Yes, I used to be a high school librarian. Now I work part-time at our community library."

"I see," Clay mumbled—but he didn't. A librarian. That surprised him. Not that she hadn't looked the part when they had first met, but because he'd figured she had never worked a day in her life, not with her privileged background. Meg Andrews, it seemed, had as many facets as a precious stone but studying them would be far more intriguing.

When he said nothing more, Meg went on with her earlier explanation. "Anyhow, I have been rather, uh, unpleasant." Uncertainty held her tongue. Maybe dropping the facade she'd assumed in San Juan wasn't wise, but when Clay took her hand, her worry dissolved.

"Not unpleasant," he assured her. "Maybe not friendly, but that's probably my fault. I was rude right from the start and haven't done much since to make you feel friendly toward me. If anyone is sorry, it's me. Sorry for being rude and thoughtless. Sorry for not taking better care of you.''

''You've been very kind to me since I fainted.''

He squeezed her hand. ''It's my fault you got sick, Meg. I should've made sure you were okay. I should've made camp where we ate.'' He shoved his free hand through his hair. ''There's no excuse except I don't spend much time with women, especially ladies, and I guess I've forgotten how to treat one.''

Meg knew that wasn't true. She'd seen him treat Carlotta with respect, even deference, but she didn't say so. Instead, she focused on Hank's observations. ''Hank said you don't trust women,'' she began, then stopped as tension again stiffened his body.

Clay released her hand. ''Like I told you in the cantina, you can't believe everything Hank says.'' Clay edged back. ''Go back to sleep, Meg. You need rest.''

A chill stole over her at his abrupt withdrawal. She longed to comfort him but knew he wouldn't appreciate the gesture. A man like Clay Terhune didn't often share confidences, she was sure, or reveal any sort of insecurity. Because he had spoken of his unhappy childhood with her, she knew he was probably regretting his lapse. Pressing him for details on his attitude toward women wouldn't be wise. Besides, Meg understood the need for privacy. She understood it all too well.

Before closing her eyes, she murmured a good-night but got no reply.

Eventually an uneasy sleep claimed Meg, as did the nightmare. Clay, equally restless, jerked awake as soon as her terrified scream echoed in the rocky cavern. In one motion, he was out of the sleeping bag and on his feet. His heart raced with dread as he again knelt beside her thrashing body. Her whimpers shredded the control he had only just begun to reassert.

"Meg, Meg, sweetheart...wake up. It's Clay. I'm here," he called as he gently shook her.

The resonant baritone broke through her anguish. Meg gripped his forearms as she quit struggling. "Clay?" she whispered.

"Yes, Meg. I'm here. You're safe," he assured her. "You must've had another nightmare."

She nodded in agreement but didn't say it was the same nightmare, one that had plagued her for years. Instead, her fingers tightened on his bare flesh. His heat and hardness calmed her fears. For the moment, his strength meant protection and his nearness, security.

When her nails dug into him, Clay bit hard on his lower lip but didn't flinch. He saw the alarm shimmering in her gaze. She didn't have to tell him that this dream had been much worse than her previous one. The terror was etched in her fine features. Clay gently drew her to him and stroked her back through the blanket.

"Everything will be fine, Meg. In a few days, your brother will be safe and you'll both be on your way home." Speaking the words made his throat raw. He didn't want to think about never seeing her again. "I know you're worried and tired, but everything will be okay."

Meg stiffened when she realized that Clay quite naturally misinterpreted her anxiety. She swallowed back the truth. If he knew, how would he react? With pity or condemnation? Meg didn't think she wanted to know, so she merely agreed.

"I know," she whispered as she let her head fall against his broad shoulder and pressed closer. While she was in his arms, she felt safe and secure.

With only the sleeping bag as a barrier, Clay rapidly became aware of Meg's soft breasts pressing against the hard wall of his chest in a most disconcerting manner. He would have released her except for the tremors rippling through her. Instead, he struggled to keep his embrace light and undemanding despite the white-hot need scalding his veins. Even as the depth of his response alarmed him, he cradled

Meg like a precious doll and crooned encouragement into
her ear. She needed reassurance and comfort, and he was
powerless to deny her.

After a time, her shaking ceased. Clay eased back a bit.
"How are you feeling?" he asked.

"Okay," she mumbled against his throat. As long as he
held her, she wasn't afraid. Her hands tightened on him.

Her warm, moist breath sent prickles of awareness jolt-
ing along his nerve fibers. His blood flowed like molten lava
through his veins as heat seared him, yet a particle of sense
intervened. "Then I guess we ought to get some more sleep."
If he didn't move away soon, she was sure to notice the extend of his arousal. Dull color crept into his cheeks as he
wondered how he'd explain his adolescent reaction.

At Clay's suggestion, panic darted through her. She didn't
want to be left alone with only ugly memories for company. She wanted Clay to hold her, protect her, reassure her.
It no longer mattered what his occupation was. Meg knew
him to be a man of tenderness and compassion; she knew
him to be caring and kind. He was a decent man, a strong
man, and she wanted him with her. She lifted her head and
let him see the apprehension she had fought so long and so
hard to suppress.

Clay sucked in a long breath. If he had a shred of sense,
a particle of self-preservation, he'd ignore the anguish in her
turquoise eyes and go back to his own bed where he might
have a chance of survival. But her next words ended any
hope of that.

"Please, Clay...please don't leave me. I'm so scared."
Her voice quavered so badly that she hardly recognized it.
Neither did she recognize the plea. She had never admitted
her fear to anyone but Cathy.

Her plea was his complete undoing. If he'd ever had any
hope of escaping unscathed, he lost it when he looked into
her eyes. A man could get lost there, he thought. "I'll hold
you until you get back to sleep," he promised. Doing so
without revealing the desire clawing at his insides would be

difficult but not impossible. He was usually good at hiding his feelings. The problem was, with Meg, he had more feelings than ever before.

A month ago, a week ago, even a day ago, such an offer would have frightened Meg worse than her nightmare, but not now. Not with Clay. The tenderness in his touch made her forget the potent power of him. Or maybe she just accepted both as part of him. All she knew for sure was that she trusted Clay as she did no man except her brother. On the heels of that thought came the realization of how deep her emotions regarding this man were becoming.

She tore her gaze away from him before he noticed her inner turmoil. Worn and weary, she swept the muddled ideas from her head. When she felt better, more in control, she would examine these feelings. Then maybe she could harness them.

Feeling somewhat relieved, she let her eyelids droop shut and sagged against Clay. Soon her breath was deep and even.

A rueful smile curved Clay's usually hard mouth. He wasn't sure whether to be grateful or annoyed by her patent trust. Something in her manner suggested she didn't give trust easily, which increased Clay's contentment. Meg Andrews sparked something warm and wonderful inside him, something far more powerful and profound than lust. Something he feared and fought, but to no avail.

As his lips brushed her soft curls, he cursed his weakness. Meg Andrews was out of his reach despite the reckless hope his heart refused to relinquish. When the mission was over, she'd go home, back to her safe, secure, sunny world... back to her long-distance relationship with Dave Thornton.

A frown settled over Clay's face. Funny how Thornton had never mentioned Meg when he spoke about her brother. Not that he and Thornton talked that often. Clay knew almost nothing about Dave's personal life, nor had he known anything about Ted's. He hadn't known he was married, or that his wife had died, so why should Thornton discuss his relationship with Meg?

A ragged sigh escaped him. No, he couldn't expect personal information from Dave, not when he so carefully guarded his own privacy. All the same, Clay was consumed by curiosity and, if he were honest, jealousy.

Dave and Meg would make one of those perfect couples, which made him wonder again why Thornton had let her go alone to Puerto Rico, and why there wasn't a ring on her hand.

Clay peered through the deep shadows to study Meg. He'd promised to hold her until she fell asleep, but he wasn't ready to relinquish the pleasure of having her in his arms, not when they had such a short time together. Not when he needed to store up memories for a cold, lonely future.

He buried his face in the heavy fall of hair curling around her neck even as he called himself every sort of fool for his stupidity. When she went home, she might be another man's, but for a few hours in the inky night, she was his.

A shiver rippled through Clay as goose bumps broke out over his skin. Despite the pleasantly warm weight draped over his lower body, he felt cold, but he didn't move. Not until the weight shifted. Then his eyes snapped open.

The first thing he saw was Meg's copper hair strewn across his bare chest. His breath caught in his throat. He couldn't see her features clearly, but he knew she was still asleep and unaware of his body's purely male response to her. He closed his eyes and tried to relax, but each breath pushed his muscular chest against her lush breasts. Even with her lower body encased in the sleeping bag, he was very aware of soft thighs brushing his lean ones. He was also aware of the aching emptiness deep in his soul, an emptiness requiring more than sex to fill, an emptiness echoing in the vacant chambers of his heart.

Desire dispelled the last traces of slumber as he struggled to extricate his body without waking Meg. When she shifted again, he couldn't stop the low moan that rumbled out of his chest.

"Clay..."

Her soft, sultry voice, thick with sleep, made him tremble with suppressed longing. Just that one word, his name on her full lips, provoked a flood of feelings. Yearning, need, tenderness—things he had long dismissed as weak and foolish—filled his heart and soul. In the solitary life he had chosen, emotions weren't permitted. At least, he hadn't permitted them until he met Meg and found they seeped in under his barriers.

Over their brief acquaintance, she had shown no real signs of being spoiled and vain like Annette. And she had apologized for not being friendly. A soft smile lifted his lips. He couldn't remember another soul ever apologizing to him for anything.

No, Meg wasn't like Annette. He felt sure of that, but she was from a separate world, one dramatically different from his own. For a space in time, their lives had collided, but soon, too soon, they had to go back to their own orbits. As much as Meg attracted and entranced him, Clay knew they had no future and very little present.

Despair choked him. The hopes and dreams of his boyhood hadn't died, but merely withered. Under Meg's warmth, they again flourished, growing larger and larger until, like sunflowers in summer, they stood tall and straight.

He sucked in a deep, steadying breath before responding. "Sorry I woke you. I guess we both fell asleep and got tangled up." He should have returned to his bed the second she'd fallen asleep. But, where Meg was concerned, his self-control was nil. He levered his hips away from her.

Meg's lashes fluttered against her cheeks. "Mmm..."

"I guess I ought to get back to my bed."

"Mmm..."

He glanced at her and wondered if she'd already fallen back to sleep. His discomfort was becoming acute. Even if he did escape, he wasn't likely to sleep anytime soon.

"Meg..." His voice was a low groan.

The dark copper lashes opened a crack. "What?" she asked in the same seductive whisper that had earlier mesmerized him. Slowly, as the layers of slumber peeled away, she became aware of the heat and hardness emanating from the body tangled with hers. Drowsy, Meg was weakened by illness and fatigue, and not even fear permeated the cocoon of security and serenity ensconcing her. In the semidarkness, Clay's eyes glowed like warm honey, and Meg found his attention just as sweet and soothing. When he exhaled sharply, his warm breath fanned her face, sensitizing her flesh and eliciting tingling awareness. Her mouth, only inches from his, opened as if of its own volition and her tongue darted out to trace her lips.

Clay stared at her mouth as the coil of desire in his belly wound tighter and tighter until it became a physical pain, an ache that couldn't be denied and one he dared not quench. But longing and emptiness made a powerful one-two punch, one that left Clay reeling.

Meg, cast adrift in the hazy world where dreams and reality mesh, reacted instinctively to Clay's heat and hardness. Her arms snaked around his neck and her lips hovered over his. Beneath her touch, his flesh damped and his pulse pounded.

"Meg, do you know what you're doing?" he asked in a rough whisper. When she made no reply, he shook his head. "This is a mistake," he muttered, as much to himself as to her. "But I'm no saint. I'm a man. If you don't want me to kiss you, you'd better move."

Sweet, fierce desire provoked Meg. Dazed by newfound yearning, she leaned forward to brush her lips over his but for Clay, whose restraint was shattered, it wasn't nearly enough. His hands cupped her head, but the kiss he delivered was like a summer breeze, light and undemanding, warm and gentle.

Her mouth trembled, or perhaps it was his. Clay didn't know and he didn't care. With infinite tenderness, he stroked her bare back while his tongue traced her lips as if to chart them for further exploration. When her mouth again opened, his tongue darted inside to taste the sweet, hot moisture of her mouth. Heat turned his blood to liquid fire as his mouth mimicked what his body craved. Her kisses were sweeter than honey, more intoxicating than champagne. Clay savored each one and hungered for more.

Lost in sensation and drugged by the richness of his kisses, Meg drifted away from reality. As the pressure of his mouth increased, so did her response. Her slender arms clung to his broad shoulders while her breasts flattened against the unforgiving wall of his chest. His warmth reassured her. His touch relaxed her.

When Clay shrugged the sleeping bag down past her hips, she shifted to ease the task. Torrents of pent-up desire buffeted her. Pelted by need, she clung to Clay. If she was dreaming, she hoped she never woke up. The relentless yearning formed a fog from which she didn't care to escape.

Her mouth grazed the hollow of his neck before trailing a string of kisses over his stubbled jaw. His dense whiskers tickled her lips in a surprisingly sensuous way. From somewhere deep inside her, a moan of longing emerged.

Arousal pounded through Clay like a jackhammer. He tried to tell himself to slow down, back off, but he couldn't. He wanted Meg beyond all sense, all logic. And if her ardent attention was any gauge, she wanted him, as well.

For one fleeting moment, Clay thought of all the reasons he should get up and walk away, then her mouth recaptured his in a deep kiss that drove rationality to the farthest recesses of his brain.

While their mouths clung, Clay rolled Meg to her back and straddled her hips. He carefully braced his weight on his forearms and as he lifted her into his arms, his arousal prodded her. "I want you, Meg," he muttered in a voice hoarse with passion.

As soon as she felt his hardness, Meg froze. Then as he began to kiss her bare breasts, her body jerked spasmodically. As the haze of passion lifted and panic replaced it, she forgot who held her, and her euphoric dream turned into the familiar nightmare. Frantic, Meg pushed against Clay. Like a trapped animal, she fought instinctively and with every weapon at her disposal.

Shock immobilized Clay as the sweetly responsive woman in his arms became a snarling wildcat. Her nails scored his chest, her body bucked and her legs kicked out so quickly and ferociously that Clay, unwilling to fight back for fear of hurting her, took several battering blows before he could roll away. Even so, she kept kicking and hitting him until he was out of range.

"Let me go. . . leave me alone," she cried in a voice filled with terror and misery.

Her panic and anguish tore at his heart. Never in his life had he provoked such a violent response in any woman. Her reaction wounded him in a way her blows never could.

Clay prided himself on control, and in his limited liaisons with the opposite sex, he had always assured his partner's comfort along with her pleasure. Meg's attack baffled him. One minute she had loved him so well and the next . . . He shook his head. Maybe being touched by a man like him repelled her. Or maybe she had remembered Dave, although Clay couldn't see how either could provoke such a brutal resistance. *No* would have sufficed.

His fingers touched his sore cheek. One particularly harsh blow had caught him right beneath the eye. From the way it felt, it was sure to produce a shiner.

In the uncomfortable silence, Meg curled into a tight ball beneath the covers, her back to him.

Clay's gaze moved over her and fresh remorse hounded him. "I'm sorry," he muttered. "I thought. . . I made a mistake." A big one, he decided as his insides coalesced into a sinking mass of disgust and dismay. He had to admit she'd been half asleep while he'd been wide awake. He'd known exactly what he was doing but had honestly thought she did, too. When he got no response, he went on. "I honestly didn't mean for things to get out of hand." Self-reproach put an edge in his tone. Seeing her hunched form made him feel like a schoolyard bully picking on a smaller child. "You're under my protection, so there's no excuse. I know I may not seem a particularly moral man to you, but I wouldn't have done anything you didn't want, which doesn't excuse my touching you in the first place. I had no right."

Meg's own misery and humiliation were so great that she scarcely heard Clay's words. There was no sense in trying to explain her behavior, or any in admitting the truth. To do so would complicate their situation beyond measure and not accomplish a thing. No man could understand her anguish.

Clay ground his teeth. No response, but what did he expect? His presence must sicken her. Whatever her reasons, she didn't want him touching her, and that was her prerogative. "Go back to sleep, Meg. You have nothing to fear. Not from me." He stumbled to his feet and into the inky night without a backward glance.

Meg observed his departure with disappointment and dejection. For a time she had responded to his intimacies, had even initiated some. Right up until Clay loomed over her, his male body reacting to the passion binding them, she had forgotten her fears. Then, abruptly, the man towering over her had been not Clay but a memory.

Hot tears spilled from her eyes as she wondered if she had hurt him. Her actions had been feral and fervid, yet he hadn't fought back. He had even taken the blame himself when he had done nothing but pleasure and treasure her. He had mistakenly assumed she didn't want him, and she hadn't had enough courage to admit the truth. A truth she was certain would drive him away as effectively as her attack.

Her heart and soul in chaos, Meg rolled over and closed her eyes. Just as she was getting to know the depth of Clay Terhune, Meg had virtually assured that he'd never let her close again.

Sleep was a long time coming.

Chapter 5

Rose and coral began lighting the gray dawn when Clay returned to the cave. A sleepless night, spent reliving those precious moments before Meg had attacked him, left him more exhausted and depressed than ever. Although a dip in the nearby pond had cleansed the grime from his body, nothing could wash the regret, or confusion, from his mind.

The sight of Meg, curled in the same ball as when he had left, provoked fresh guilt and protectiveness. The hours spent alone in the dark, with only his sorrow for company, had made Clay see how stupid he had been. The chasm between him and Meg Andrews was unbreachable. In his head, he'd known that from the first, but whenever he got near her, his heart filled with hope.

When he had taken her into his arms, then felt her sweet mouth cover his, he had forgotten they had nothing in common. Even now, in the clear morning light, her image haunted him.

So did her unexpected attack. Over and over, he had tried to understand her reaction but nothing made sense. If she hadn't wanted him to continue, all she'd had to do was say so, and no matter what her excuse, no matter how difficult he found agreeing, Clay would have stopped.

He sighed wearily. The bottom line was that he had no business touching Meg Andrews and he knew it. He'd do well to keep the thought in mind.

As he crossed the narrow cave, his shoulders slumped with fatigue and frustration. With a single backward glance at Meg's still form, he crawled into his sleeping bag, then closed his eyes. Within minutes, he fell into a troubled sleep.

Meg awoke feeling groggy and disoriented. As she rolled to one side, she caught sight of Clay. Anxiety invaded every muscle in her body. When had he returned? she wondered. Several times after his departure she woke up to find him still absent. On each occasion, she found it difficult to go back to sleep, but she fought the urge to go after him, to apologize and try to explain.

Sick with regret, she cursed her lack of control, along with her flagging courage. Clay hadn't deserved to bear the brunt of her terror or retribution. He had offered solace and she had repaid him with brutality and rage. The ugly scene replayed itself in her head. While she had battered him, Clay hadn't even fought back or tried to restrain her. Instead, he had accepted the punishing blows as if he deserved them.

In the gathering light, she could make out a purple bruise just below his eye and several long lacerations on his bare shoulder. Bile rose in her throat as she realized she had put the marks on him.

Meg sat up, unmindful of her aching head or bare torso. As her gaze riveted on him, the bitter gall of guilt churned in her belly. Never in her life had she harmed another living being. No amount of apology could atone for her abuse of him, or ease her stinging conscience.

Clay, who had responded to her plea to hold her, who had reacted to her kiss with tenderness, who had let her batter him when his superior strength could have easily subdued her, deserved an explanation, an apology.

Tears pooled in her eyes. After her bizarre behavior, Meg doubted he'd even listen to her, and she couldn't blame him. He was a complex, complicated man with levels she hadn't begun to plumb, but he was a private, solitary man, as well, one who might well retreat behind the barriers he'd only lowered in the soft, seductive night.

Unable to find peace, Meg rolled to her feet and donned her clothes before going out into the pale, thin morning light.

Bright sunshine streaming into the cavern woke Clay from a restless slumber. He blinked rapidly to clear his vision. His body, stiff and sore, protested as he struggled to his feet. "Too damn old for this stuff," he muttered under his breath. He ought to consider retiring. In his line of work, forty-two was considered over the hill but Clay had no idea of what else he could do.

Settle down, a tiny voice whispered. Settle down with someone like Meg Andrews. No, it amended, not someone like her. Settle down with Meg.

As Clay recognized the stupidity of that thinking, he snorted with humorless laughter. Men like him didn't have the chance to settle down with someone like Meg. Hell, men like him seldom had the chance to settle down at all. The only retirement he was likely to have was a cemetery plot, if he was lucky.

Clay shoved the troubling thoughts from his head and glanced around the murky interior. When he didn't see any sign of Meg, he grimaced. Where in hell was she? he wondered as he hobbled outside, still trying to get his taut muscles to cooperate.

Clay stopped dead when he saw her perched on a wide stone ledge a few feet from the cave's entrance. Sunlight danced over her hair, turning the strands to gold and copper. His breath caught in his throat when she turned to him with a tremulous smile on her lips. With the sun behind her, the cloud of auburn curls formed a bronze halo that made her resemble a Christmas angel. His angel, he thought before common sense intervened. By Christmas, they'd again be worlds apart. By Christmas, she'd be someone else's angel. Probably Dave Thornton's.

His mouth flattened into a grimace. If he could have escaped, he'd have run as far and fast as his legs could carry him, but even then he doubted he could elude the web of longing she had woven around him.

Since he couldn't afford to make her aware of the invisible bonds ensnaring him, Clay gathered the shredded remnants of his restraint around him as he approached her. Cool and calm, he reminded himself. He could manage a few more days in her company without self-destructing. She need never know how profoundly she affected him.

Meg's smile faltered as he neared her. The bruise on his face looked much worse in the brilliant daylight, as did the angry abrasions on his shoulders and chest. As remorse spilled through her, she bowed her head.

A multitude of conflicting emotions buffeted Clay as he pondered how to proceed. Maybe ignoring last night would be best. It would certainly be less embarrassing for both of them. Awkwardly, he cleared his throat.

"How do you feel?" he asked in a low murmur. "Is the headache better?"

Her head was the least of her worries, but because she didn't know how to word her explanation, or how he would react to it, Meg responded to the question. "It's much better, thanks."

"Do you think you're up to moving on, or do you want to rest today?" Clay desperately hoped she wanted to get going. At least on the trail, he wouldn't be expected to make small talk. If he stayed ahead of her, he could pretend he was alone.

His voice, devoid of emotion, slashed through her. From his chilly civility, she might have imagined last night, but one glance at his bruised face reaffirmed she hadn't. It was all too real. "I'm ready if you are," she mumbled.

An odd expression crossed his battered face before a shutter fell over it. "Let's get packed up. We'll eat before we leave, then we won't waste time stopping for lunch. If we're lucky, we'll make it in a few hours." Without glancing at her, or waiting for agreement, he spun on his heel and strode away.

Meg, her heart heavy, followed.

The last leg of their trip proceeded at a more sedate pace, but by mid afternoon, Meg's nerves were flayed and raw. Since leaving the cave, Clay hadn't spoken at all. It was as if she no longer existed. He probably wished she didn't, Meg thought with dismay.

A dozen times she had started to apologize, but since she wasn't prepared to give a full explanation, what good was saying she was sorry?

Tears of worry and weariness stung her eyes. She wanted so badly to reestablish the tenuous ties her attack had snapped, but fear proved stronger than regret. Despite his gentle understanding and tender concern, Clay was a man, a man she barely knew. The dark demons haunting her came with companions—terror and rage and shame. It was the shame keeping her silent, making her wonder how Clay, or any man, would react to her most closely guarded secret. How could she discuss that private pain with a man she'd known for days when she'd never even told her brother? How could she bear his disgust or, worse, his pity?

The answer was simple, she couldn't, but her weakness haunted her as badly as the memory itself.

Lost in her troubled thoughts, Meg didn't hear the approaching vehicle. Abruptly, Clay grabbed her arm and yanked her into the dense trees beside the dusty road.

"What do you think you're doing?" she asked as she stumbled against him. Contact with his hard male body sent shivers of awareness through her.

Clay pushed her behind him. "Waiting to see who the hell's coming up the road," he muttered with unconcealed irritation. Despite his hours of silence, he remained incredibly aware of Meg. He'd retreated into himself in an effort to suppress his runaway emotions, but his efforts proved feeble. Meg drew him like honey drew bees, and nothing seemed to keep him from wanting her. He was angry at himself for his vulnerability and stupidity, and his voice came out sharper than he intended. "It may not be a friendly face. At this point, the odds are about fifty-fifty."

Meg, insulted by his condescending tone, yanked free. "You could have just said so without hurting me," she replied, rubbing her arm with unnecessary concern. It wasn't injured, but her pride was.

The harshness left his face as contrition softened the carved, masculine features. "I'm sorry," he muttered before turning back to look at the approaching vehicle.

Meg immediately felt penitent. She was the one who ought to apologize. His light grasp hadn't been painful. He hadn't hurt her, not ever.

Her gaze flickered over the obscene purple bruise stretching his skin. He hadn't hurt her even when she'd attacked him. Her hands balled into fists as she fought the urge to caress the mark.

As Clay stepped away from her and into the dusty road, she gasped in fear. Fear for Clay, she realized, as the driver, clad in faded fatigues, drew to a halt in a cloud of dust. Meg dashed out of hiding and to Clay's side as if somehow her presence might protect him. Her gaze went from Clay to the stranger.

The guarded expression on the man's face softened as he and Clay began to converse in what Meg now recognized as Spanish.

Feeling bereft and abandoned, Meg stepped closer to Clay. Not by word or deed did he acknowledge her presence, but the other man's obsidian gaze drifted over her and his thin lips lifted into a smile before he turned back to Clay.

Some of Meg's anxiety abated. The man seemed friendly and he was undeniably handsome. His black hair, high cheekbones, straight nose and olive complexion all indicated his Latin heritage. The way the features combined made Meg think of a Spanish noble, although, judging from his broad shoulders and trim waist, this man was no idle aristocrat. He was obviously a man of action, someone who didn't spend time behind a desk. Yet, though he possessed extraordinary looks and friendly charm, Meg experienced no increase in her heart rate, or any of the excitement Clay's mere presence elicited. Even her wild warrior's smooth baritone, speaking words she couldn't understand to a man she didn't know, made her pulse quicken in a way that was foolish and futile. After what she'd done to him, he'd never want to touch her again.

An ache took root in her heart. By leaving her safe rut, she'd hoped to put the past behind her. Instead it seemed to be destroying her first hope of happiness in years.

Meg watched as a dark flush crept over Clay's lean cheeks. Then saw his fingertips brush his swollen cheek. When he muttered something in Spanish, she knew he must be explaining the bruise and went scarlet. From the other man's benign reaction, Meg was sure Clay hadn't told him the truth but that didn't ease her conscience. If anything, she felt worse. She certainly didn't deserve his gallantry.

"This is Juan, one of the men I told you about. He's been driving this stretch of road looking for us," Clay said as he turned toward Meg. "He can take us into town."

Juan leaped out of the vehicle and came around to stand before Meg. He bowed slightly and offered his hand. "Welcome to my country, Señorita Andrews. I am sorry it is under such unfortunate circumstances but rest assured we will liberate your brother."

"Thank you, *señor*," she murmured as she extracted her hand from his warm grasp.

"You must call me Juan," he insisted with a friendly smile.

"Then you must call me Meg," she responded with an answering grin. After Clay's protracted silence, Meg felt warmed by this man's attention.

"Could we get moving?" Clay muttered. "The sooner we get started, the sooner we'll get your brother. And that's why we're here." His irritation, he knew, stemmed from profound jealousy, which only increased his irritation. Glancing from Juan to Meg, Clay wished she would smile at him instead of the other man. An acute sense of loss left him feeling emptier and more alone than at any time in his adult life. In the hot afternoon sun, a chill rippled through Clay as he realized this was how he was going to feel forever. Without Meg, he'd be struggling in the cold darkness with no hope of light or warmth, no flicker of fire or ray of sunshine. Because he was sure his misery must be written on his face, Clay strode to the rear of the Jeep where he deposited his gear.

Meg watched with a frown, but Juan chuckled as he relieved her of the backpack and assisted her into the Jeep. "A beautiful woman is always welcome, no matter what the reason."

Meg's smile resurfaced. "Why, thank you."

Clay cleared his throat. "Could we get into town before some army patrol comes along and decides to give us a ride all the way to prison?" he asked in a guttural tone that masked the desolation slashing his heart to ribbons.

Juan chuckled as he jumped back into the driver's seat. After Clay swung in beside him, he gunned the engine and took off. "I guess I don't have to ask if your journey was pleasant," he said with a sidelong glance at Clay.

Clay sent him a killing stare before hunching down and closing his eyes. ''Pleasant doesn't begin to describe it,'' he mumbled.

Meg, in the back seat, felt the sting of his comment like a physical blow but she withheld comment.

''I am afraid our accommodations are rather primitive,'' Juan murmured apologetically as he parked in front of a rambling stucco house.

Although the structure appeared much the same in style as Carlotta's, the resemblance ended there. The black wrought-iron fence surrounding the front yard badly needed a coat of paint. Unkempt grass, withered and yellowing, was visible through the rusty gate hanging haphazardly from one hinge. A brick wall, extending from street to door, was almost obliterated by weeds.

As Juan led them up the cracked walk, shabbiness became more apparent. Massive clay pots, chipped and crumbling, contained only dead stems. As they entered the house, Meg saw the interior was little better.

The wide foyer was bare of furnishings, its parquet floor scuffed and dull. An aura of decay and despair pervaded the place. Once the expensive structure must have been magnificent, Meg thought sadly.

After Juan ushered the pair into what once must have been a handsome study, Meg sank gratefully into a worn leather chair and let her gaze travel around the room.

Across one wall ran an expanse of bookcases filled with hard-bound tomes and framed photographs. In front of it rested a massive desk. An impressive, though empty, stone fireplace flanked twin wing chairs on the exterior wall.

Although no fire blazed in the hearth, Meg felt warmed by the room's cozy atmosphere. Unlike the entry or exterior, it maintained an air of vitality as if it were the soul of a weakened body.

Clay collapsed in another chair and thrust his long legs out in front of him. Briefly, fatigue overwhelmed him and he let his eyes drift shut. When they again opened, he trained his attention on Juan, who had moved behind the desk. He noted Meg's relaxed posture and gritted his teeth. She and Juan seemed to hit it off immediately, and though he knew it would prove helpful, he didn't like their easy comradery at all.

His troubled gaze moved from one to the other as he recalled their own meeting in San Juan. She hadn't smiled at him or offered her hand. In fact, her disgust had been palpable. Disgust for him.

Over their brief acquaintance that disgust appeared to dissipate, but now Clay wondered. His fingers moved to his black eye. He couldn't picture her attacking Juan and, heaven knew, he didn't want to picture Juan touching her as he had.

Clay forced his attention back to the present.

"I regret that the house is not in better condition," Juan was saying. "It belongs to my parents, but they left our country some time ago." His gaze went to Clay before returning to Meg. "I returned only recently myself, hence the lack of care."

The haunting shadows in his ebony eyes made Meg's heart soften. "Where are your parents?"

"In your country, where they can be safe. For that, I am most grateful." Regret roughened his voice. "If you will excuse me for a few moments, I will see that your rooms are ready. You must be tired from your journey."

"Thank you," Meg murmured as Juan departed. She glanced at Clay, who stared straight ahead. The tight set of his features made her quiver, but eager to somehow heal the breach between them, she plunged ahead. "Juan's parents must have been very wealthy. This is a lovely home, or must have been."

He looked at her, then around the room. Juan certainly had more in common with Meg Andrews than he did, which only intensified his frown. "It was beautiful. Juan's father was a diplomat under the democratic government. Juan was an army officer. He went to Costa del Palma's West Point," he informed Meg. "Unfortunately, no one in his family could be bought or intimidated."

Meg pursed her lips. "What do you mean, unfortunately?"

His gaze returned to her. "People who stood up to the drug lords ended up in prison, dead or exiled."

"And Juan's parents chose to leave?"

"I wouldn't say it was a choice."

"Did Juan leave, too?" she asked, recalling how he'd said he'd only recently come back.

"No, he didn't leave Costa del Palma. He fought the drug lords, fought their corruption, fought their illegitimate government. He was, is, a leader of the resistance. He's one of the people my . . . the U.S. government tries to help." Bitterness twisted his mouth. "Not that they helped much. Juan was captured and imprisoned. He only escaped very recently."

Meg's eyes widened. "Was he in the same prison as my brother?"

A pensive shimmer shadowed his eyes as warning bells clanged in his head. Clay needed to weigh his words more carefully. He'd nearly slipped, not that Meg seemed to notice. All the same, he needed to be more circumspect.

"Yes," he replied. "The same place, but Juan was out before Ted was arrested."

A frown crinkled Meg's brow. "How was Juan arrested if this place is as safe as you said? If they found him here before . . ."

"They didn't find him here, Meg. They wouldn't have found him at all if someone hadn't taken a bribe to disclose where he was meeting with . . . some others. They were all part of an effort to get the drug lords out of power."

"How did a bunch of drug dealers get in control of a democratic government, anyhow?"

"Time, money, violence. They killed, imprisoned or intimidated anyone who stood in their way. When they had a base of power, they took over. Even though it was nearly hopeless, Juan and some others maintained a solid resistance for a long time. Until someone betrayed them. Those who weren't captured or killed came here. Most of the rest are still in prison, or executed."

Apprehension rippled through Meg. "Was Juan going to be killed?" she asked in a high, thin voice.

"He and some others were scheduled for execution," Clay replied. "Luckily, they were rescued by some of the same men who'll help us get Ted."

"And all these men live here now?"

"Yes, they live in this isolated region because the entire area resisted the drug lords. Besides, it's remote with rough terrain, so penetrating it wouldn't be easy. Juan and his men are safe as long as they stay here." His voice dropped a fraction. "It is safe here, Meg. Completely safe."

She pressed one hand to her trembling lips. "Going to the capital isn't safe. Going into that prison...that's not safe."

The uneasiness smoldering in her eyes surprised Clay, but assuming it was meant for Juan, he looked away. "These men aren't fools. They aren't doing anything they don't want to do."

Neither was Clay, she knew, but that didn't lessen her anxiety.

"Ted should never have come down here," she mumbled as her thoughts returned to her brother.

"It wasn't particularly wise, but he wasn't the first American journalist to come down here. He had no real reason to worry. I'm sure he's been in just as dangerous places and survived well."

"Yes, he has but he's never been kidnapped by drug lords before." She licked her lips. "What if...what if they think he's a spy or an agent or something? Remember what happened to that drug agent in Mexico a few years ago..." The American Drug Enforcement agent had been kidnapped, then tortured to death. A shudder racked her as the harsh realities of the situation closed around her.

"I remember," Clay mumbled. His mouth flattened into a thin, white line as some suppressed emotion darkened his gaze. "Ted isn't a federal agent, Meg. He's a well-known photojournalist. These people know that."

Her gaze, filled with hope and tension, clung to him. "Then you think he's okay?" she asked in a whisper.

Clay nodded and forced a reassuring smile even though he wasn't sure of anything except the need to comfort her. "I think he's fine and you have to think so, too. In a short time, everything will be back to normal. Once you're home, this will all be an unpleasant memory."

The words tasted as bitter as lemon. No doubt he'd be among her most unpleasant recollections. The idea made his stomach clench into a knot. At the very least, he had wanted her respect, but after the episode in the cave, he doubted if even that was possible. He was surprised she carried on a civil conversation with him. Surprised but grateful. Her attack still didn't make sense, but he didn't blame her. A man like him wasn't her type. She needed an educated gentleman, someone refined and sensitive. Someone like Dave or Juan. If one of them kissed and caressed her, she wouldn't be terrified or repulsed, he was sure. Regret and resignation filled him even as he struggled to keep his expression relaxed.

Meg studied Clay's face and saw that the tentative smile never reached his gaze. His red-rimmed eyes and bruised cheek made her uneasy. She owed him some sort of excuse, but nothing short of the truth came to mind. She laced her fingers together and bowed her head. The only course of action open to her, the only safe topic of conversation, was her brother and his rescue.

"I guess since Juan and his men know about the prison, that will make your job a little easier."

Clay fought to vanquish the emotions clouding his mind and return his thoughts to the task ahead. He couldn't afford to be distracted. "Any firsthand information is valuable, but we don't know exactly where Ted is being held. The prison is huge." When he saw fresh apprehension cross Meg's face, he went on quickly. "But we have someone in the capital who should be back late tonight or tomorrow. He should be able to find out exactly where your brother is, which will make our job much easier."

"That's good," she whispered but couldn't shake the anxiety plaguing her. She hated thinking of Clay risking his life, hated thinking that if she hadn't hunted him down, he'd be enjoying a holiday in Puerto Rico instead of leading a dangerous mission in an unstable country like Costa del Palma. Telling herself that was his job, one he'd chosen, didn't help. Neither did the reminder that he'd come voluntarily. She still felt guilty and frightened. Frightened for Clay.

"Meg, your brother will be fine," Clay whispered. Seeing her undisguised fear made him hasten to reassure her. "I'll do everything I can to see that he gets here safe and sound."

Her head jerked up. "I know you will, Clay," she said in a broken whisper. "But can you promise you'll come back safe and sound, too?" Hot tears shimmered on her russet lashes as, for the first time, she let him see part of the emotion she'd tried to hide.

Shock froze his face. "Meg?"

"I'm sorry, Clay. Sorry I've put you in danger, sorry I hurt you." Torment, raw and aching, gnawed at her insides. There was so much she wanted to say, so much she wanted to tell him.

Her words struck deep into the fortress surrounding his heart and soul. Suddenly, he was catapulted back into the dim cave where his world had consisted of her taste, her touch, her texture. Then and there, he forgot all that stood between them. Then and there, he forgot everything but the woman in his arms and how right it was to have her there.

Even in Juan's sun-drenched library, Clay felt the cool, damp air of night and the hot, scorching need of wanting Meg. He knew his thoughts were reflected in his gaze, as Meg's were in hers, but he didn't look away. He couldn't. It was as if her gaze was metal, his magnet. For long, silent moments, they stared at each other.

As Clay was about to speak, about to forget his resolve, about to forget their differences, Juan reappeared to announce that their rooms were ready. When their host offered his arm to Meg, Clay nearly reached out to brush the offending limb away but stopped in time. Still, jealousy stole over him as he trailed up the winding staircase behind them.

When Meg disappeared into her room without a backward glance, Clay didn't know whether to be angry or grateful.

Chapter 6

Later, as Meg sat on the bed combing out her freshly shampooed hair, she recalled her conversation with Clay. Juan's reappearance had effectively ended their budding intimacy. Meg wasn't sure if that was good or bad. In the brief time they were alone in the cozy confines of the library, they had regained lost ground as barriers fell away and expectation and awareness crackled between them.

But where could it lead? she wondered. Did the warmth in Clay's eyes result only from desire or did it spring from something deeper, something stronger? Meg couldn't be sure and the doubt troubled her. How could she bare her soul for a brief interlude?

She bit her lower lip as she mulled over the content of their talk. Clay knew a good deal about Juan and his family and about the politics of Costa del Palma. Were all mercenaries so well informed? she wondered. And why was someone as intelligent and articulate as Clay involved in such dirty work?

For the money, an inner voice whispered.

Meg frowned. Clay Terhune, despite his tenderness and talent, was a hired gun, a soldier of fortune. In San Juan, he had taken pains to inform her of his high price.

Her frown deepened. Yet he hadn't wanted an advance, and nothing he had done since leaving Puerto Rico seemed particularly mercenary.

Her fingers tightened on the brush. The man was a puzzle, an intriguing puzzle with many intricate pieces. But would she have the opportunity to see them in their proper place? Would she ever see the puzzle solved?

A ragged sigh left her. On the surface, they had nothing in common. Not background, or education, or interests, or goals. Even so, Meg felt as if she had known Clay forever and, at the same time, as if she would never really know him. The emotions crowding her heart were unfamiliar, yet they seemed to grow deeper with every passing moment.

She tossed the brush aside and glanced in the mirror. Clad in a clean shirt and fresh trousers, she looked and felt much better. After scrambling to her feet, she tucked her shirt more securely into her waistband and smiled at her reflection. She looked good, she thought with an uncharacteristic tinge of feminine vanity. Although her attire was far from provocative, the loose garb flowed over her soft curves in a pleasing manner while her complexion glowed with natural color. Her hair, still damp, framed her face in a becoming way. For the first time in ages, she felt comfortable looking feminine.

After slipping her feet into a pair of sandals, she went in search of Juan and Clay. Meg wandered through the house until she located the pair on the terrace. With them was a petite woman about her age. The trio was engaged in a loud conversation, conducted in Spanish, and didn't notice Meg's approach.

Halting just outside the French doors, Meg studied the newcomer with open curiosity. Dressed in snug jeans and a clinging sweater that showed off her slim, slight figure to best advantage, the woman was strikingly beautiful. Of the same coloring as Juan, she radiated both aristocratic aloofness and exotic beauty.

Envy washed over Meg as her newfound confidence wavered. Compared to the petite female, she felt as dowdy and dumpy as she'd tried to appear when meeting Clay. The difference was that then she had wanted to appear unattractive. Now...well, now she wanted him to notice her, not a stranger.

As Meg listened to the rapid-fire conversation, she tried to catch a word here and there but found it impossible.

Trepidation grew inside her as she observed the group. Although languages varied, facial expressions proved universal. Juan glanced repeatedly from the woman to Clay and back. Occasionally he mumbled a few words before the woman launched into an impassioned monologue. But it was neither the woman's agitation nor Juan's uneasiness that most upset Meg. It was Clay's reaction.

Fury blazed like golden fire in his eyes. Like a jungle predator, he was alert, intense, dangerous. Whatever the woman said obviously disturbed him. Meg's discomfort escalated with with every passing moment. Who was this woman? What was she saying?

Finally, Clay muttered something to his companions. When the woman replied, he nodded in weary agreement. Then he turned to Meg and gestured for her to follow him. When she came to his side, he grasped her elbow and led her down the patio's shallow steps and along a narrow path to a gazebo.

Dusk fell quickly in this hilly region, Meg discovered as they moved off the terrace. By the time she took the bench Clay indicated, deep shadows hid his expression, but the tension lacing his lean body was clear. Meg shifted restlessly on the wooden seat.

"Clay, what's wrong? Has something happened to Ted?" Her voice quavered with apprehension. "What did that woman tell you? Who is she?"

Clay braced one shoulder against the nearest pillar. "Ted's okay, Meg. He's still in the prison, but he's okay." He wasn't sure how to answer her other questions or how she'd accept the woman's news. From Meg's earlier revelations, he knew she was very close to her brother. After all, she took care of his home and his sons, her life revolving around his. That she loved both her brother and her nephews was clear.

A grimace formed on his mouth. The way Ted Andrews relied on Meg, took advantage of her generous nature and allowed her to forgo a life of her own seemed selfish; the way he had betrayed his sister's devotion and risked his life was insensitive. As soon as the rescue was over, Clay planned to tell Ted so. In the meantime, he had to disclose that her brother hadn't spent all his time in Costa del Palma working. While Meg had been in Ohio assuming Ted's responsibilities and sacrificing a personal life of her own, he'd been rather busy.

"Clay, why did you bring me out here? Something must be wrong."

"I guess that's a matter of opinion," he mumbled.

"Clay, you're scaring me. Who is that woman? I know whatever she said upset you . . ."

Clay levered away from the post, still unsure how to proceed. "She knows Ted."

Meg swallowed hard. "She's seen him recently?"

"Not since he was taken, but she knows his exact location." His tone remained remote and guarded. The woman knew a great deal about political prisoners, but it was only Ted Andrews who concerned Meg, only Ted Andrews who was Clay's primary focus.

"That's good, isn't it?"

"Yes, it will make getting him out easier."

Meg's shoulders slumped with relief. If it was easier, it would be less dangerous and Clay would be less likely to be harmed. "I'm glad," she murmured.

Clay moved to sit beside her. Gently he laid one hand over both of hers. "That's not all she said. Meg, that woman...well, she says—and she has proof—that she's married to Ted. She says they got married several weeks ago."

Briefly, Meg's jaw dropped, then a smile curved her mouth. "So that's what he meant," she murmured.

Amazement rounded Clay's eyes. He'd expected shock or surprise, doubt or dismay. He'd expected anxiety or astonishment. Never had he expected calm, almost pleased, acceptance. Her approval grated on his nerves, as did the suspicion that the wedding wasn't a surprise. From the moment he'd met Ted's wife, Clay's only concern had been for Meg. He'd worried and fretted over how to tell her what he figured would be shocking news, but his anxiety had been useless. That anxiety quickly became anger, anger because he feared he was being played for a fool. "Just what does that mean?" he asked in an icy tone. Feeling stupid for wanting to protect and shelter her, even from being hurt by her brother, goaded him. "Did you know Ted got married?" When she failed to reply immediately, he continued in a harsh whisper. "Dammit, you did know."

His accusation stung an already stunned Meg. Clay's lack of trust raised her ire. Meg, to whom honesty was not only a virtue but a necessity, resented being accused of lying.

A niggling voice reminded her how she had let him assume she and Dave were involved, but she pushed it away. She hadn't actually said so, and even if she had, it wasn't the sort of information that made any difference to the mission. Thinking she was cold or snobbish or involved wasn't going to affect anyone's safety.

A gulf of silence, as deep as the waters of the sea, lay between them. When Meg still failed to respond, Clay went on the offensive. "I don't appreciate surprises or complications. Is there any other little detail you haven't told me, something else you and Dave Thornton figured I didn't need to know before I put my neck in the noose?" His outrage, he knew, stemmed more from frustration than from her re-action to her brother's marriage, but that knowledge didn't alleviate the rage erupting inside him like a volcano. "Is that why Thornton didn't come? Because there's more?"

Meg's teeth toyed with her lower lip. Although Clay's anger upset her, she wasn't afraid of him. He'd already proven he wouldn't hurt her, not even when provoked. She lifted her chin and held her ground. "You know Dave's in London. He wanted to help, he just couldn't."

Clay snorted with disbelief. "I'm sure he'd love to come down here. What federal agent wouldn't want to come to a tropical paradise like Costa del Palma?" he asked with a sarcastic sneer.

Meg sucked in a long breath to steady her nerves but it did little good. Her own anxiety led to her response. "You didn't have to come down here, either. Dave would've found someone else to help me."

Clay's nostrils flared with a sharp intake of breath. "Good old Dave. I guess you figure he can do about any-thing. I guess you figure his advice is sacrosanct." Clay jumped to his feet and went to stare at the shadow-filled woods. "I suppose he suggested that hideous outfit and ugly hairdo. Just to make sure you didn't attract any male atten-tion, since he couldn't be with you," he muttered. The thought of Thornton, or any other man, touching her sent a spear of potent jealousy straight to his heart.

Meg ran one hand over her face. How she wished for the words to make peace between them, but her deceit stood like a shield, as did her past. "Dave doesn't have anything to do with how I dressed," she whispered.

Clay spun back to her. "He's a fool. A damn fool. If you were mine, I wouldn't have let you come down here all by yourself."

His hoarse admission unleashed a torrent of longing. If she was his... What would it be like to belong to a man like Clay Terhune, to have him belong to her?

In the dark, dank cave, she had enjoyed a hint of his passion. If she hadn't gotten lost in the old nightmare, what would have happened? What sort of lover would he be? The question caused her blood to heat and her pulse to race. Meg searched his handsome face. Angry amber fire blazed in his eyes, but so did something more. Something hot. Getting lost in the passion and promise would be so easy, but the past loomed over her like a thundercloud. Even if she explained about Dave, how could she reveal her ugly secret? And if she did, how could she expect Clay to understand?

"I don't take orders from anyone, Mr. Terhune," she said with far more courage than she felt.

"There better not be any more little secrets, Miss Andrews. This job will be difficult enough without loose ends. I won't ask Juan and his men to take any additional risks."

Fear, stark and vivid, assailed her. Clay would be in as much, maybe more danger, than the others. The thought of his being hurt paralyzed her. If something happened to Clay, it would be like losing a part of herself—the only part that felt vibrant and vital. How could she live with herself if something happened to him? How could she bear it if she didn't let him know part of what she felt?

When she didn't respond, anger, like waves in a pond, rippled through him. As Meg stumbled to her feet, he yanked her toward him. His free hand caught her waist and held her facing him. Her feminine warmth and fresh scent filled his senses. Despite her attitude, he still wanted her, and that knowledge sharpened his tone. "You've baited, teased me, taunted me, attacked me . . . all for no good reason, as far as I can see. I don't know what Thornton told you about me, but if he said I was harmless, he lied. I've taken a lot from you, maybe too much, but I'm not about to risk my neck or anyone else's without knowing everything you know. If you've got any more secrets, it's in your best interest to tell me now." The words, harsh and guttural, sounded as if they'd been torn from his throat.

Tears flooded her eyes and leaked out beneath her lashes.

At the sight of the moisture trailing down her cheeks, Clay released her. Unrelenting remorse destroyed his righteous anger. He hadn't meant to upset her, only to get the truth. No, not even that. His own defeat and disappointment fed his anger. So did his lack of judgment. It wasn't like him to lose control of his emotions, but that wasn't Meg's fault. Despite her strange behavior, she didn't deserve his indignation. She hadn't forced him to care for her. He stepped away. "I'm sorry, Meg. I'm edgy, I guess."

Her wet lashes fluttered open. "I'm the one who should be sorry," she mumbled. "I didn't know Ted was married, Clay. Not until you told me."

Shock filled his gaze. "What?"

"I didn't know," she repeated. "The last time he called, he said he had a surprise, a pleasant surprise for me and the boys, but I had no idea what he meant. Not until now."

"Why didn't you just say so?" Baffled, he searched her face for some clue.

She shook her head. "I don't know." Her jumbled emotions kept her from thinking clearly, but she didn't want to explain that. "I guess I didn't like you accusing me of lying and hiding things, important things that might hinder the rescue or put you in danger."

He stared at her in confusion. Again, her words left the impression that he mattered, but those words didn't match her actions. The previous night she had kicked and hit him with every bit of strength in her, but she didn't want him calling her a liar? It didn't make sense, yet Clay was discovering quite a lot about her didn't make sense.

"I was under the impression that my opinion didn't matter to you," he murmured.

Color warmed her cheeks. "I really am sorry, Clay. I know it doesn't make the scratches or bruises disappear, but I didn't mean to hurt you. I really didn't."

"I could have stopped you," he admitted.

"I know. Why didn't you?" she asked in a whisper-soft voice.

He lifted one shoulder in a half shrug. "Because I'm bigger, stronger. Because I might have hurt you, even unintentionally." That was something he could never, would never do. He wanted to cherish and protect Meg as she deserved. No words could explain the overwhelming tenderness filling his heart.

"But I hurt you," she mumbled in a voice filled with contrition.

His hand went to his battered cheek as the semblance of a smile curved his mouth. "This? It's nothing. Hardly worth noticing. I'd forgotten about it."

A half smile tugged at one corner of her mouth. "I don't believe you."

His dark brows lifted a fraction while his eyes twinkled. "Well, maybe just a little," he admitted, his expression contemplative. "But you can believe this—I may not be like the men you're used to, I may not be like Ted or Dave, but I'd never harm you, Meg, or let any harm come to you." His voice, hushed and solemn, made the words a vow, an oath, a solemn promise.

The reverence and sincerity in his tone filled Meg with awe. A hardened loner like Clay Terhune didn't form attachments easily, and he didn't make pretty speeches for effect. If he gave his word, he kept it. In spite of his work, he was a man of honor and integrity. A man worthy of trust and more, so much more.

"I know, Clay," she whispered. "I know you're a good man."

Her reassurance both pleased and alarmed him. With Meg, his veneer of indifference and insolence fell away, leaving him strangely, and uncharacteristically, vulnerable. Despite his deeply ingrained defenses, longing slipped past them to pierce his heart. As if of its own volition, his hand reached out to stroke her soft cheek. "I'm not sure I deserve that sort of confidence," he murmured.

Her hand caught his wrist as if to bind him to her. "You'll be careful, won't you? I couldn't bear it . . ." Her lashes lowered to cloak the anguish threatening to swamp her. "I don't want you to get hurt." A nervous giggle escaped as she looked at his bruised eye. "That sounds stupid when I've already done damage myself."

Clay sighed. She had done damage, quite a lot and probably irreparable, but it wasn't physical as she thought. The very real damage wasn't visible to the naked eye.

"I'll be fine, Meg," he replied without conviction. But how could he be when he finally knew what his lonely life had long lacked? How could he go on now that he'd seen the embodiment of his faded hopes and dreams? Yet how could he do anything else? He had no way to hold Meg Andrews, or any right, either.

Clay cleared his throat. "Don't worry, Meg. Everything will be all right."

Her gaze searched his face. "But I am worried." Her hands fell away from him as she turned around. If he saw her expression, he'd recognize the depth and source of her concern. He'd know what she was feeling. "I can't help but worry," she mumbled.

Clay shoved one hand through his hair. "We'll be very careful, Meg. We all know the situation. We all know what to do and how to do it."

The urge to wrap her arms around Clay, to keep him safe and secure, to keep him from going with the others became a palpable force. On its heels came acute embarrassment. Such a gesture would be futile, as well as foolish. A man like Clay didn't need protection—he provided it. He was strong, resourceful, hardened. He was a warrior, a man who lived by his gun, a man accustomed to violence. Her feeble attempts to hold him would be useless.

When she swiveled back, he remained in the shadows, a solitary figure, near yet so very distant. Resignation stiffened her will. Once Ted was safe, they'd never see each other again, she realized as sadness ate at her. "When will you leave?" she asked in a strangled voice. Distressed and miserable, she bowed her head.

Clay ground his teeth. After the rescue, she'd return to her world, a place he could never enter. "Tomorrow night probably. It'll be easier to get into the prison in the dark."

When she faced him, her features, carefully schooled, gave no hint of her terror. "Are you sure you'll be ready by then?" She licked her lips. "I mean, I know you're tired. You were tired in San Juan and you haven't gotten any rest. I don't want—" Meg stopped abruptly; she had already revealed too much. If she said any more, repeated her worries, he'd realize . . . realize what? That she was in love with him?

Sudden realization flashed in her heart like a Fourth of July firecracker. She loved Clay Terhune. Loved him with all the passion so long denied, so deeply buried. Although she had known her feelings went beyond infatuation, she hadn't dared to label them love. She hadn't dared to label them at all, hadn't wanted to feel them. Nevertheless, love for Clay swelled her heart, took root in her soul. Even if, as she feared, she never saw him again, Clay would remain part of her.

Looking at him filled her with awe—and panic. She couldn't let him know of her love, not when so much stood between, not when she doubted he would ever feel the same. Somehow she had to hide her growing affection. In an effort to camouflage her love, she said the first thing that came to mind. "I know you're exhausted. I don't want you to . . . well, fall flat on your face, or something."

Clay recoiled as if struck. The color drained from his face and the hope from his heart. What a fool he'd been to think her concern was personal. Her foremost interest would naturally be for the mission, for her brother. Yet, only moments earlier, she had sounded as if she cared what happened to him. Despite the lessons of his past, Clay had been ready to believe Meg's anxiety included him, but he'd evidently been wrong. Dead wrong.

"I can assure you I won't fall flat on my face, at least not until after your brother is safe. I may be tired, but I'm not incompetent and I'm quite accustomed to working on little or no sleep, so you don't need to worry. I'll do the job you hired me to do," he muttered before spinning on his heel and striding away.

Meg, stunned by his reaction, watched as he disappeared into the house. Despondent and dejected, she collapsed on the bench. In trying to hide her love, she had only succeeded in widening the breach between them.

Bracing her elbows on her knees, she buried her head in her hands. Falling in love with Clay Terhune complicated her situation immeasurably. Of all the men on earth, she couldn't have found one more unsuitable or unattainable, not that she'd been looking. The idea of giving her heart to a man, any man, had long ago disappeared. Other than her brother, Meg hadn't allowed any male close to her in years. Her trust didn't extend to being alone with a man. At least it hadn't until Clay.

Her mind rewound and replayed their conversation. He had been correct about one thing. He wasn't like the other men of her acquaintance. Rugged and untamed, primitive yet sensitive, tender and compassionate, he was an endlessly fascinating paradox.

She knew violence was common in his work, yet he hadn't defended himself when attacked. Instead, his primary concern was not hurting her in return. Because of that, and so much more, Meg trusted him. Trusted him, loved him, even wanted him.

Her heart stutter-stepped as she recalled the heated sweetness of his mouth, the gentle persuasion of his hands. For a time, she had responded. For a time, she had forgotten her nightmare. For a time, she had reveled in being a woman, Clay's woman.

Had she ruined any chance of knowing his touch? Even if he never cared for her as she did him, Meg knew he would be a wonderful lover. Demanding yet giving, strong but gentle, passionate and tender. Instinctively she knew exactly how it would be between them, and the knowledge increased her longing.

To be with him, if only for one night, to know his passion and fulfill his needs. A hot blush stained her cheeks. The unusual eroticism of her thoughts embarrassed Meg but didn't stop them.

She loved Clay. She needed him. There could be no shame in that, nor any regret.

Meg knew she had only one option. With the determination that made her leave the security of home, then insist on accompanying Clay, she jumped to her feet and followed the path he had taken. Even if he threw her love back in her face, she had to confront him, had to resolve the misunderstanding lying between them. Courage, she reminded herself as her trembling legs took her into the house and after the man she loved.

Chapter 7

Confronting Clay wasn't as easy as Meg figured. For one thing, after talking to an elderly servant who spoke little English, she discovered he and the other men were in a meeting. The woman also managed to convey that dinner would be served in an hour.

Eager to look her best, Meg returned to her room to redo her hair and pace the floor. When she came downstairs an hour later, she was disappointed to learn that the men were eating in the library and her brother's new wife was resting.

After a lonely meal, Meg lingered at the table until it became apparent that no one else would appear. Finally, she retreated to her room and waited for Clay's footsteps in the hall. As time passed, her anxiety increased but her resolve remained firm. Nothing would stop her from talking to Clay tonight.

It was almost midnight when she heard him enter his room. After again checking her appearance, she went to his door. Small tremors rippled through her as she peeked through the narrow opening. A single light illuminated the room and the tall, lean figure moving about the shadow-filled corner. When Clay swung around, shock froze his features into a hard mask.

Trembling with apprehension, Meg fought the urge to return to the safety of her room. She knew safety was no longer what she craved. Safety held no appeal. Only Clay did. All she wanted was this wild warrior and whatever he would offer, be it one night or a lifetime. She took a tentative step forward.

"I thought you'd be asleep by now," he mumbled in a tight, strangled voice. His body felt as taut as a bowstring. After their parting earlier, he hadn't expected her to seek him out, and he wasn't sure how to feel about this surprise visit. Why had she come? he wondered. In the dim room, her expression was unreadable.

"I—I couldn't sleep," she murmured. "I'm too worried, I guess." She took more hesitant steps, then stopped as she waited for some sign from him.

His shoulders sagged with weariness and despair. "I already told you, everything will be okay."

"I know, it's just that...I know it's dangerous, very dangerous," she managed in a tremulous whisper. Hesitant and anxious, she didn't know how to continue. With his brooding gaze on her, Meg's carefully rehearsed speech flew out of her head, leaving only anxiety and need in its wake.

"So you've said before," he muttered. An edge of bitterness slashed his tone. She had already expressed doubt in his fitness. Was that why she sought him out now? To make sure he was in decent shape? Anger spurred his imagination. Did she think he'd been partying all evening? He gritted his teeth against a nasty outburst.

He had spent the past few hours with Juan and his men, mapping out strategy and going over every detail of the rescue. Bone-deep fatigue weighed every cell of his body like wet cement. Although he doubted he'd sleep, he wanted nothing more than to collapse on the soft mattress and let his weary body relax. His mind whirled with the intricacies of the job ahead, and thanks to Meg's presence, his body was wired with desire. Didn't she have any idea of the tumult her nearness caused? Was she trying to torture him? He'd already admitted he wanted her, and been rejected. His fingers went to his cheek. No, worse than that, attacked.

Guilt spread through Meg at his gesture. Another apology was on her tongue, but she held it back. She had to gain control of the situation, then state her case. Sorrow wasn't the primary emotion she wanted to convey. "Well, yes, I know," she murmured.

"Look," he said hastily, "this will all be over by this time tomorrow. Your brother will be here with you, safe and sound, and the danger will be over."

A puzzled frown knitted her brow. "What do you mean? You said you weren't leaving until tomorrow night." Dismay thundered through her.

Clay sighed. "Well, things have changed. Juan's contact got back a couple of hours ago. From what he said, it looks like Ted may be moved soon. We don't want to wait until tomorrow night. We know exactly where he is now. If they move him . . . well, it's just better if we get there before they do." He didn't want to tell her that if Ted was moved, they might never get him out.

"But you said you needed darkness." Panic squeezed her heart like a vise. In only hours, Clay would be gone. Gone into grave danger because she had found him, because she had hired him to find her brother. She bit hard on her lower lip. If anything happened to Clay, she could never live with herself.

"We'll manage. We worked out a good plan." *Good but not foolproof,* he thought, but didn't say so. She didn't need any added stress. "Quit worrying, Meg, and try to get some sleep."

Meg didn't move. "I told you, I'm too nervous to sleep." She advanced another couple of steps.

Now that the light illuminated her face, Clay found sending her away even more difficult and, silently, cursed himself for a fool. He and Meg Andrews had nothing in common. Rough and refined. Dark and light. Good and bad. They were two distinctly different people from two separate worlds, something she had the sense to accept even if he didn't. And accepting it proved impossible when she was so close that her sweet scent filled his nostrils and ignited his need. Because he couldn't trust his restraint where she was concerned, because her presence confused him, he knew he had to get rid of her before he made an even bigger fool of himself.

"Go to bed. The past few days have been hard on you. At least try to rest."

"I don't want to go yet," she said, playing for time. "I wanted to talk to you, Clay."

He bowed his head. "I don't see what else there is to say," he muttered. If she stayed, he knew he'd say things he shouldn't, maybe make promises he had no way of keeping, probably humiliate himself and embarrass her.

"I—I wanted to say that, well, what you said earlier . . . I mean, what I said. Well, that is, you misunderstood me, Clay. What I'm trying to say is, you seemed to think I was only concerned about my brother, I guess, and that's not true. I'm just as worried about you." She searched his face for some reaction, but his features grew hard and unyielding, as if they were etched in ice. Had she been wrong to seek him out? Maybe he didn't care what she thought, or how she felt. Maybe he simply wanted to get this job over with and move on.

Having been misled once, Clay was unmoved by her words. "It's nice of you to worry about the rest of us, but it's only natural that Ted is your primary concern. After all, he's your brother."

"He's my brother," she whispered, "but he isn't *all* that matters." She took a deep breath before going on. "I truly hope no one is hurt, but Ted isn't my only concern anymore. You are, too."

His hands tightened into fists. Her words gave him hope, foolish hope. "Why are you doing this? What do you hope to gain by saying something like that, Meg? I'm going to get your brother. You don't have to be nice or pretend to give a damn about me. And you sure as hell don't have to come to my room at midnight and—" He exhaled sharply. With his control wavering, he had to dismiss her before she drove him crazy. "I don't expect any prepayment, Miss Andrews. Or any bonus. None is needed. None is wanted." Lies. Both lies. He needed and wanted her beyond anything in the world, beyond the world itself, but he couldn't afford to let her know. He'd shown his vulnerability to a woman once and it had nearly killed him.

His words struck at the root of her anxiety but with love instead of logic guiding her, Meg stood her ground. "I'm not trying to influence you, Clay. I'm not here for any reason except—I'm here because I want to be with you."

With those words, she reminded him of Annette, of pain and betrayal and resolve never to be so stupid again. "You shouldn't be here," he muttered. "Dave wouldn't like it." Saying the words nearly killed him. Meg wasn't Annette, yet he knew he wouldn't refuse her as he had Annette. Despite his resolve, despite his experience, tonight he'd take whatever Meg Andrews was willing to give him. What he had felt for Annette, so long ago, was nothing compared to his affection for Meg. He wanted her more than anything in his life, more than life itself, and he dreaded the day, fast approaching, when she'd walk away, without a backward glance.

Meg saw the intense emotions cross Clay's face and knew real fear. She should never let him believe there was something between her and Dave, should have corrected the misconception immediately, but her fears had held her captive. Now her fear was losing Clay before she ever had him. Her promise to Ted's boys was to bring their father back. Her promise to herself was overcoming the terror holding her hostage much too long. So far, her efforts had been feeble. Now she had a chance to sever some of those bonds with the sword of truth.

Meg lifted her chin and held Clay's gaze. "Dave has no reason to care what I do, or with whom."

A dark scowl shadowed Clay's face. "What do you mean?"

Although somewhat apprehensive, Meg replied in a steady voice. "I mean, Dave is an old army buddy of my brother's and nothing more. I hardly know him."

His frown deepened as he accepted the extent of her deceit. Anger and frustration gripped him. "Why the lie, Meg? Did you think a boyfriend would keep me from making advances? I do have a certain amount of decency—all you ever had to do was say no." He paused to stare at her. She hadn't said no, she'd responded, then attacked him. "If it wasn't Dave, what was it? You knew damn well that I wanted you. You gave me every reason to think you felt the same way. Why the games, Meg?" His features hardened until they resembled carved granite. "Did you enjoy teasing me? Did it give you a sense of power to have me hard and aching for you? Is that how you get your thrills—getting men aroused and then beating them away?" He knew he was being cruel, but the drive to hurt her as she had him prodded him on. "I guess it'll be fun to tell your friends how you had a dirty, money-grubbing mercenary at your mercy, how you almost had me begging for you." In his anger, he forgot her undisguised terror when she'd lashed out at him in the cave, forgot her genuine misery, forgot her actions were far from teasing.

The color drained from Meg's face. "It wasn't like that, Clay." With every beat of her heart, anguish pumped through her veins.

"Wasn't it, Meg? What was it like? What's going on now? Tell me because I don't understand. All I see is that I'm just a hired gun to you."

"That's not true, Clay," she insisted. "It's not true at all. I know I shouldn't have let you think there was something between Dave and me. I know I should've explained that he and Ted were in Vietnam together, that I only met him when they first got back." Clarifying that misunderstanding was only the first step, she knew.

Clay's dark lashes drifted shut. "I guess I can't blame you for that. You never exactly said you and Dave were...a couple. And, as for Vietnam, I already knew." He opened his eyes. "I didn't tell you that I knew your brother and Dave there, either. I don't know why, I just didn't."

Her jaw dropped open as she stared at him. "You couldn't have been in Vietnam. You're too young."

"Well, I'm younger than Dave and Ted but I was there." Suppressed emotion darkened his gaze. "We met in a POW camp."

"Did you escape with them?" Meg knew the story well. It had been big news in her hometown when her brother and two other Americans escaped.

"Yeah, you could say that. It was more like they dragged me along with them." Ugly recollection crowded his head. "We sort of formulated an escape plan from the time they arrived. I'd been itching to try from the first day but nobody else wanted to. But your brother and Dave were game."

Meg sensed there was more to the story. "Is that why you agreed to rescue Ted? Because he and Dave agreed to escape with you?"

A rueful smile lifted Clay's lips. "Not exactly."

"You said they dragged you along? Didn't you want to go?"

"Hell, yes, I wanted to go," he replied. He shoved his hands in the pockets of his pants. "I wanted to go, but they shouldn't have bothered to take me."

"I don't understand," Meg mumbled as she searched his face for some clue.

"I'd been there for a year or so before your brother and Ted were captured. By the time we had a solid plan and a good chance, I was a little worse for wear." He cleared his throat. Half-dead was closer to the truth. "I told them to go ahead without me..." Memory closed in on him. Between Ted and Dave, they'd half carried him out of North Vietnam, had given him the will to live when he had none of his own. More than the will to live, he recalled. They'd given him a sense of belonging, something he'd never had before, or since.

"So you feel like you owe my brother," she observed, knowing he'd glossed over his own suffering.

"I do owe him," Clay replied. "I owe him and Dave. They saved my rotten neck."

On trembling legs, she crossed the remaining distance between them and laid one hand on his chest. Rewarded by the frantic pace of his heart, as rapid as her own, she smiled up at him. "I'm glad," she whispered.

Searing heat seemed to leap from her palm into his heart before spreading through his body like wildfire. His blood flowed like warm molasses, thick and slow and sweet. Trying to concentrate on her words proved difficult when his body craved a different sort of communication.

"It was a long time ago," he mumbled. "I don't think about it much."

Meg studied his face. Maybe he didn't think about it often, but when he did, she knew those thoughts were unpleasant. "You must have been very young when you joined the army."

Clay's hand closed over hers before moving it away. He took a step back. "Seventeen and right out of high school. Four months later, I was in Nam." He turned to stare out the window, though in the ink-black night he saw nothing but haunting memories.

"How long were you there, before you were captured?" she asked in a tremulous whisper.

"Five months."

Meg saw tension invade his lean body and forgot her own nervousness. She walked up behind him, then reached out to massage his taut shoulder muscles. Beneath her light touch, the stiffness ebbed.

Recollections of her brother's return from Vietnam came back full force. For months, he had been aloof and antagonistic, rebuffing all attempts at kindness, ignoring his well-meaning family and friends, taking no pleasure in his former hobbies. Slowly, over a long time, he seemed to evolve into a reasonable facsimile of the young man he'd been.

Dread curled in the pit of her stomach. How much worse had it been for Clay, just a boy, to be thrust into the violence of war, then the brutality of imprisonment? Her heart turned over as her mind replied, *Hell on Earth*. No wonder he had chosen such an alien life-style. Especially after what he'd already described as a less-than-ideal childhood. When she asked his reasons for joining the army, Meg wasn't surprised at his answer.

"To get away from home." His jaw tightened. The past so rarely intruded on the present that he forgot its power to wound him. He was so different from that unloved, unwanted boy... or was he?

His brow furrowed. He liked to think he had overcome his poor start in life, but had he really? Poverty was no longer a problem, but he was alone as in his youth. Alone and, now that he knew what his life lacked, much lonelier.

Tension reentered his muscles. Maybe he'd been fooling himself all along by taking pride in his isolation and self-control. Maybe he'd just been covering the emptiness in his soul with the facade of remoteness.

"I'm sorry, Clay," she murmured as she felt him tense up. Her own family, happy and close-knit, had been the mainstay of her young life. Leaving home to go away to college had been a major upheaval. Even then, she'd stayed in close contact with her parents right up until their untimely deaths.

"I don't want pity, Meg. I don't need it," he muttered. "I left because I wanted to and I've stayed away for the same reasons."

When he turned to face her, her slender hand cupped his jaw. Pity wasn't what she wanted to offer him, she knew as she leaned forward to press a soft kiss at the throbbing pulse in his neck. "I don't pity you, Clay," she whispered against his warm flesh. "I'm just sorry."

A shudder racked him as he fought the urge to yank her against him and cover her mouth in a deep, demanding kiss, but he still didn't understand her violent withdrawal in the cave, and he wasn't prepared to risk such rejection again.

"There's no reason to be sorry. I didn't have it any worse than a lot of other guys, including your brother and Dave." His voice was a low growl. Her warm breath sensitized his skin in a way that made thinking difficult. "We were just like thousands of other American soldiers, caught in a bad situation, but we were lucky. We survived and escaped."

Meg's shimmering gaze saw potent pride, undeniable strength and firm determination in his handsome face. Only when she looked deep into his amber eyes could she discern any trace of vulnerability.

His experiences, beginning in childhood, might have destroyed any remnant of softness in a weaker man. Looking at him, Meg understood that real tenderness and compassion, especially in a man, were rooted in strength of character. And Clay was a real man, both tender and strong. Still, her heart ached for the lonely boy and the captured soldier.

"Ted and Dave were twenty-three when they went to Vietnam. They'd already finished college. They were adults."

Clay's mind locked on only one fact. "I didn't go to college. I almost didn't finish high school."

She moved her head back so she could see his face better. "I know." A perplexed frown crinkled her brow. "You don't think something like that would make any difference to me, do you?"

The unguarded warmth in her turquoise eyes reignited the banked fires of longing deep inside him, but he formed his reply carefully. "I think you *think* it shouldn't matter."

"I know I seemed like a snob at first but I thought by now you'd know me a little better. I thought you'd realize that I don't judge people by their educational levels, or their occupations," she said pointedly.

He bit hard on his lower lip. Every second in her presence weakened his will, sapped his resistance. He bowed his dark head. "Maybe you ought to go back to your room now, Meg."

A frown settled on her face. Suppressed emotion resonated in his deep voice, an emotion she couldn't quite identify but one that gave her a fresh burst of courage. "Do you want me to go, Clay?"

His jaw tightened until a muscle twitched. "No," he mumbled, "I don't want you to go. But it's better if you do."

"Better for who, Clay?" she asked, her courage growing. "Not better for me."

Longing further dulled logic as he struggled for control. "Meg, you don't know what you're suggesting." He released a pent-up breath. "I'm not the sort of man who...well, who has a lot of women friends. Hell, I hardly have any friends at all. I'm not a real sociable type so, if you're looking for someone to talk with...well, I think your sister-in-law would be a better choice."

Meg's tongue darted out to moisten her dry lips. "What happened in the cave won't happen again," she managed in a hoarse whisper. "You said you wanted me, Clay. Wasn't that true?"

A flash fire of desire consumed him. "Of course, it was true. I wanted you then...I want you now." He shook his head. "But it's no good."

"Clay, I told you, I won't forget again," she murmured. Her hands closed around his forearms. "I won't fight you."

His gaze narrowed on her flushed face. Somewhere in her words was the reason for her attack, but he couldn't figure exactly where. "What do you mean forget?" he asked in a low murmur. "You said you're not involved with Dave.... Is there someone else?"

She shook her head. "There's no one else," she whispered. Anxiety rose up before her like a restraining wall, but Meg knew she somehow had to scale it. After all she'd accomplished in the past week—leaving home, finding Clay, accompanying him here—she couldn't back down now. But despite the difficulty of those tasks, her next job was far more onerous. Her mind scrambled for just the right words to explain, words that wouldn't bring his pity or disgust, words that would make him understand.

Meg's gaze moved to a point above his right shoulder so she wouldn't see his expression, for better or worse. "In the cave you said that all I had to do was tell you no...but not all men believe a woman when she says no." The observation was wrenched from the depths of her soul, from the seed of her memory, from the source of her nightmares. Saying them made her throat raw and sore. Hearing them hang in the air made her ears ache for Clay's reply.

Cold sweat broke out over his back while shock froze him. The implication of her statement, along with his recollection of her sudden and seemingly illogical attack was like a kick to his gut. His stomach clenched into a hard knot.

"God, Meg," he muttered. "I must have scared the hell out of you." As he rested his hands lightly on her narrow shoulders, they trembled badly. "If I had known...I wouldn't have let things go so far." Then, remembering the ugly accusations he had flung at her earlier, he continued. "I'm sorry, Meg. For being so stupid and for saying what I did."

She swallowed hard. His reaction gave her faith. No trace of pity or disgust tainted his voice or his expression when she found the courage to face him.

"You didn't scare me, Clay, the memory did. I don't know, I guess I got confused. After the nightmare, well, I guess I forgot who was holding me," she mumbled. "I was okay as long as I could see your face, as long as I knew it was you. I wasn't afraid but somehow I got all mixed up."

His fingers massaged her taut muscles. "You were sick and tired, Meg. You had that awful nightmare a couple of times. You were half-asleep..."

"No," she corrected him. "I was wide awake when we...kissed. I knew what I was doing, Clay. And I wanted to kiss you. I wanted you to kiss me."

Relief sang through his veins. His touch hadn't repulsed her.

"Then it was probably just a one-time thing, anyhow. Because you didn't feel well. You haven't reacted like that other times, I guess, with other guys." The knot in his belly doubled. Why had he asked? If she said she hadn't, he'd only feel worse. Maybe he reminded her of her assailant. The idea revolted him.

Meg ducked her head as pink crept into her cheeks. Her innate sense of privacy made explaining difficult. "I...well, after the...assault, I didn't date much." She cleared her throat. "The truth is, you're the first man I've gotten into that sort of situation with since...it happened. I guess that's what triggered it...I knew in my head you wouldn't force me but...being in the same position, when your face was in the dark, I got scared and confused, I guess."

"That's understandable," he whispered. If they ever got in that situation again, he'd make sure she knew who held her.

She lifted her gaze to his. "The thing is, lots of men, you know, they think if a woman gets them...aroused, she should, you know, be prepared to do something about it." Discussing such a topic was alien to Meg, but with Clay, it seemed natural. "I know you're not like that," she hastened to assure him when she saw storm clouds mute the warmth in his eyes.

He tucked her head under his chin and held her in a loose, undemanding embrace as a surge of pure protectiveness welled up inside him. Sweet, gentle Meg should be cherished and adored. Any man with a brain could see that. "A lot of men get aroused just looking at a woman, but that doesn't give them any rights. Women don't owe them a damn thing."

Meg burrowed her nose into the strong column of his neck. The masculine scent of him tickled her senses even as his words filled her with relief. "But, when we were close like that...when we didn't go ahead, you must have been uncomfortable."

Not much more uncomfortable than he was at the moment, Clay thought. "I was, but only because I find you very attractive. Because you're desirable, I react to you in a certain way, but that doesn't give me any rights. Even if we kissed and caressed and you changed your mind, I would never force you, sweetheart. I couldn't do that, not to you or any other woman. I wouldn't want to and I sure as hell wouldn't have the right."

"Not all men are like you, Clay. Some of them don't care if the woman is screaming no," she whispered.

"Do you want to talk about it, Meg?" he asked as his hands skimmed her back. "If you're going to let me hold you, well, I want to make sure I don't scare you again."

She took a deep breath and inhaled his enticing male scent. In his arms, she found contentment and passion; she found her rightful place in the world. His words made her heart spin like a top. She wanted much more than just being held in his arms and was relieved at his indication that, despite everything, he did, too.

"It happened when I was in graduate school," she mumbled. "I'd been dating this guy, another student, for a few weeks. I liked him but it was casual, a friendship. Most of the time we went to the library, or went to activities on campus with other students we knew. We weren't alone very much. A couple times he sort of pressed for a more intimate relationship, but when I said no, he seemed to accept it. He teased me about being a goody-goody, having hang-ups, that sort of stuff. Maybe I was stupid, but I really didn't think I was leading him on or teasing him. I sure didn't mean to. I went to his place to study for an exam. When I got there, well, I guess he'd had a few beers.''

Clay continued to stroke her back. With difficulty, he remained placid, knowing instinctively that his anger would be misconstrued. ''What happened, sweetheart?'' he asked, though he dreaded her reply.

''I should've left right away, I suppose, as soon as I knew he'd had too much to drink,'' she mumbled against his neck.

''What happened wasn't your fault.'' He hugged her tighter in an effort to absorb some of her anguish. For one of the few times in his adult life, Clay felt truly helpless and he didn't like the feeling—didn't like it at all.

''He said I'd held out long enough.'' She shuddered at the memory. ''It happened so fast...'' Tears streamed down her face to wet his skin. ''He was too strong and he held me down. I tried to scream...but he covered my mouth. I could hardly breathe.''

Rage surged inside Clay, but he just held Meg, soothing her with incoherent murmurings and gentle touches. His lips skimmed her silky hair. ''I'm so sorry, sweetheart.''

She went on in a low monotone. ''I struggled but he slapped me, hard enough that I must have lost consciousness while he...raped me. When I came around, he was laughing... I hurt so much and all he did was laugh, said he hadn't figured on getting a virgin but at least I'd never forget him.'' Her tone remained flat and emotional, as if she repeated a dull, everyday event instead of a very real, personal tragedy.

''Dear God,'' Clay mumbled as his own tears filled his eyes while hers continued to wet his neck. Impotent fury raged through him. It was worse than he'd figured. If he could only get his hands on that bastard for five minutes . . . Knowing such a sentiment wouldn't help Meg, he held her close. "Did he go to jail?"

"No, I never reported it." She pulled away to look up at Clay. "I couldn't. We'd been dating. I went to his place voluntarily. No one would have believed me, Clay." Her voice took on a plaintive, melancholy tone. She hated the pleading note, but she wanted so desperately for him to understand why she'd kept the ugly secret.

Clay ground his teeth. What could he say? Knowing the treatment rape victims had to endure in court, he realized Meg would have been the one on trial. Breath hissed through his teeth. Meg, who had done nothing wrong except give her trust, remained a victim long after the assault was over.

She wiped the moisture from her face and for the first time noticed the tracks of tears on his hard face. Her hand reached out to trace the path. "Are these for me?" she asked in a voice filled with awe.

His hand went around her wrist. "I just hate thinking of anyone hurting you, Meg. It makes me sick inside." He moved her hand to his mouth and pressed a gentle kiss in the palm. "You deserve to be protected and cherished. You deserve tenderness and affection."

Her thumb caressed his upper lip in a feather-light motion. "Do I, Clay?"

Her innocent question sent longing through him. "Yes, sweetheart. You deserve a man who appreciates you, a man who will treasure you."

The warmth in his gaze melted her heart. "What do I do when I find such a man, Clay? How do I get him to . . . make love to me if he knows my ugly secret?"

"Nothing about you could ever be ugly, Meg. Don't even think that. You're beautiful, inside and out." Emotion nearly choked him. When he looked at her shimmering gaze, filled with promise and need, he yearned to tell her how much she meant to him, how dear she was, how important. He yearned to reassure her, but he hesitated. As soon as Ted was safe, she'd go back to Ohio. Back to where she was safe and secure while he returned to his job, a dangerous, dirty, deceitful existence that someone as good and kind as Meg could never understand.

"You didn't answer my question, Clay," she whispered.

"Meg, you don't really know me," he muttered as he removed her hand from his mouth and turned away. "You don't really know anything about me. You don't know the things I've done, the life I've led."

"I know you're a mercenary, Clay, and I don't care. You're a good man, a strong man . . . you're kind and sensitive. It doesn't matter what you do for a living."

He wished to God it didn't, but he knew better. "I live by my gun, Meg. I wear it the way most men wear a watch."

"Only because you have to. You're so much more than just what you do, darling. You're so special."

"I don't think you see me for what I am."

"I see a man who wouldn't protect himself for fear of hurting someone weaker. I see a man who'll risk his life for someone he hasn't seen in over twenty years. I see a man who's been hurt and disappointed yet still has an inner core of goodness. I see someone I trust, someone I respect . . ." She drew a deep, reassuring breath before pressing ahead. "I see the man I love."

Clay spun to face her. The open admission in her gaze humbled him. "Meg, do you know what you're saying?" he asked in a raw whisper.

Meg bit her lip as Carlotta's warning rang in her ears. "Someone hurt you, very badly."

"I'm not discounting what you think are real feelings, Meg, but I . . . well, I allowed myself to be deluded once but I was young and foolish and filled with romantic notions that don't have much to do with real life."

"But you aren't anymore," she said sadly.

"No, I'm not. Sometimes, when we're with people in unusual circumstances, we get, well, strange ideas. Maybe you see me as some sort of hero because I'm going after your brother," he explained, "but I'm just a man and not a very good one at that."

He went to the bed and braced his elbows on his knees. Fighting his desires was difficult. Fighting hers, too, almost impossible.

Meg knelt in front of him. "I already told you, my vision is twenty-twenty. I'm not a schoolgirl, despite my lack of experience. I know the difference between love and infatuation."

"You think you do, just like you think you love me but you're in a strange place, under difficult circumstances. When you get home, you'll see I'm right."

"What I feel has nothing to do with proximity or circumstances, Clay. What I feel for you is real. What I feel is something I'll remember for the rest of my life, no matter where I am. I love you, Clay. I need you. I want you."

"Meg, you don't know what you're saying, what you're suggesting," he muttered in a strangled voice.

Shocked by her audacity and anxious over his response, Meg moved to halt more of his self-recrimination. She wrapped her arms around his neck and covered his mouth in a potent kiss.

Blood coursed through Clay like a raging river. When the tip of her tongue traced his lips, he shook. When it darted inside, he shuddered. Finally, after she made a thorough inspection of his mouth, he yanked her up against him.

"Meg, you send me reeling. I can hardly think straight." He tried to gather his scattered thoughts, but only one idea permeated the fog in his head. Meg loved him. She wanted him.

She burrowed against him. "Neither can I, but I like it, don't you?"

"I like it far too much," he whispered into her soft curls. Freshly shampooed, her hair held the scent of some exotic flower. The fragrance tickled his nose with every breath.

Anxiety and inexperience softened her voice until it was nearly inaudible. "I want to be with you, Clay."

"I'm leaving early in the morning, Meg."

She heard the warning note in his voice. He hadn't returned her vow of love, but as much as she wished for it, she'd take whatever he was willing to give. She'd been prepared for rejection, prepared to have nothing, or one night. "Forever" was a foolish wish, a schoolgirl's whim. Holding a man like Clay Terhune would be like chaining a jaguar to a doghouse. Such an exotic creature would die in captivity.

"I know, Clay, and I understand. I don't expect promises."

She might not expect them but he wished he could make them. He wished he had something to offer her but he didn't. He was leaving in a few hours, leaving and, despite his reassurances to Meg, maybe not coming back. Lifelong restraint collided with yearning. He hadn't been so close to losing his control in years. The last time he'd lost it, disaster had followed. Clay started to pull away but Meg wouldn't let him.

Her head fell back as her arms tightened around him. The ambivalent emotions crossing his face telegraphed his need, and the shackles he placed on it. "Clay..." Lacking both experience and confidence, Meg didn't know how to proceed. All she knew for sure was that she loved this man and wanted to be with him.

Looking down at Meg's flushed face was like taking a blow to the gut. Seeing his own need reflected in her eyes loosened but didn't destroy his self-imposed restrictions. Because he knew letting her go was the best course, for both of them, he clasped her hands and drew them away from his shoulders as he took a half-step backward. The emotions growing between them were something he wanted to pursue but not when he faced a dangerous mission within hours. "Meg, it's late," he mumbled.

Her eyes widened with dismay. "I want you, Clay," she whispered. Her teeth caught her trembling lower lip. "You said you wanted me, too."

A shuddering sigh escaped him. He pulled her back into his warm embrace. As he stroked her soft hair, he pressed his lips to her temple. "I want you more than my next breath," he murmured with complete honesty. "I want you so much I ache but, more than that, I want to be the one who shows you how lovemaking should be between a man and woman." He brushed his lips across her brow. He wanted that and more, so much more. Maybe too much.

Relief made Meg relax. "That's what I want, too." Although he hadn't reciprocated her vow of love, Meg knew Clay cared about her. She also knew, from Hank and Carlotta, that he lacked trust in the opposite sex. Meg could have told him she was trustworthy but she knew firsthand no amount of talking could convince anyone as gun-shy as Clay. After all, hearing words of reassurance about him from Hank and Carlotta hadn't eased Meg's mind about this potently masculine mercenary. Only his actions had done that. She only hoped he'd give her the same chance she had given him. By offering the gift of trust, Meg hoped to eventually secure his. "I want you to make love to me, Clay." She swallowed hard. "I never thought I'd say that to any man...not after the rape but I do want you." Her voice sounded odd, as if it came from a distant stranger, a stranger familiar with the dark desire and pounding passion Clay's touch evoked.

Her admission sent a sharp lance of longing through him while at the same time humbling him. Meg, who had every reason to be terrified of intimacy, offered a gift greater than gold, a gift Clay wasn't sure he deserved but couldn't deny he wanted. But he didn't want to take advantage of her heightened emotions, or hurry what should be something special, for both of them. For Meg, it needed to be perfect.

Clay's lips skimmed her hair as his fingers trailed up and down her bare arms. "I want that, too," he murmured, "but not tonight, not when I have to leave you in a few hours."

When Meg let her head rest against his hard chest, she heard and felt his pounding heart. The staccato beat gave her confidence. "When?"

Her simple query drove past his last vestige of common sense, past his last rein of control. Fighting his feelings was no longer possible. Somehow Meg had slipped past his defenses. If he got back with her brother, Clay knew he couldn't walk away from her.

His mouth moved over her face, stringing kisses over every inch before settling on her lips. At first his kiss was coaxing and cajoling but when she responded like spark to tinder, he again took possession of her willing mouth.

"When, Clay?" she asked again when he tore his mouth from hers.

For several moments, he stared down at her, then let his hands slide down her arms to grasp her fingers. "Meg, when I get back," he began in a ragged whisper, "when I return with your brother, I have some time left before I have to go back to work. What I'm trying to say, if you wanted, you could stay in Puerto Rico for a couple of weeks, at least until I have to leave."

Relief spiralled through her. Clay wanted to be with her for as long as possible. Although it wasn't the declaration of love and trust she hoped for, it was a start. A smile lifted her lips. "Of course, I want to stay, for however long you have, I want to be with you."

Clay tugged her against him and pressed a kiss to her temple. He still needed to be sure she understood that what he was offering wasn't permanent. He had to make himself realize it, too.

"Are you sure, sweetheart? I could understand if you want to go home right away." He not only understood, he thought it might be better for both of them if she did. "You've been through a lot."

With one forefinger, Meg traced his furrowed brow. Despite his invitation, she knew he believed her feelings resulted from infatuation, not love. She also knew he still withheld a part of himself from her, as he did with everyone. The knowledge that she might not pierce his defenses saddened her but she kept her smile in place. At least he was giving an opportunity to try, even if he didn't realize it.

"I love you, Clay. I want to be with you," she murmured.

His callused fingertips skidded over her soft cheek. He studied her open expression and wondered if he could afford to be as open and honest. By inviting her to stay in Puerto Rico, he ran the risk of exposing himself emotionally. By inviting her to stay, he committed himself to a course that might spell disaster.

If Meg learned the entire truth about him, how would she react? And if he didn't tell her, how he could accept the gift of trust and love she offered?

Even if she knew and accepted the truth, they still came from different worlds. Worlds apart. Even though he yearned for more than a brief interlude, how could he ask her to share the future when he never knew if he would have one? How could he saddle her with the burden of waiting and worrying, maybe forever? In his line of work, he might disappear without a trace, be held hostage, or worse. How could he ask Meg to endure that sort of hell? She deserved better. She deserved a man who could stand with her in the sun, not pull her into the darkness.

"Nothing will change how I feel about you, Clay," she promised.

How he wanted to believe her assertion. How he wanted to forget the obstacles separating them.

Clay's failure to respond disturbed Meg but his expression troubled her more. The lines of fatigue scoring his heavily shadowed eyes sent a spear of guilt through her. His earlier fatigue had become exhaustion. While he desperately needed rest to face the dangerous job ahead, she was keeping him awake. Her fingers lightly traced the bruise beneath one eye.

"You need to get some rest," she whispered. Her heart hammered against her ribs. Would he ask her to leave? Or would she be allowed the luxury of sleeping in his arms?

Because he knew he ought to lie down before he fell down, Clay agreed. "I guess we both could use some sleep," he murmured as he gently stroked her inner wrist. If he had any sense, he'd insist she leave but Clay had already learned that logic had no place in his dealing with Meg Andrews.

"Meg, do you want to stay here?" His voice was a rough, ragged whisper he barely recognized. He knew he was being a fool, but he was unable to send her away. He'd have to do that soon enough.

"That's why I came," she admitted in an equally hoarse voice.

Clay sighed. Knowing what it had cost to confront a man, any man, in his room, Clay was powerless to deny her. "We're both tired and worried now. It'll be better if we wait," he said as he gently stroked her back.

"I suppose," she mumbled as fresh awareness trickled through her, making her quiver in his arms. She laid one hand on his chest and felt the rapid thud of his heart. Never in her life had she felt closer or more bound to another human being. Never in her life had she wanted a man with such fierceness. No one but Clay had ever, would ever, evoke such a strong response.

Feeling her tremble and mistaking its source, Clay loosened his hold and stepped away. Although he felt a bit like a man on the way to the gallows, he smiled down at her. "I think we better get you under the covers," he whispered as he helped Meg into the cozy bed before discarding his shirt and joining her.

When he opened his arms, she entered his embrace. Then, as her bare legs met denim, she tensed slightly. "Are you going to sleep with your pants on?" she asked in confusion even though she still wore her shorts and top.

A low chuckle rumbled out of his chest. "I think that's best, if I expect to sleep at all," he said, although he doubted he'd get much rest. With her soft curves cradling his hard angles and his anxiety about the future crowding his mind, Clay felt wired and restless. Still, he tucked her closer and tried to sound calmer than he felt. "Now, try to get some sleep, sweetheart. Dawn is only a few hours away."

Apprehension impinged on Meg's peace. She didn't want to think about Clay leaving. She didn't want to think of him in danger, but she couldn't ask him to stay beside her. He wasn't the sort of man who would ever stay on the sidelines. He wasn't a man who could be content outside the arena of action. "You'll wake me before you go, won't you?" Her voice trembled with concern while one hand stroked the strong column of his neck. Her forefinger tested his pulse, finding it strong and steady, as strong and steady as the man himself. But, despite his vigor and virility, Clay was a human being, a human being who hurt and bled, a human being who could suffer and die.

Tears pricked her eyes, but she blinked them away. At least until he left, she had to be as strong and sure as he was. At least until then, she had to be brave.

Clay hesitated. In the morning, he would again assume his professional persona, an identity that had already disgusted and dismayed Meg. Did she recall her reaction to him in Hank's cantina, or did proximity and passion dull that memory? He couldn't be sure. All he really knew was that he couldn't bear to see her eyes cloud with loathing.

When he became Clay Terhune, mercenary, would she forget the Clay who had dropped his barriers to be vulnerable for the first time in years? Would she forget the Clay who had opened his heart to a woman he shouldn't want and probably couldn't have?

"Of course I'll say goodbye," he promised, although he took care not to say he'd actually wake her. "Now rest, Meg."

The remaining tension drained from her as she settled against him like a trusting child.

But long after Meg slept peacefully, Clay continued to stroke her back and wonder what the future held for them.

Chapter 8

During the long hours of darkness, Clay held Meg and worried. Possibilities and problems spun wild webs of confusion in his mind.

He was good at what he did, he knew. That competence had always been a source of pride, but now that it kept him from the one person who mattered, Clay cursed his talent. His prowess at handling difficult, dangerous situations might well keep him from Meg forever. His skills weren't the sort to transfer to another, more suitable, line of work. And even if he found another way to make a living, didn't Meg deserve a man as untainted as she, a man untouched by violence and deceit?

A heavy sigh escaped him as he gently stroked the copper hair strewn across his pillow. Already the leaden sky turned to silver. Outside, he heard movement and soon, too soon, he had to leave her.

Before disentangling their bodies, he brushed a featherlight kiss across her brow and prayed to find some way to reconcile the differences threatening their relationship. Reluctantly, he rolled away and left the comforting warmth of her presence.

The morning air cooling his flesh was warm compared to the ice freezing his heart. An inexplicable sense of grief and loss filled him as he looked down at Meg's lovely face. She really was too good for him. He'd known it from the first but it hadn't stopped him from wanting her. Only her rejection could do that. If she turned away from him, from what he was, Clay would walk out of her life forever, even though he'd be leaving his heart behind. After several long moments, he turned away and began to dress.

Meg awoke slowly, but when her arms reached out and found nothing, her eyes flew open in alarm. In the dim light of dawn, she saw Clay's muscular body silhouetted in the window and relief flooded her. He was still with her. He was still safe.

"Clay..."

Her sleep-thickened voice sounded sultry and seductive as it floated to him. A hot thread of yearning wound through his veins until it reached his aching heart. How easily she aroused him, he thought with a trace of amazement. Ordinarily he found ignoring his wants simple but *want* didn't even scratch the surface of what he felt for Meg.

"It's not daylight yet, sweetheart," he muttered. Fear compelled him. "Why don't you go back to sleep." It took every ounce of self-control he possessed to continue dressing.

"When are you leaving?"

"Soon," he mumbled, keeping his back to her.

"When will you be back?" Anxiety expanded in her chest until she could barely breathe.

"Later today, tonight probably. Maybe not until tomorrow morning. It depends on how things go. It's difficult to predict." As difficult as it was to predict what her reaction would be when she saw him in work garb.

Meg shifted to sit against the headboard. "I—I hope it goes well," she whispered. She wished she knew what to do or say to bring his attention to her. His behavior rattled her confidence and undermined her courage. Why didn't he look at her?

The concern in her voice made his heart turn over. "Thanks," he muttered as he snapped on the light and began smearing his face with a dark substance that matched the camouflage clothing he wore. She obviously wasn't going to cooperate and go back to sleep, he thought with irritation. Well, so be it. She might as well see him for exactly what he was. And, glancing up so he could see her reflection in the mirror, he might as well see her, too.

The dismay on her face didn't surprise him but the fear that had stalked him in the night settled over him like a shroud. Something deep inside died as he bowed his head.

"This is what I am, Meg. This is how I dress to go to work. Not in a three-piece suit, not carrying a briefcase." His stomach churned violently.

Before he'd ducked his head, Meg had looked into his eyes and seen a flare of anguish. She hastened to correct his assumption. "I know what you do, Clay. I knew when I walked into the cantina. What you do for a living isn't what you are. What you wear or carry with you doesn't change how much I love you."

Maybe. But when he looked into the mirror, he knew the truth was there. While Meg appeared delicate and fragile, he looked wild and dangerous. In the reflection, they were complete opposites—hard and soft, darkness and light, good and evil.

In the gaping silence, Meg grew increasingly uneasy and uncertain. As she studied Clay, his bowed head and tense shoulders, she wondered if he was sorry he'd let her stay. She wondered if he was sorry he'd asked her to come to Puerto Rico. Then a more devastating thought flashed in her mind.

"Clay," she began in a hoarse whisper. "Last night...did you let me stay here because you felt sorry for me?" Her voice was barely audible but its tremor was clear. Maybe he didn't really want to make love to her, after all. Maybe he was just trying to let her down easy. Maybe, when he got back he'd find some excuse to rescind his invitation.

His heart clenched like a fist as he swung to face and saw the pain in her eyes. Because he couldn't bear to hurt her, Clay hastened to reassure her. "No, Meg. That wasn't why I let you stay."

She closed her eyes against the hot moisture burning in them. "I don't believe you," she whispered. If her legs hadn't been shaking so badly, she would have run away, as far and fast as possible, away from humiliation, away from embarrassment, away from the aching agony of loss. What a fool she was to think any man who really wanted her would invite her into his bed and then do nothing more than hold her. Clay's action had been nothing more than kindness.

Clay took an involuntary step forward. In the gathering light, Meg looked delicate, fragile, almost ethereal yet he now knew that was deceiving. Inside her was a core of steel, a determination he admired, a courage he respected because he knew it had been forged from the ashes of devastation. Yet he also knew she was vulnerable. "I let you stay because I couldn't bear to let you go."

Delicate color warmed her cheeks as she said, "I was afraid you didn't want to hurt my feelings by, you know, rejecting me after I came to your room."

"Reject you? Are you kidding?" he asked in surprise. "I wasn't rejecting you when I said we should wait, Meg. I was fighting every instinct and hormone in my body." His fingers burrowed through the silk of her hair. "When I said I wanted you, I meant it. It took every ounce of self-restraint I've got not to make love to you last night."

Warmth and relief spread through her. Meg reached out to trap his head in her hands. When she pulled his mouth down to hers, he didn't resist. Hot shards of longing exploded inside her as he deepened the kiss.

As soon as their lips touched, Clay forgot about restraint. His mouth grew more urgent, more possessive, more persuasive. Both the past and the future faded to black as desire ruled him. The rest of the world disappeared until Meg was his only reality, pleasing her his only concern.

Meg was equally oblivious to the outside world. Just as her hands slid down to his open shirt, a sharp rap at the door intruded.

"Clay," Juan called through the barrier of the door, "it's almost time to leave. Are you ready?"

Cursing under his breath, Clay eased away from Meg's warmth and tenderness. "I'm ready," he called back. "I'll be right down."

"Fine, I'll see you in the library."

When his footsteps retreated, Clay glanced back at Meg. Her flushed face and glazed eyes reminded him of how completely he forgot his duty, how easily he lost control. He shook his head as if to clear it of the fog. There was so much he needed to tell her, so much he had to explain but he didn't have time. His jaw tightened.

Meg saw his features harden into an implacable mask, the mask he wore for the role he played. The role of a cold, hard warrior. Looking at him—face caked with grease, body clad in camouflage, sidearm strapped to his lean thigh—she could almost believe the image he presented, almost but not quite. Not when she knew the tender, sensitive man dwelling inside this wild warrior.

Clay looked at Meg and again felt amazement that this woman might care for him. Emotions exploded inside him as he fought for control.

"Be careful, Clay," she whispered.

"Meg, there's so much I want to tell you," he began before her fingers against his lips stopped further comment.

"We'll have lots of time to talk later," she said, reassuring herself as well as him. Her fingertips gently stroked his damp lips.

His hand cupped her jaw while a frown crinkled his brow. "I got dark cream on your face."

"It'll wash off, Clay."

"I suppose," he mumbled, but the sight of the smudge he'd left on her pale skin reminded him of the gap between them. It reminded him all too clearly how his presence might soil her life.

"I'll be waiting for you, Clay."

Deep in his soul, Clay felt something give. An entire lifetime of solitary self-sufficiency left him unprepared for the need coursing through him, a need to believe in the pretty fairy tale of her love, a need to believe in white knights and fair maidens and happily-ever-after.

As he reached out to her with both hands and she placed her slim fingers in his, Clay knew he might be making a critical error. Still, when he looked into her eyes and saw his longing reflected there, he knew he couldn't turn his back on her, or all she made him feel. Even if, later, she left him, at least he'd have a few precious memories.

"We can talk when we get to Puerto Rico," he whispered. When he was rewarded with her dazzling smile, he forgot his misgivings, forgot everything but his feelings for this remarkable woman.

"Yes, we will," she agreed with relieved enthusiasm.

Clay lifted her hands to his lips and placed a kiss in each palm. After tucking her beneath the covers, he got to his feet. "Try to get some more rest, sweetheart. I'll see you soon."

Meg trembled as she watched him gather the rest of his supplies. Despite their confident exchange, she knew he was risking his life by going after her brother, risking his life because she had asked him. "Clay, please be careful," she said in a broken whisper.

"I will," he promised. Then, with one last longing look, he was gone.

After tossing and turning and punching both pillows, Meg finally fell into a light sleep. When she awoke again, sunlight flooded the room...Clay's room. She sucked in a deep breath and found his male scent everywhere...on the linens and in the air. She burrowed her face into the pillow that had such a short time earlier held his head, but she found no comfort there.

Finally, unable to bear reminders of his absence, she jumped up and tossed on her clothes. After a quick bath, she went downstairs.

The somber silence of the house drove her outside. Feeling alone and lonely, she wandered down the path to the gazebo. In the brilliant sunshine, the structure's blemishes were completely exposed, but Meg didn't mind. It offered serenity. Yet, as she mounted the steps, she realized she wasn't alone in her quest for tranquillity.

Maria glanced up in surprise but a welcoming smile lifted her lips as Meg joined her.

"I hope you don't mind," Meg said as she sat down beside her new sister-in-law, the sister-in-law she had nearly forgotten existed since last night.

"Of course not," Maria replied in slightly accented but perfect English.

"Are you feeling more rested?" Meg asked. "The housekeeper said you didn't come to dinner because you were tired."

"Yes, thank you. It was rude of me not to come down, not to speak with you but I was very tired," she hastily explained.

"I understand," Meg assured her. "You must have had a long, hard trip getting here."

Maria nodded. "Leaving the capital city unobserved was not easy." She sighed. "And I was not certain I was doing the right thing. Not when Ted was still being detained. But since I could not do anything myself, I came here in the hope of securing help." She smiled again. "Of course, I was not expecting to find that you had already made arrangements for Ted's rescue."

"I'm glad you came here," Meg told her. "And I know Ted will be glad, too."

"Thank you," Maria murmured. Her dark gaze glittered with hope and anxiety. "I hope you are not unhappy about this surprise. Ted wanted to tell you in person."

"I understand, and I'm very happy for both of you. I hope we'll become good friends."

"That is my hope, as well. Ted has told me a great deal about you and I know you are a close family." Tears filled her ebony eyes. "I hope you will not blame me for keeping Ted here. If not for me, he would be safe in America."

"Of course I don't blame you."

Maria caught her lower lip between even white teeth. "Ted talked about going home; he wanted to go but I would not go with him." A shuddering sigh left her. "I could not go. You see, it was my brother who called him."

A frown crinkled Meg's brow. "Your family owned the newspaper?"

"Yes, we did."

"You were very courageous to keep publishing, to keep speaking out against the drug lords and their corruption of the government."

Maria shrugged. "Only a few years ago, my country was a proud democracy. Then, our economy faltered. Many people were out of work, the farmers suffered as crops failed and prices fell. At the same time, the drug trade grew rapidly in neighboring countries. Many have tried to crack down on the cartels but with little success. The drug lords fear nothing, except extradition to America. Even when they are arrested in South America, they often continue their business from prison. And in Costa del Palma, they do not even have to worry about prison because they control the government."

Meg shook her head. "I don't know much about your country's problems. I didn't realize how bad things were."

"We are a small nation, which is part of why the drug lords gained control so quickly, so completely. With our economic troubles, they found ample opportunity to spread their influence, and their evil. People who are hungry often forget their values. So do people who are afraid.''

''But your family didn't.''

Maria gave her a sad smile. ''When the drug lords first came to my country, my father was still alive. He was well-known and respected, both as a journalist and as one who had fought for our country's independence many years ago. He was always a man of principle, a man of conviction. He spoke out against the drug cartels, and those who appeased them.''

Maria's words reminded Meg of the things Clay had told her. ''He wouldn't accept money or cave in to threats.''

''Yes,'' Maria agreed. ''Those who could not be bought or intimidated were killed, or imprisoned. It is an ugly truth of life in Costa del Palma, and much of Latin America.''

''Your father was killed by the drug lords?''

''Indirectly,'' Maria replied. ''Several months before our paper was bombed, he died from a massive heart attack brought on, I believe, by stress.''

''I'm so sorry,'' Meg murmured. ''You've been through so much.''

Tears filled Maria's dark eyes but her smile remained in place. ''I do not know how I would have gotten along if not for Ted. He has been a source of strength for me.'' Her smile faltered. ''I am only sorry I have kept him from his family for so long.''

Meg gave the other woman's shoulder a reassuring pat. ''It won't be long until he is here with us,'' she said softly.

Maria nodded as she wiped the moisture from her eyes. ''I know it must be very difficult for you, having two men you love in danger.''

Color warmed Meg's cheeks. ''I hardly know Clay,'' she mumbled, unable to deny the truth yet unable to admit it, either. ''We only met a few days ago...''

Maria's expression softened with understanding. ''But I knew Ted only a few days when I fell in love with him,'' she murmured.

"It's not the same situation," Meg said as she got to her feet and went to stare into the dense woods.

"No," Maria quickly agreed. "You are not in love with a man from another country, a man with a family including two little boys who may not want a new mother."

Meg spun back to face her sister-in-law. "The boys will love you, Maria. I know they will. And you'll like Ohio, too."

A slow smile curved the other woman's lips. "I look forward to meeting them, and seeing your home. It will be good to have a family again." Her gaze skimmed Meg's expression. "Wouldn't your Clay like Ohio?"

Meg sighed. "I don't know. We haven't discussed the future...not the distant future, anyhow. I don't think he's ever had a real home, and I know he doesn't let many people get close to him."

"But he has let you close," Maria observed. "It was in his eyes yesterday when you came out of the house."

Meg's heart danced a jig but her head swirled with confusion. "He doesn't seem to have much faith in love, or much trust in people," she said almost to herself.

"Then you must be especially patient with him. You must show him love and trust so he can believe in their power."

As Meg nodded in agreement, she knew the task ahead required far more courage and determination than leaving home or journeying to Costa del Palma had. It required every ounce of strength and faith she possessed, and some she hadn't yet acquired. Still, doubt assailed her. Could she, as Maria suggested, convince Clay they belonged together for longer than the interlude in Puerto Rico he had promised? And, more worrisome, would she have the chance?

Chapter 9

Through the long hours of the day and night, Meg and Maria waited. While they got better acquainted, an unspoken undercurrent of anxiety stretched between them. They slept briefly, awakening before dawn to find their men not yet returned, nor was any word about them available.

By midmorning, a steady drizzle fell from the leaden sky and the pair retreated to the library where the housekeeper had lit a cozy fire. Although the blaze warmed the room, it did nothing for Meg's chilled spirits. The men were late, very late, she realized, although she said nothing to her sister-in-law.

When shouts broke the echoing silence, both women darted into the hall and then outside. Standing in the fine mist, they watched as a small band, surrounded by a clique of greeters, approached. Terror and hope strangled Meg, but when she felt Maria's hand grasp hers, she forced a thin smile. With visibility hampered by gloom and drizzle, she found identifying any of the men impossible.

"There," Maria murmured, "there he is." She released Meg's hand and raced away.

Meg watched as Maria barreled into one of the men and the two figures became indistinguishable. Joy spiraled through her as she recognized her brother's rangy form, but her gaze searched the street for another, equally important, figure.

Before she could look for Clay, Ted and Maria were beside her, pulling her into their enthusiastic embrace. Momentarily, she allowed herself to be swallowed by their warmth, but over her brother's shoulder, her gaze swept the street. When she finally saw Clay, the terror that had haunted her finally disappeared and real relief, pure and potent, took its place. Clay was safe.

Meg broke away from her family and darted toward Clay, who stood alone in the middle of the street.

Clay saw Meg coming toward him and tried to meet her, but his feet refused to budge. Rain soaked his hair and plastered his clothing to his clammy flesh as he kept his attention fixed on Meg's lovely face. Chills raced down his spine and exhaustion weighted his limbs. He took a tentative step toward her, but the straps of his pack digging into his aching body and the accompanying pain radiating through his chest and shoulder stopped him. Meg's figure blurred and the voices around him became garbled. While he struggled to focus on her smile of warm welcome, he shook his head in an effort to dispel the grogginess. Instead, the motion sent agony ripping through his shoulder. Sudden dizziness made him sway. As he slid one hand inside his jacket, his fingers met with a sticky residue. Clay sighed. The makeshift bandage he had applied hours earlier was saturated with blood.

In the hours since the rescue, lightheadedness had threatened but not broken his control. Now waves of vertigo broke over him. Clay gritted his teeth against pain and nausea. Again, he tried to move but couldn't.

Meg was only inches away when she saw him stagger. In concern, she reached to grab his arm. "Clay, what's wrong?"

Fiery pain flamed up his arm. Its roaring intensity drowned out her words. Bile choked him, and he shut his eyes against the giddiness.

"Clay..." Meg became frantic when she saw his ashen complexion and dulled gaze up close.

He forced his eyes open for an instant, but her image remained fuzzy, her words indistinct. Clay stared at her, trying to root himself in the present, trying to fight off encroaching oblivion, trying to say something that would drive the terror from her garbled voice but the task was impossible. "Meg..."

She watched in horror as he collapsed at her feet. Frozen by shock, she stared down at his crumpled body for several seconds. By the time she snapped out of her dazed astonishment, Ted was on his knees beside Clay.

"Damn fool," her brother muttered as he tore away the other man's jacket.

Meg felt the color drain from her face as Clay's heavily bloodstained bandage was revealed. "No..." Her voice was a plaintive cry.

Ted scowled. "The idiot must have been shot during the rescue, not that any of us knew it," he muttered. "He stuck this on it," he said as he removed the saturated cloth from Clay's torn flesh.

Fear lay like a lump on Meg's heart. "No..." she repeated in a high, taut voice.

Briefly, Ted glanced up at his sister's pale face before turning back to the wounded man. "Tell Juan that Clay's been shot. I'll need help getting him to bed and taking care of the wound."

Getting Clay settled in the upstairs bedroom proved to be an arduous task. Although he didn't regain consciousness, his low moans tore at Meg's heart. She trailed after the men carrying him, feeling acutely guilty and very anxious.

Once Clay was placed on the big bed they had shared so briefly but so beautifully, Meg edged into the room and stood at the foot. In the glaring artificial light, his complexion was a sickly gray and the fresh blood soaking his undershirt glowed scarlet. She couldn't help but wonder how much of the precious fluid he had lost in the long hours since the rescue. Dismay flickered through her as she knew it must have been a great deal.

"I'll need bandages and whatever medical supplies you might have available," Ted told Juan.

"One of the men has gone to the local pharmacy to get medicine and your wife is gathering the necessary supplies." He glanced from Ted to Clay, his dark gaze troubled. "But we have no doctor now and no way to give a blood transfusion."

Ted bit his lower lip. "If only Clay had told us he'd been hit instead of ignoring it until he fell flat on his face." Frustration and fatigue roughened his voice.

Juan nodded. "I know, but we have all done foolish things."

"You're right about that," Ted admitted, "but walking miles with a bullet and losing blood the whole time goes beyond foolish."

"You are sure the bullet is still in him?" the other man asked.

"I'm afraid so," Ted said on a resigned sigh. "I wish to hell it wasn't."

"At least no organs were hit," Juan murmured.

Ted sighed again. "If any had been, he'd be dead."

Panic reasserted itself in Meg, squeezing hard on her heart. "He'll be okay, won't he?" she asked in a hoarse whisper. Dismay coalesced into a sinking mass of dread. Seeing Clay so pale and still terrified her. Clay was usually so vital and virile, which only made his current condition more frightening. Hot tears flooded her eyes.

Ted recognized his sister's anxiety and tried to reassure her. "He's strong and healthy, Meg. That's in his favor."

Before Meg could form a reply, Maria, arms filled with supplies, entered the room. As Ted relieved her of the burden, he managed a tired smile. "Thanks. I'm going to need your help. The bullet's still in him and it looks like it's pretty deep."

"I can help you," Maria offered. "I took nurse's training before I received my degree in journalism."

"I didn't know that," Ted said in surprise.

Maria smiled. "You do not know everything about me," she whispered.

"I can also help. I have tended many such wounds," Juan said.

Ted glanced at him. "Is there any sort of painkiller we could give him before I try to take out the bullet?"

Maria was the one who responded. "The pharmacy has nothing appropriate for presurgery, but we can give him something after we get the bleeding stopped."

An uneasy sigh escaped Ted. "Maybe we ought to tie him down..."

"No." Meg stepped forward. "You can't do that."

Three pairs of eyes shifted toward her, but she saw only Clay. Clay, weak and vulnerable, in pain and at their mercy. The same protective instincts she often felt in regard to her nephews surged forth. "Don't tie him up," she urged in a tremulous whisper.

"Meg," her brother began, "we have to keep him still. We can't have him thrashing all over and maybe doing more damage."

Maria slipped a reassuring arm around Meg's shoulders. "Why don't you go downstairs and help the housekeeper make some sandwiches? I will be down as soon as I can."

Meg shook off Maria's arm and advanced on the bed. "I can help here," she protested.

"Meg, you've never seen a bullet wound, much less watched a bullet removed under less than perfect conditions. I don't think you need to witness this right now. I think you'd be more help in the kitchen. Later, when we're done, you can sit with Clay."

Her attention shifted from Clay to her brother. In the glaring light, he appeared almost as gaunt and ashen as Clay. The will to argue with him deserted her. "Okay," she mumbled with reluctance.

"I will be down when we are done," Maria promised.

Meg's expression softened as she faced her sister-in-law. "Thank you," she murmured before, after one last look at Clay, she turned and left the room.

As soon as the door closed behind her, Ted looked back at Clay. "Let's get this over with."

Late that night Meg sat in the bedside chair holding Clay's limp hand and praying for some sign of improvement. In the hours since the bullet was removed, he had remained unconscious and unresponsive. From time to time, he murmured incoherently while shifting restlessly on the wide bed. When she gently stroked the damp locks of hair from his forehead, he seemed to relax a bit before growing still again.

Over and over, she wished he would open his eyes. Over and over, she prayed he would show some sign of recovery. The thought of losing him tore at her heart until she experienced a very real physical pain—an aching anguish that made each moment agony.

She scanned his fatigue-lined face. The loss of blood left him with alarming pallor. Only the deep smudges ringing his eyes gave his complexion any hint of color. As her apprehension continued to grow, Meg tightened her grasp on his broad hand as if, by that action, she could somehow transfer some of her strength to his weak and wounded body.

During their brief acquaintance, Meg had seen many facets of Clay's complicated and often contradictory character—aloof stranger, gentle protector, tender lover, wild warrior—but seeing him as he was now, incapacitated and unconscious, terrified her. For all his lithe strength and lean muscle, Clay was flesh and blood and very vulnerable. Tears flooded her eyes. Despite the love and acceptance she offered, Meg had no way to infuse him with physical fortitude, no way to ensure his recovery from a bullet wound.

Even if he survived and they went on to Puerto Rico for the two weeks he had promised, could her love induce him to offer more? Would he let her into his life on a more permanent basis?

Tears flooded her eyes. She could only hope she had the chance to persuade him, to show him that they had something worth pursuing beyond the immediate present. Warm moisture splashed down her cheeks as she linked their fingers. Compared to hers, his felt cold and stiff. Fresh misery spurred her.

"Don't leave me, Clay. Please don't leave me. Not before we ever have a chance. Not like this," she mumbled in a broken whisper. "If you die now—" she cleared her throat "—I'll always feel responsible, always blame myself. Please, Clay, you've got to get better. Please, darling, fight...."

Overwhelmed by fear and fatigue, she slumped forward until her head rested next to his. Soon, she fell into a restless slumber.

"Meg, you ought to get some rest," Ted said as he pulled a chair alongside hers and sat down. "You won't do Clay any good if you get sick yourself."

Her worried glance collided with her brother's. "He's so pale," she murmured in a hoarse, husky voice, "and he's been unconscious such a long time."

Ted laid one hand on both of hers as they lay clenched in her lap. "He lost a lot of blood, but there's no sign of infection. He's resting comfortably, which is the best thing under the circumstances."

"I suppose," she mumbled, but her tone lacked conviction.

"Meg, your worrying won't make him heal any faster. He'll be fine."

"You really think so?" she asked anxiously.

Ted hesitated only briefly before responding. "I really think so. He'll be weak for a while and I don't think his shoulder will feel very good, but he'll survive."

Her gaze went back to the still figure on the bed. "I hope so," she said in a fervent whisper.

Ted scanned her face. "You seem very concerned."

Color invaded her cheeks. "I'd be concerned about anyone who got hurt rescuing you."

"Would you have sat beside anyone else, Meg? Held his hand?" he asked in a low murmur. "Stayed here all day and most of the night?"

The color in her face intensified. Meg hadn't had time to consider how her actions might appear to Ted. After the way she had avoided any contact with men for years, Ted undoubtedly found her current behavior unusual. Since she didn't know how to explain, she offered an excuse, "I hired Clay, so in a way I'm responsible. If it hadn't been for me, he'd be safe and sound in Puerto Rico instead of lying hurt and unconscious."

"Are you sure that's all there is to this, uh, concern?" Ted inquired in a concerned, brotherly voice. "I saw your expression when we came back, when you went to him. It didn't seem like the reaction of an employer, Meg."

She caught her lower lip between her teeth. How could she explain the ties between her and Clay?

"I don't feel like an employer," she admitted. "I know he's a mercenary but, I don't know, he doesn't seem like the sort of man who'd do anything for money..."

"I know," Ted agreed.

Her gaze shot back to her brother. "He said he knew you and Dave in Vietnam."

He nodded. "We all knew each other. Dave and I met him in the POW camp."

The tension tightening her brother's weary features made Meg's heartbeat accelerate. When she spoke again, her voice was barely audible. "Clay told me that he escaped with the two of you, that you and Dave saved his life. I guess that's why he felt he had to take this job, because he owed you."

Ted's brow furrowed. "Vietnam was a long time ago," he mumbled.

"But Clay didn't forget what you did for him. He seems to think a lot of you and Dave."

Her brother shrugged. "He would've done the same thing for either one of us." He released his sister's hands and slumped back in the chair.

"Did you know Clay very well?" she asked, eager for any information about the man she loved, even if it was over two decades old.

"Not really. He wasn't easy to get acquainted with. He was pretty much of a loner in the camp, didn't confide in anyone, or even talk much when there was an opportunity, which was seldom." He ran one hand over his face. "Later, I found out he grew up pretty much on his own. From what I could gather, he had little family and his father wasn't exactly what you'd call caring."

Although Meg had learned that, and more, from Clay, she kept silent. She was more interested in what her brother might know about the aloof man who had stolen her heart. "He told me that he and his dad didn't get along."

Ted sighed. "I think it went way beyond not getting along. From what I gathered, the old man was a drunk and an abuser. Clay never actually said so, of course, but he was pretty sick when we escaped. He had malaria and was out of his head with fever at times. From the things he mumbled, well, his home life must have been hell."

Anguish clawed at Meg's heart. "He just said they didn't get along, that he'd been glad to get away and had no reason to go back."

"I'm sure he didn't," Ted muttered.

Meg looked back at Clay. "No wonder he can be so remote at times," she observed. Her brother's revelations gave new insight into Clay's complex character. She only wished he knew something about the woman who had hurt Clay but that, she knew, had taken place after Vietnam.

"He no doubt had to be to survive. You know how abused children are. They put up walls to keep from being hurt anymore. Even in a POW camp, where most guys reach out for some sort of support, he stayed aloof. The only time he ever leaned on anybody else was when he was too sick and weak to stand on his own."

"He's still that way at times—most of the time, I guess." But not always. He had opened up a little, had been far from distant when she came to his room but she wasn't going to share that knowledge with her brother.

"I suppose he has to be, as a mercenary," Ted said. "I always figured he'd stay in the military. From what I saw, he was a good soldier, even patriotic."

"I guess he's still a good soldier," Meg observed. "A soldier of fortune. As for patriotism, he has worked with Dave, and Dave said Clay is one of the best."

"Clay mentioned Dave had sent you to him, but we didn't have time for much of a discussion." Ted's mouth twisted with ironic humor.

"I'll bet."

"At least Dave was right about Clay being good. He and the others were great. I didn't think I'd ever get out of that place." His expression softened. "I wouldn't have if it wasn't for you."

A weary smile lifted Meg's lips. "I didn't know where to turn when the government wouldn't help. I called Dave as a last resort."

Ted frowned. "I'm sort of surprised Dave didn't offer to contact Clay himself."

"He would have, but he was on his way to London. Since I had no proof that you'd been kidnapped or arrested, he couldn't do anything officially." Remembered anxiety darkened her gaze.

"I'm sorry, Meg, sorry to put you through all this and sorry I've taken advantage of you for the past few years."

"You haven't taken advantage of me," she protested. "I haven't done anything I didn't want to do."

He shook his head. "You haven't had much time for a social life, or for yourself."

Meg shifted restlessly on the chair. "I didn't have much of a social life before I started taking care of the boys," she said. She glanced back at Clay's ashen face. She hadn't realized just how dull and restricted her life was until he came into it. She hadn't figured she'd ever again open her heart and soul to any man. Yet this hardened loner had won not only her trust and respect but her love. Meg pressed her trembling lips together. Clay didn't believe in her love, she knew, and she had only a couple of weeks to prove the depth of that emotion, two weeks to convince him of the awesome power of true love, two weeks against a lifetime of barren solitude if she failed.

"All the same," her brother was saying, oblivious to her preoccupation, "you've assumed responsibilities that are mine. You deserve a life of your own, Meg."

"I have a life," she muttered with a trace of annoyance.

Ted frowned before continuing. "Yes, well, you won't have to be saddled with my duties anymore. I plan on being home more, a lot more, with my wife and my children and my sister." He scanned her face. "I guess my marriage came as quite a shock."

"Sort of," Meg agreed, "but I'm very happy for you and I know the boys will love Maria."

"They love you, Meg," he hastened to reassure her.

"I know, and I love them, but I'm not their mother and they know it. They'll be glad to have Maria as a mother and I can still be their favorite aunt," she said with a grin.

His gaze narrowed. "Then you're not . . . well, upset or anything?"

Meg's grin widened. "Of course not. I'm happy for you and Maria. She seems very nice."

He smiled back. "She is. I didn't expect to fall in love again but it happened so suddenly that I hardly knew what hit me." He glanced from his sister to Clay and back. "Sometimes it's like that, Meg. Sometimes it happens so fast you can hardly believe or accept it."

Acceptance wasn't her problem, it was Clay's. "How are you sure when it's really love and not just infatuation, Ted? How can you be sure it isn't physical attraction or chemistry or proximity?"

"I've only been in love twice, and I've experienced the other stuff quite a few times. At first, I guess, attraction is foremost but then, well, you feel things inside that you don't feel for anyone else in the world—not your family, not your best friends." He shook his head. "I guess that makes it about as clear as mud," he finished with a laugh.

"No, it's clear to me," she murmured. She understood and accepted her feelings, but what about Clay? Would he ever feel the same, and if he did, would he ever admit it?

She hadn't needed her brother's revelations to realize Clay had formed a hard callus of indifference as a child, one that had thickened and toughened over the years, one that might make him impervious to love. Recalling his tenderness and passion, Meg knew he possessed a wellspring of emotion, but would he ever release it? Hope and love, need and longing, made her want to believe so.

Ted's troubled expression remained on her. "Meg, I just don't want you to get hurt. Clay is a good man, he's brave and determined but . . . he's been a loner all his life . . ."

"I know, Ted. I knew that from the first, but I'm not sure he wants to be a loner. I think he's just always been alone, and there is a difference." She knew that was true because, despite the fact that she hadn't trusted men for a long time, she had often wished for someone special, someone to trust and treasure, someone to love. Now she had met that man and she wasn't ready to give up without a fight, even if the fight was with him.

"Maybe you're right," he replied. "Just be careful, Meg."

"You're the one who just got married," she reminded him with a genuine grin. "You're the one who said sometimes these things hit you out of the blue."

Dull color crept into his freshly shaven cheeks. "Yeah, I guess I did at that."

Meg stifled a yawn.

"Why don't you take a nap?" he asked. "That's why I came in, to see if I could relieve you for a while."

Meg rubbed her gritty eyes with the heels of her hands. She was tired, so very tired. A nap sounded like heaven, but how could she rest while Clay lay sick and helpless? "I don't think so, but thanks."

"You'll feel better if you rest. I know I do."

Meg shook her head. "I couldn't sleep away from him." Her troubled gaze went to Clay's too-still form. "I can't leave until I know he's okay."

"Meg, getting sick won't help," he pointed out again. "You're exhausted and you know it."

"I remember lots of times when you were exhausted, but you didn't leave Cathy," Meg reminded him in a soft whisper.

Ted's broad shoulders slumped forward as he searched his sister's face. "He means that much to you," he murmured.

Meg bit her lower lip. What was the sense in denying the obvious? A weary sigh left her. "He means a lot to me, Ted, more than I can say," she admitted in a barely audible voice. "He asked me to go back to Puerto Rico with him, and I plan to go."

Something akin to shock flared in Ted's azure gaze. When he spoke, both his voice and expression were devoid of judgment. "You're entitled to make your own decisions. I just want you to be happy, Meg. If Clay's the right guy, well, I wish you both luck."

"Thanks," she said, "but wishing us luck is a little premature. He hasn't suggested anything beyond the next couple of weeks. When he goes back to work, I guess I'll be coming home for good."

Ted's expression hardened. "If he lets you go, he's a damn stubborn fool."

Meg smiled, a sad smile that failed to reach her eyes. "He's stubborn, all right. As for the rest ... well, that remains to be seen."

Chapter 10

When Clay woke several hours later, pain fogged his brain and flamed in his bound shoulder. Forcing his weighted lids open proved difficult, but as his gaze scanned the dim room, the mist lifted.

Curled in the bedside chair and wrapped in a blanket, Meg was like a beacon of light in a dark tunnel. Meg, sweet and gentle yet strong and determined, represented everything he'd wanted, everything he needed. She had waited for him. Waited and worried and, if the dark smudges beneath her eyes were any indication, hadn't left his side since his ignominious return. Despite her obvious exhaustion, she looked more beautiful and desirable than ever. For her comforting presence, he'd gladly take a thousand bullets and more pain than he was in now.

As he shifted to obtain a better vantage point, a low moan escaped him. Abruptly, her lashes lifted and Meg leaned forward in an automatic gesture to touch his forehead with comfort and concern.

"Clay, are you all right?" she asked as she brushed an errant lock of hair from his damp brow.

Her tender touch banked the fire of pain scorching his shoulder. "Sure," he muttered in a rusty voice he barely recognized.

"You've been out for a long time," she observed. Was he really okay? she wondered as she again searched his ashen face.

Meg reached for the pitcher on the nightstand. "How about some water?" she suggested as she poured the liquid into a tumbler.

"Yes, thanks," he managed to croak out.

While holding the glass in one hand, she reached out to support Clay's broad shoulders, being careful not to jostle his wounded side. As his eyelids drifted shut, she held the tumbler to his dry lips.

The effort to sit up, even with assistance, left Clay shaking and exhausted, yet he managed to down half of the water before collapsing against the pile of pillows at his back. "Thanks," he mumbled.

Fresh anxiety assailed her. Seeing him so weak frightened her. "Is there anything else I can get for you?"

Clay forced his eyes open. When he saw the fear tightening her lovely features, he hastened to reassure her. A boyish grin lifted his lips. "Don't look so worried, sweetheart. One bullet isn't going to keep me down for long. I'm a pretty tough guy. I'll be up and around in no time."

His cockiness reminded Meg of their initial meeting, but now she knew that arrogance was only a cover. That he was flesh and blood had been clearly illustrated to her, and it was something she wouldn't forget anytime soon. With one trembling forefinger, she traced the edge of the pristine bandage but saw the bloody rag he'd applied himself. "You shouldn't have ignored a bullet wound," she murmured. "You lost a lot of blood and risked a serious infection by letting it go so long."

"I didn't ignore it, Meg. I bound it as best I could under the circumstances."

She shook her head. "You took a terrible chance," she replied in a voice thick with unshed tears. "You should have told someone, let someone take care of it."

"Meg, it wouldn't have helped to tell one of the others. We had to get out of the city fast. We didn't have time to stop."

Her fingers stilled on his shoulder. "I don't know how you stayed on your feet long enough to get here." The reassuring, natural warmth of his flesh tickled her sensitive skin. He had made it, she reminded herself.

"I'm not sure myself," he said in rueful tones. A half smile tugged at one corner of his hard mouth. With every agonizing step, he'd thought of Meg and his promise to return. As the veil of unconsciousness threatened to obscure the path ahead, he'd remembered her vow of love and acceptance of his invitation. When he'd thought he couldn't go on, he'd pictured her and forced his tired and tormented body to continue. For the moment, at least, Meg needed him, needed his safe return, needed his reassurance, needed his loving, if only for a brief interlude.

Clay's smile faltered. Despite her care and concern, Meg would eventually recognize what she felt for him as infatuation, not love. That his injury had probably complicated their situation wasn't lost on Clay, but he couldn't afford to believe in anything.

"I was so scared, Clay, so worried. Then, when you passed out—"

Meg's words only reinforced his observation. If she had painted him as a heroic figure before the rescue, she now saw him as a knight in shining armor, a wounded knight. Many men, Clay knew, would take advantage of Meg's heightened emotions, but experience had taught him how easily such feelings could turn into a double-edged sword, one that might end up slashing both of them to ribbons. So, instead of playing on her vulnerability, Clay made light of the situation.

"I don't faint for just any woman, you know," he said with a chuckle.

"Silly," she whispered as she took her hand away. Suddenly, she felt embarrassed and foolish. "You were badly hurt, you could have..." She stopped as she bowed her head to conceal the tears flooding her eyes. What an idiot she was being, Meg thought with dismay. If she continued this emotional display, Clay, who had already made it clear that he wasn't in the market for a permanent relationship, might withdraw his invitation.

Seeing Meg's struggle and knowing the source of her dismay, Clay reached out with his good arm. Gently, he stroked her cheek. "I appreciate your concern, Meg, I really do, but I'm back and I'll be fine."

When her head came up, anxiety still clouded her gaze. "I was so terrified, Clay, so afraid for you."

Knowing her worry for him had put the dark shadows beneath her bloodshot eyes made him queasy. "This isn't the first time I've been injured, Meg," he muttered, revealing the ugly reality of his life. A reality she had to face even though it might end their relationship before it really began.

"That doesn't make me feel any better," she managed in a husky whisper.

He wasn't trying to make her feel better, he was trying to make her see reality. "What I do... it's dirty and deceitful. Violence is very much a part of it. I've been hurt before, and I've hurt others."

Meg's mouth trembled. "Only if you had to," she whispered.

When he looked back at her, Clay experienced a surge of protectiveness, one that made him want to spare her, but he couldn't. He couldn't let her think he was some sort of paragon, a storybook hero. "I guess I'd like to think so," he replied, "but a lot of what I've done... well, it's been ugly, too ugly to tell you."

"You've only done what you had to do," she repeated.

"I've killed people, Meg. More than I care to remember."

Her gaze searched his schooled expression, then she saw a flicker of suppressed emotion deep in his eyes. "I almost got you killed," she whispered. "If it hadn't been for me, you'd be enjoying your vacation in Puerto Rico."

Prepared for her disgust, he wasn't sure how to handle her understanding. "Meg, you didn't force me to go after Ted. This job wasn't any different from a hundred other rescues. I wasn't in any more danger." In his confusion, Clay didn't realize how much he had revealed until Meg responded.

Her penetrating gaze narrowed on him as sudden comprehension struck her. "When Dave said you were the best, I didn't think he meant rescue specifically, but he did, didn't he? You're not an ordinary mercenary, are you? You rescue hostages."

The little color in Clay's face drained away. Before he could form a reply, she continued.

"You specialize in saving kidnap victims. People hire you to retrieve family members, just the way I did."

"Not exactly," he muttered. Things were rapidly spinning out of his control, and in his confusion and weakness, he had trouble regaining the proper equilibrium.

"I knew you weren't the kind of man who would sell himself to the highest bidder." Relief spread through her.

The benevolent smile she bestowed on him made Clay increasingly uneasy. "Meg, you don't really know me," he muttered in frustration. As much as he wanted to accept her love, as badly as he wished to believe the admiration softening her voice, Clay hesitated. Fever and fatigue intensified his befuddlement. "Meg, I'm no hero," he repeated.

"You are to me," she whispered.

"Meg, the way things have been, well, you're bound to be carried away by emotion, to see me as something more, someone better, than I am."

His words and manner reminded Meg of his earlier assertion that the circumstances surrounding a rescue heightened and confused feelings; people mistook gratitude and proximity for something more profound. Clay had, although he refused to admit it, evidently retrieved a number of hostages. The blazing heat of fear sparked in her belly.

"The woman who hurt you," Meg began in a tremulous whisper, "was she someone you rescued?"

Surprise forced his attention back to Meg. Ensnared in the web of deceit he'd woven to protect both of them, he released a long breath. Although he hadn't planned to tell Meg about Annette, or his own foolishness, he now saw no alternative. Maybe, if she knew, she'd understand his reluctance to believe in her illusions.

He licked his lips before speaking in a low monotone. "Annette's father was a wealthy businessman who had holdings all over the world. The family had a home in Europe, and she spent a good deal of time there. Anyhow, he owned several companies, one of them in Libya. This was back before the U.S. cut off relations, but there was already trouble. A group of terrorists kidnapped Annette. Since they wanted a large ransom, not publicity, her father was able to keep it quiet, but he didn't want to pay them for fear of the same thing happening again, to Annette or one of her sisters. Besides, he wasn't sure he could trust them to let her go once they had the money."

"So he hired you to rescue her," Meg interjected.

"Pretty much," Clay agreed. Although that wasn't the precise truth, it was enough to keep his guilt at bay. "I had some dealings with them and knew the place they were hiding her pretty well. It was a very remote area in the Alps." He sighed. "Freeing her wasn't nearly as difficult as eluding her captors afterward. We spent over two weeks on the run." His features hardened into an icy mask as memory swept over him. "In that sort of situation, it's easy to get emotionally involved, to delude yourself that what you feel is something more than hormones and adrenaline."

The implication of his words struck at the root of Meg's anxiety as she understood why he refused to believe her. Even so, she knew what she felt was real, real and permanent. "Maybe if you're very young," she suggested.

"We were young and scared. And I was foolish and stupid, as well." The memory of his ignorance humiliated him as nothing else in his life had, or could. He'd allowed himself to believe in love, something he was in grave danger of doing again.

"You became lovers," Meg mumbled as jealousy roared over her like a freight train out of control. Annette had shared something with Clay that Meg hadn't and, when she studied his set features, wondered if she ever would. If he rescinded his invitation, how could she crack his reserve and resolve? If she didn't, how could she go on without him?

"Yeah, we did." Clay stared up at the cracked ceiling. "Like I said, we were both scared and running on adrenaline. We turned to each other for comfort and reassurance, but by the time I got her home, I was sure that fate had brought us together. Once I met her family, saw their home, I should've realized that I'd never fit into her world, but I was too dazed to accept reality." He chuckled humorlessly. "I was pretty surprised to meet her fiancé. Afterward, I asked her when she planned to tell her folks the marriage was off, but she just laughed. She said she had every intention of going through with the wedding. Her fiancé was acceptable as a husband and I wasn't. According to Annette though, that didn't have to change what we had. After all, I was a better lover." He shook his head to dislodge the painful memory of rejection. "I was shocked by the idea."

No wonder Clay had been so angry when he'd thought she was involved with Dave Thornton while dallying with him. She must have, all along, reminded him of Annette.

"I wasn't that far gone," he muttered. "Annette didn't like being refused, of course. She made it quite clear that she was used to getting what she wanted and she was willing to pay whatever was necessary to bend me to her will. She offered fancy cars, a luxurious penthouse, about anything you can imagine, which only appalled me more. I was in love, or thought I was, and I didn't like the idea of being bought for stud service." Revulsion twisted his insides. "The more she carried on, the surer I was that she didn't care about me at all. She just wanted to be in control . . . of me, of our relationship."

Meg's mind locked on his admission. He had loved Annette, maybe he still loved her. A lump of dismay formed in her throat. "But, eventually, she gave up?"

"Not exactly. When I told her we were through, she threatened me, said she'd see me in jail, or worse." And it very nearly had been worse, he recalled. "She offered more money . . ."

Meg's stomach clenched. No wonder he'd taken an instant dislike to her. When she offered any price, she reminded him of Annette, just as she had when she kissed him in the cave. A shuddering sigh left Meg. "Did she have you arrested?"

"No," Clay replied. "She didn't have to. Her father had money and power. She used both against me." His jaw clenched. Meg didn't need to know the rest of the hideous details. "If I hadn't let emotion cloud my judgment, I wouldn't have gotten into the situation to begin with."

Meg's heart convulsed. "I'm not Annette," she whispered.

"I know, Meg." She was nothing like Annette, he now knew.

"I'd never betray you, or threaten you, or harm you," she promised in a solemn, subdued tone.

"I know, sweetheart, I know."

"Then, why...why do you keep warning me off? I know you must care for me, at least a little. Why are you so sure a relationship between us can't work? Why won't you try?"

He bowed his head. Any further explanation would only add to the heroic image she'd created in her mind, he feared. "If you don't want to come to Puerto Rico with me, I can understand," he mumbled, "but the terms haven't changed, Meg. They won't change."

Emotion, stark and strong, ripped through her. Despite his words, she held a remnant of hope in her heart. To permeate the barriers he'd erected would take action, not talk. Knowing that her chances of breaching such defenses under any circumstances were poor at best, Meg persisted. As long as she was with him, the improbable remained possible.

"I'm still going to Puerto Rico," she said aloud. To herself she added, *You're not getting rid of me that easily.*

Clay offered a weary smile, and seeing his growing fatigue, Meg hastily changed the subject. "I've let you talk far too long. You need your medicine and you need to rest."

Hampered by weariness, he took the pills and closed his eyes. As he drifted into a deep sleep, Clay tried to tell himself he was still in control of the situation.

When Clay awoke again, his gaze shot to the bedside chair. Instead of finding Meg, he saw her brother. Disappointment shuttled through his aching body even as the other man leaned forward.

"Good afternoon," Ted murmured. "How are you feeling?"

"Afternoon?" Clay blinked in confusion. Groggy and disoriented, he had lost all track of time. Had he lost contact with reality, as well? he wondered. Had he dreamed Meg's presence, imagined their conversation? Had she ever been there at all?

"How long have I been here?" he inquired as he struggled into a sitting position despite the protest of his wounded shoulder.

"We got back yesterday morning. Since then, you only woke up once."

Clay studied the other man's face. "Did I say anything?"

Ted shrugged. "You talked to Meg. She was with you until about an hour ago when I made her leave. Not that I hadn't tried before, but she wouldn't leave your side until she knew you'd be okay."

"She's all right, isn't she?"

Amusement twinkled in Ted's gaze. "I think she'll be fine after she rests. She was really relieved when you woke up."

Hazy recollections of their conversation flashed in his head. He had told her about Annette, he remembered, but she hadn't seemed upset as he'd figured she might be. On the contrary, she had reaffirmed her decision to go with him to Puerto Rico. He licked his cracked lips as he studied the other man's expression. Did Ted know his sister's plans? His face gave no clue. "Could I have some water?" he asked as much to stall for time as to quench his thirst.

"Sure."

After downing the contents of the glass Ted held for him, Clay leaned back against the pillows. "Thanks," he murmured.

Ted replaced the tumbler on the nightstand. "I'm the one who should be saying thanks. I didn't have much of a chance during the rescue or on the way back, but if it wasn't for you, I'd still be in that hole with little hope of getting out."

"I owed you," Clay said.

For a moment, Ted remained silent. When he spoke, his voice was carefully controlled. "Meg said Dave recommended you."

"Yeah," Clay agreed, but he closed his eyes.

"She said you've worked with Dave."

A muscle in Clay's jaw twitched. "I work for a lot of people, even Uncle Sam, if the price is right."

"Really?"

"Really." Clay's was flat, guarded, unemotional.

"And I guess you agreed to rescue me because my sister offered you a lot of money."

"She offered whatever I wanted," Clay replied. "She was anxious to get you back." The memory of their meeting fluttered through his head. How wrong his first impression had been. A rough sigh left him as he returned his attention to Ted. "When she told me your name, when I realized who you were and why Dave sent her to me, I never planned to take her money."

"But your time is valuable. If you hadn't come after me, you could have accepted another job, a paying one," Ted pointed out. "Besides, I wouldn't think you'd want to get a reputation for doing charity work—not in your business."

Clay's eyes smoldered with some indefinable emotion. "I'm not destitute, and I don't call repaying a debt charity."

Ted shrugged. "You didn't owe me anything."

"I owed you my life," Clay said. "If it hadn't been for you and Dave, I would've died in the prison camp and you know it. Hell, if it hadn't been for the two of you, I wouldn't have made it a mile."

"You're the one who had the escape plan," Ted reminded him.

"You're the one who insisted on taking me along even after I got sick, even when it was clear I'd be nothing but a burden."

Ted shrugged again. "I'd still like to pay you something."

"It isn't necessary," Clay ground out between gritted teeth. "I didn't pay you to haul me out of the camp, or most of the way to Saigon."

"I figured you'd stay in the army, make a career out of it," Ted said, redirecting the conversation.

Clay's glance skittered away. "I did for a while, then it didn't seem like I was doing anything particularly worthwhile."

Ted's gaze narrowed. "And wandering around the globe is."

"I'm good at what I do, very good," Clay shot back.

"So Meg told me. She also said you're some sort of expert at hostage retrieval."

"That's putting a nice name on it," he muttered. "She wants to see me as some sort of hero, but I'm not."

"I think saving my hide was pretty heroic. Juan and his men seem to feel pretty much the same way," Ted commented, "and I know Dave would never have sent Meg to you if he didn't trust and respect you."

"He knew I could handle the job."

"Well, I'm very grateful."

"Consider it a fair trade."

Several seconds of silence ticked away. "I do."

Clay's gaze shot back to Ted. Something in the man's expression made him edgy. He shifted restlessly on the bed. He'd tried to warn Meg off but hadn't succeeded. Now, looking into her brother's eyes, eyes so like Meg's, Clay wondered if he hadn't overlooked what might be a more effective barrier than anything he'd previously considered. "Maybe that was a poor comparison. I'm sure as hell nothing like you."

"I wouldn't say that," Ted murmured. "See, I remember you in that POW camp, Clay. You were just a kid, but you had more guts than half the guys there. I remember how stubborn you were, how strong your beliefs were. No matter what they did to you, you didn't crack." Ted exhaled sharply. "If we hadn't escaped when we did, well, you wouldn't have lived much longer because you refused to do what they wanted. You refused to betray your country, even to save your life."

Clay clenched his teeth. "I hope to hell you didn't tell Meg that story," he said.

"I haven't, but I don't see any reason not to," Ted replied in a calm, controlled voice.

"There's every reason not to. From the first, no...not the first, but for a while, she's had this misbegotten notion I'm a knight in shining armor, a storybook hero. And I'm not."

"She cares for you, Clay."

He ran one hand over his face. "She cares for an image, a false image. She hardly knows me. She doesn't know what my life has been like. She doesn't realize that my world is filled with deceit and depravity. It's an ugly world, Ted, one that would sicken her. Hell, it would sicken you."

"She says you invited her to go to Puerto Rico with you, to stay with you until you go back to work."

Clay's hands tightened into twin fists. "Yes, I did," he said.

"Does she mean anything at all to you, Clay? Or is she just a pleasant diversion?"

The cool cadence of Ted's tone whipped him like a lash, cutting deep into his conscience and unleashing a torrent of self-defense. "She's not a child. She doesn't need big brother to run interference for her."

"She doesn't need to have the little trust she's got in men shattered, either." He jumped out of the chair and began to pace the room. "I know Meg wouldn't like me interceding. After all, like you say, she isn't a kid, and I know I'm being overprotective." He paused to look back at Clay. "Meg's very independent in most things, strong and self-sufficient. I don't know what I'd have done without her these past few years. She's taken care of me, my boys, the house, everything." He cleared his throat. "But, when it comes to relationships with men...well, she's very fragile. She hasn't dated much for a long time—"

Clay's voice, as rough and ragged as Ted's, cut him off. "I know about the rape."

Shock froze the other man's features. "Meg told you?"

"Yeah, she did." Since he didn't think it wise to reveal under exactly what circumstances, he voiced the rage he'd hidden from Meg. "I'd love to get my hands on that bastard for five minutes."

"So would I," Ted agreed. He studied Clay for several moments. "Meg never told me, you know. I found out from Cathy, my first wife. She and Meg had been best friends for years. They were roommates when it happened." He swallowed hard, as if over some bitter pill. "Cath explained why Meg didn't tell me, why she'd agreed to keep it a secret. I was pretty volatile back then and I might have done something stupid," he admitted.

"I don't see how you could've stopped yourself," Clay observed. "Any man wants to defend his loved ones."

"Meg trusted you with something she couldn't even tell me. I wonder if you understand how significant that is, how important."

Ted's observations only increased Clay's discomfort. "She seems a lot stronger and determined now than even when we met, and she was vehement about finding you, about coming to Costa del Palma herself. Maybe the past few months have helped her. She said something about not staying in her safe rut anymore, about not just existing but living." He paused. "I think she'll tell you about what happened to her when she's ready."

"Maybe so," Ted agreed, "but that doesn't change the fact that she told you, or that she's willing to stay with you in Puerto Rico."

"She trusts me."

"It's more than that, Clay, a lot more."

Clay shook his head. "Sometimes, when people are thrown together in a life-and-death situation, well, circumstances and chemistry can confuse you, make you mistake attraction and appreciation for love."

"Maybe for some people, but not for Meg. She doesn't open up to many people, especially men, but her feelings run deep and true. She's very loyal, very loving ... very special."

"You don't have to sell her to me," Clay retorted without forethought. "She's terrific. Braver than most men, too. I've never met anyone like her." And he greatly feared he never would again.

Amazement rounded Ted's eyes. "Well, I'll be damned. You're in love with her."

Upset by his lack of control, Clay felt his face become an icy mask but still his gaze blazed with unbridled emotion. "I admire Meg. I respect her. But love . . . I'm not sure it exists outside novels and movies." The words were as much to convince Ted as himself. If he let himself hope, if he recognized the emotion crowding his heart as love, how would he survive when Meg went back to her world and he went back to the shadows of his?

"I don't believe you," Ted said in a flat voice as he dropped back into the chair and stared at Clay.

Clay lifted his good shoulder in a half shrug. "It doesn't make much difference what you believe." The problem was inside him. What he felt for Meg frightened him. If he lowered the last of his defenses, then lost Meg, as he knew was inevitable, how could he go on?

Ted scowled. "What about what Meg believes? Do you care about her feelings at all?"

As tension wired his lean body, Clay stared at the ceiling as if the answer to his dilemma might be discovered in the cracks and crevices. "What she believes . . . well, it's make-believe," he murmured. "The man she thinks is me doesn't exist outside her head."

"She's not a fool or an idiot. She may be inexperienced, but she knows her own mind," Ted informed him. His voice lowered a fraction. "She knows her own heart."

Pent-up breath whistled through Clay's clenched teeth. "It's no good," he muttered. "I've got nothing to offer someone like your sister. I live out of a suitcase or a field pack. My lifestyle doesn't lend itself to domesticity and, even if it did, I've got no experience with relationships. I've never had to consider another person's feelings. I don't know if I could." Excuses, all excuses, he knew. "It's just no good. I'm no good, not for Meg. She needs a guy who comes home every night, briefcase in hand, ready to grill steaks, bounce the baby on his knee and tell Meg about his dull, routine day. She sure as hell doesn't need a guy who's separated from her by thousands of miles, inaccessible by mail or phone, in some dark alley or dirty foxhole." His fingers touched the thick bandage at his shoulder. "Or a guy who might bleed to death in some dark corner of the world she doesn't even know exists."

"For someone who doesn't know if love exists, you've given a lot of thought to one of its less heralded drawbacks."

Clay's brow crinkled in perplexity. "I don't know what you mean."

"You seem to be willing to sacrifice your own wants for what you see as Meg's best interests."

Dull color invaded Clay's stubbled cheeks. He hadn't realized how his words might be construed, hadn't realized just how much he was giving away. "I—I'm just stating the facts," he mumbled as he glanced away.

"Well, whatever your reasons, I think Meg deserves a chance to be part of the decision," he said, "but you'll have plenty of time to discuss your differences. Here and in Puerto Rico."

Ted's tacit approval barely registered with Clay. "I won't be able to travel for a few days. Maybe you should get Meg and Maria out of here." Ted's observations and his fear for Meg's safety combined to make Clay doubt the wisdom of taking her to Puerto Rico. Neither Meg nor Ted seemed to accept Clay's firm belief that a man like himself and a woman like her had no sort of future.

"I don't think that's necessary," Ted murmured as he searched Clay's taut features. "We're safe enough here. Besides, there's no way Meg will leave without you."

Clay couldn't stop the swelling of his heart but he didn't let what he felt surface in his voice or expression. "We're safe if we don't stay too long," he muttered. "But I think we should leave as soon as Juan can arrange it."

"Clay, you've lost a lot of blood. You need a few days to rest before you're fit to travel."

Clay turned on Ted. "I don't want Meg in unnecessary danger."

"Neither do I," he assured him. "I don't want Maria in danger, either, but Juan says we're perfectly safe here and I trust him."

Some of the tension drained from Clay's body. "I suppose you're right," he mumbled. Fatigue and pain sapped his energy to argue. Besides, he didn't really want Meg to leave without him. He wasn't *that* noble. "We'll all leave together as soon as I can travel," Clay finally agreed with a suppressed yawn.

Ted grinned as he got to his feet. "I've kept you talking too long. If Meg sees how tired you look, she'll post herself to your bedside."

Despite pain, doubt and fatigue, Clay couldn't help but smile back before he drifted off to sleep.

Chapter 11

When Meg returned to Clay's room, she found him sitting up in bed. Although his complexion was nearly as white as the sheets, and lines of pain and fatigue still bracketed his eyes, his mouth curved into a boyish grin as soon as he saw her.

"Hi," he murmured.

"Hi," she replied as she stood at the side of the bed and looked down at him. To keep from reaching out, as she had so often when he was unconscious, she clasped her hands in front of her. The doubts he'd expressed earlier continued to buzz in her head. Somehow she had to convince him that what she felt wasn't infatuation, that what she felt was real and right, strong and steadfast. Somehow she had to convince him that they belonged together, not for a limited time but for forever.

"How are you feeling?" she asked softly.

"Better." His gaze scanned her face. The dark smudges beneath her eyes had lightened, but worry clouded her gaze.

"How about you? Do you feel better now that you've rested?"

"Yes." Sleep, a shower, fresh clothing and a hot meal had fortified her body, and seeing Clay's clear improvement now buoyed her spirits.

"You needed the rest."

"I guess so," she said, "but I don't usually sleep so long."

His smile deepened. "You don't usually sit up all night with a total idiot, either."

Tiny tributaries of hope flowed through her. "I wanted to be with you," she whispered. "I still do."

The smile faded. "You want to be with the man you think I am, with the hero you've created in your head," he responded. His voice grew rougher with each word, so rough it was like sandpaper abrading his throat, scratching it raw. "If you knew me, really knew me, your feelings would change."

It was then that she reached out to cup his bristled jaw and force his gaze to meet hers. "My feelings won't change Clay. Even if I never see you again, I'll always love you. Nothing can change that."

His jaw tightened beneath her touch. "Meg, you don't understand," he said in a strained voice.

"Yes, I do. I understand that you've had very little reason to believe in love."

He shook his head. "You don't understand," he repeated. How could he explain that he knew she'd eventually change her mind about him, about them? How could he make her realize she wasn't seeing him as he was? Not by admitting the entire truth, he knew. If he did that, her romantic notions about him would only grow bigger and stronger. By letting her close, closer than anyone else in his life, he had struck a match that might easily flame out of control, burning them both. Clay had known the mutual awareness and attraction between them was dangerous but his conversation with Ted had increased his apprehension. Much to Clay's surprise, Ted Andrews didn't see anything wrong with a relationship between his sister and Clay. Ted thought he knew what Clay's world was like. But he didn't. Not really. Ted Andrews had lived in the shadows for a few months. Clay had lived there his entire life.

"Meg," he began in a rough whisper, "we come from two different worlds. Worlds we'll be going back to very soon. If you come to Puerto Rico, you need to know that whatever happens between us begins and ends there. No matter what you feel, or think you feel, I've got nothing more to offer."

Although his words slashed her heart like a knife, Meg forced a smile and pressed her fingers to his lips to keep him from saying more. Somehow, in difficult and dangerous and unlikely circumstances, she had found the man of her dreams, the hero she hoped for during so many long, lonely nights. Because of Clay she felt whole again.

"I'm not expecting anything beyond the next couple of weeks," she said in complete honesty but she didn't add, she hoped for more. Much more.

As Clay scanned her calm countenance, he saw no trace of subterfuge. Evidently Meg meant what she said, which ought to be a cause for relief. It wasn't.

Inviting Meg to stay with him had been a mistake. He saw that even if neither she nor her brother did. For the first time, Clay had the notion he might end up paying the highest price for his lapse of control. Not the same price he'd paid with Annette. No, the cost of this weakness might be much higher than a battered body and bruised pride. When Meg walked away, she'd be taking a huge hunk of his soul and spirit with her.

If he had any remnant of sense left, he'd send her home with her brother and sister-in-law and he'd do it immediately. But he knew he wouldn't, knew he couldn't. Whatever time she gave him would be cherished and prized, held in his heart during the dark days and nights ahead.

Clay caught her wrist. "You're sure you can settle for a brief...interlude? You're sure you won't regret it?" He couldn't bear recriminations or remorse later. Not when he was so weak where she was concerned.

She gently stroked his stubbled cheek. "Whatever happens, I'll never regret loving you, Clay, and I'll treasure whatever time we have together. I told you that before and I meant it."

"You'd be safer if you went home now." They both would.

Her thumb traced the sensuous curve of his lower lip. "I've been safe far too long."

His grasp tightened, but not painfully so. "Then we'll go to my place as soon as I can travel."

"I can't wait," she whispered.

Despite doubt and apprehension and fatigue, Clay grinned back. "Neither can I, sweetheart. Neither can I."

For the next several days, Clay continued to recuperate while Meg continued to spend most of her time at his side. As he grew stronger, Clay left the seclusion of his bedroom to join the others downstairs where, to his surprise, he felt more accepted and at ease than he thought possible. Juan treated him like an honored guest and Ted and Maria acted as if he was an old and dear friend. If Meg's brother had any misgivings about Clay, he hid them well.

Clay's only discomfort came from observing the newlyweds. Seeing their happiness and catching the hint of envy in Meg's eyes jolted him with jealousy—and remorse—but he pushed both emotions aside. Just as he cloaked his ambivalence and apprehension. Yet, more than once, he wondered what it would be like to share the future with Meg. More than once, he wished he was a different man, the man Meg believed him to be.

Although Clay's condition had improved he resisted Meg's not-so-subtle hints that they share his bed. His excuse, that he was still weak, seemed to satisfy her.

When, nearly a week after the rescue, he could stay up for an entire day, he met with Ted and Juan to discuss their departure. After the meeting, Juan left to arrange for a driver and guards to escort the foursome to the north coast where a plane would be waiting. Ted and Clay remained in the sun-drenched library.

"You're sure you're up to the trip?" Ted asked just as Clay was about to escape.

Clay paused near the door. "The trip shouldn't be that difficult. I'll be fine."

"But you're still weak, and I know your shoulder's bothering you."

Clay absently massaged the offending joint. "I've had trouble with it off and on since Nam. Taking a bullet didn't help, but it's okay, I'll manage. Besides, we've waited too long already. The longer we stay, the more danger we're in, all of us." Because he knew Meg wouldn't leave without him, Clay had resolved to leave at the first viable opportunity.

Ted nodded in agreement. "I'll tell Maria to get ready." A slight smile played across his lips. "You can tell Meg."

That night, the two couples were on their way north. Although Juan's Jeep bounced over the bumpy roads, jostling Clay's shoulder, he remained silent. At the same time, his eyes constantly scanned the darkness, ever vigilant for any hint of danger.

Beside Clay, Meg felt his tension. The way he held his body, stiff and unyielding, telegraphed not only his discomfort but his anxiety. When she slipped an arm around his taut back, his sweat-drenched shirt dampened her palm, and concern darted through her.

"Clay, are you all right?" she asked in a whisper only he heard.

His dark head swiveled toward her. "Sure," he muttered from between clenched teeth.

"You should've taken a pain pill like I suggested."

"They make me groggy," he muttered.

"There are four armed men in the vehicle ahead, two with us and two with Ted and Maria."

"I know."

"Then why don't you lie down and try to relax," she suggested as she gently massaged his back. "We've got plenty of protection."

A ragged sigh escaped him. How could he explain his need to see to her safety personally without giving away the depth of his feelings, without making himself look more heroic in her eyes? "These vehicles aren't made for relaxation or rest," he said.

"I suppose not," she agreed, "but you could lean on me. It might make the trip a little more comfortable for you. Maybe you could sort of use my shoulder for a pillow."

Despite his aching arm and tired body, Clay knew he wouldn't find much comfort in being cushioned by Meg's softness. Since the night in the cave, the only time he'd escaped his desire for her was when he'd been unconscious. Just having her arm around him made his blood flow hot and heavy.

"I'm okay, Meg."

Something in his tone made her pull away. When she looked at his chiseled profile, barely visible in the pale moonlight, she folded her hands in her lap. His face appeared like a stone mask, hard and unyielding. She shifted to face forward. "Whatever you say," she managed in a throaty whisper.

He laid one hand over both of hers. "Thanks for worrying about me, even when I act like a muleheaded fool."

When Meg glanced back at his face, she saw his expression was soft as his voice. A resigned, yet rueful, smile touched her mouth. "I don't think you're a fool, Clay," she replied in an innocent tone.

A low laugh rumbled out of him. "No need for further agreement, Meg," he said as he released her hand and leaned back in the seat.

Her chuckle was lost on the breeze.

* * *

After their arrival in San Juan, Clay reclaimed his battered Jeep and drove the other three to the hotel where Meg had earlier stayed. As the foursome stood on the sidewalk, Ted, along with Maria, again thanked Clay and invited him to visit them in Ohio. He murmured something he hoped was appropriate, then turned to Meg as the newlyweds disappeared into the lobby.

Feeling as gauche and nervous as a schoolboy, he shifted from one foot to the other. "There are a couple of things I want to take care of at my cottage," he said.

Seeing his discomfort, Meg couldn't suppress a grin. "You told me that before we left Costa del Palma," she reminded him.

Crimson flamed in his lean cheeks. "Yeah, well, it'll only take a day, I guess."

Meg's smile faded. "I could help you," she suggested, just as she had when he had previously mentioned the unfinished repairs.

"There's really nothing you could do." Except provide distraction. "Besides, you'll want to spend some time with Ted and Maria before they leave tomorrow."

Disbelief clouded Meg's gaze. "I have the rest of my life to spend time with them," she pointed out. "And, since they never had a honeymoon and they're going to get the boys tomorrow, I really don't think they'd miss my company tonight."

The heat in his face spread like wildfire through the rest of his body. *Honeymoon.* That single word created an array of images so explosive and erotic Clay knew he had to get away or embarrass them both.

He dropped a quick kiss on Meg's cheek, then scrambled to the driver's side of his Jeep. "I should have everything done by tomorrow afternoon. How about if I meet you in the hotel restaurant before seven?" When Meg didn't immediately respond, Clay frowned. "Would you rather I pick you up at your room?" Proper dating procedure was some-

thing he knew little about. He did know, however, that he
wanted to do things right. Despite his invitation for Meg to
stay with him, despite her ready acceptance, Clay didn't
want her to feel pressured.

His tone and expression indicated some sort of anxiety she
couldn't quite fathom. Knowing their time was limited and
not wanting to waste it, Meg offered a reassuring smile.
"Seven in the restaurant is fine. I'll be waiting for you," she
promised. As he nodded in agreement, then drove away, she
hoped she didn't end up waiting forever.

"Are you sure you don't want to go back to Florida with
us?" Ted asked as he searched his sister's face.

Meg perched on the edge of the balcony's lounge chair.
As her attention moved from the sun-sparkled sea to her
brother, she smiled. "I'm quite sure, and stop looking so
worried. You said I deserve a vacation, that it would be
good for me."

"I know what I said," he responded.

"Then relax and stop playing big brother. I'll be fine."
She put one hand on his arm. "I really will, you know. I'm
not a child. I'm a grown woman."

He laid his hand over hers. "I know that, Meg. I just
don't want you to get hurt."

Her expression grew solemn. "It isn't your responsibility
to protect me," she said. "Sometimes people do get hurt."

His jaw tightened until a muscle twitched in it. "I know,
Meg, I know. That doesn't mean I don't feel a need to protect and defend you."

She saw the real anguish deep in her brother's gaze.
"How long have you known?" she asked in a rough whisper.

"Cath kept your secret for as long as she could, Meggie.
She kept it right up until..." He cleared his throat. "Until
we knew she wouldn't make it. Then, well, she was always
telling me to stop trying to fix you up with blind dates, always taking your side when you refused ..." His hand fell

away and he moved to the railing to stare out to sea. "I'm sorry, Meg. If I'd known I wouldn't have kept pestering."

On trembling legs she got up and joined him. "I'm sorry I didn't have nerve enough to tell you myself."

He turned toward her. "I understand, Meg. Cath explained your reasons, and you were probably right not to tell me then, because I probably would've strangled the guy."

Her mouth softened. "It wouldn't have helped, but thanks."

He put his arm around her narrow shoulders. "I'm always here for you, Meg. I always will be."

She pressed her face into the curve of his neck. "I may need you, Ted, when I get home." Despite her best efforts, her voice quavered.

"He may change his mind, you know."

She looked up at him. "You just asked me if I wanted to leave with you, and now you think he might change his mind."

Ted's mouth moved in the semblance of a smile. "That was the overprotective big brother in me talking."

"And who was talking yesterday when you invited Clay to visit you?"

"The guy who wants your happiness more than anything in this world," he replied. "If Clay's the one to make you happy, I'll roll a red carpet from here to Lake Erie."

"Thank you," Meg murmured, "but I'm not getting my hopes up. And I'm not counting on anything beyond the next week or so."

Nervous anticipation tickled Meg's spine. After Ted and Maria's departure only hours earlier, she had made good use of her free time by exploring the nearby shops and making an appointment in the hotel's beauty salon.

Following a long, luxurious soak in the bathtub, she put the finishing touches on her ensemble, newly purchased and totally unlike anything in her closet at home. After dabbing on a bit of perfume, Meg stopped to survey her efforts and smiled in approval.

The bold print of the gauze sundress emphasized her light tan while the strappy sandals enhanced her shapely legs. The face in the mirror, surrounded by lush auburn wavy hair, glowed with health while her eyes sparkled as brightly as the ocean at midday.

Years had passed since Meg had made any attempt to appear sensual and seductive. Years had passed since she had any reason to want to entice a man. The smile in the mirror broadened. Clay had changed all that. As she ran her hands over the soft fabric clinging to her curves, she wondered what Clay's reaction would be. After a day away from him, she knew her nerves were on edge. Was he planning to take her back to his cottage after dinner? If he didn't suggest it, what would she do?

With a last look in the mirror, she snatched up her purse and left the room. When her legs trembled, she decided it must be from the unaccustomed height of her heels.

In a secluded booth in a dark corner of the hotel's posh restaurant, Meg and Clay sipped Irish coffee and surreptitiously studied each other.

During dinner they had pursued only the most casual topics, much to Meg's relief. Evidently, she had sounded sensible, but she wasn't sure exactly what she had said. From the moment Clay—clad in unbelted chinos and a blue Oxford cloth shirt unbuttoned at the neck but sporting a loosened tie—appeared in the doorway, all rational thought flew from her head. Although the whiskers on his face were considerably fewer, stubble shadowed his square jaw. On the occasion of their first meeting, she had found the light beard disreputable. Now it seemed so incredibly sexy that her palms itched to stroke it. But it wasn't how he looked that made her heart stumble. It was the way he gazed intently at her.

His golden eyes gleamed with undisguised admiration and unbridled interest, and though his compliments had been commonplace and casual, Meg sensed they were camouflage for his real thoughts. Aware her emotions were surely reflected in her own eyes, she glanced at the fat candle in the middle of the table. She wished she had nerve enough to end the meal and lead him upstairs. Lacking courage and experience, she waited, albeit impatiently, for him to make the first move.

At the same time, Clay studied Meg as the flickering candlelight created a display of light and shadow that he found endlessly intriguing. The food might as well have been sawdust for all the taste he'd found in it. Meg filled his senses to the exclusion of all else. After working like mad on his cabin, he felt as if they'd been separated for a decade instead of a day.

The niggling finger of discontent touched his consciousness. If he missed her so desperately after one day, what would the rest of his life be like? Shoving the bitter thought away, he continued his perusal, wondering how he had ever found her plain and unappealing, despite her obvious efforts. With her hair unbound and her curves enhanced by the clinging gauze, she exuded a delicate desirability that took his breath away. Like the bright dress, she had brought color and light into his dark existence, had made him want to believe in the magic of her love. Like a fairy princess, Meg had cast a spell over him, one he wished could last forever.

"You're very quiet," Meg murmured as her attention returned to him. The candlelight gave a golden glow to his sun-streaked hair and turned his eyes to the color of warm honey.

Clay smiled, a tentative effort that failed to reach his eyes. "I was thinking."

"About what?" Her voice sounded hesitant and rather breathless.

"About you," he said. "About how much joy you've brought into my life, about how much you mean to me."

Her heart nearly jumped out of her chest. Outwardly, she remained calm, fearful she might be placing too much importance to his words, fearful they might be the prelude to farewell instead of the prologue to passion.

"You haven't changed your mind, have you?" she asked in a husky whisper. All her hopes and dreams, all her fantasies and desires teetered on the brink of destruction as she awaited his reply.

Clay was close to changing his mind but not in the way Meg seemed to suggest. As he reached across the table to capture her graceful fingers, he felt his final defenses crumbling. If he was making a mistake, as he feared, they might both end up paying for it. But when he acknowledged the dread on her pretty face, he wanted only to erase it.

"No, Meg. I want to take you to my cottage. I want to be with you tonight."

Although her lips trembled, the smile she gave him stemmed from pure bliss. "I'm already packed, but we don't have to go anywhere tonight. I still have the room and it's much closer."

Heat, much hotter than the candle's flame, burned through him. "Not a hotel room, Meg. Not for us," he whispered. "I want to take you home."

Chapter 12

Clay took Meg home to the cottage where no other woman had ever been. Where, he now knew, no other woman would ever be.

When they entered the small structure, he tried to see it through her eyes, as he had all day, tried to detect how someone of her background would react to the only place he had ever called home. He knew it wasn't much, certainly nothing like she was used to. But it was his. He'd built it several years earlier, rebuilt the entire deck after the recent storm. His heart and soul were in every nook and cranny, and he felt as nervous as a hen with one chick waiting for her reaction.

"It's wonderful," Meg murmured when he turned on a lamp. She glanced around the simple but tastefully decorated interior and felt warmed by a strange sense of homecoming.

A brick fireplace nestled in one corner with two couches nearby. An array of colorful pillows were scattered on the

ecru couches, and a bright rug covered most of the pol
ished wood floor.

Visible through an open arch was a small but moder
kitchen. Meg's gaze swept the living area. Books lined on
entire wall and an advanced stereo system rested inside
bleached-pine armoire. There were no photographs o
plants, which didn't surprise Meg. Clay wouldn't be hom
enough for live things, and he didn't stay in one place lon
enough to collect snapshots. That he wouldn't have famil
portraits went without saying.

"You like it?" he asked as he tossed down the bag she ha
retrieved from her pristine and luxurious hotel room. Sud
denly, he wondered if she might have preferred to spend th
night amid that elegance.

"I love it," she said appreciatively. "It's so cozy, so war
and welcoming." She turned back to him. "I thought mayt
you'd lost some of your things in the storm, but everythin
looks perfect."

A smile lifted his lips. "The damage was limited to th
outside, mostly the deck, but I fixed it."

"I'm glad," she murmured. "But I missed you."

A river of warmth flowed through him. "I missed yo
too," he admitted.

"I could've stayed here while you fixed things. I'm n
very handy, though I can cook."

"I wanted it all fixed for you, Meg. I wanted you to se
my home at its best."

As she realized he had wanted her approval, Meg couldr
contain a smile. "It's perfect, Clay. Absolutely perfect."

"Thanks," he said as his gaze shifted to the bank of wi
dows behind her. He only hoped she found everything el
perfect, as well. He shoved his hands in his front pocket
"You'll like it better in the daylight. I have a great view
the water, especially from upstairs."

Meg couldn't help but look up. Above them was a lot
Although it was shrouded in darkness, she knew it was
bedroom. Clay's bedroom. Tingling awareness ran throug

her. Meg bowed her head. How should she proceed? Should she keep letting Clay take the lead, or should she take the initiative? The questions spinning through her head distracted her. Before she knew it, Clay had crossed the distance between them and placed one palm on each of her flushed cheeks.

"You don't have to go up there, Meg. You don't have to do anything you don't want to do. Not ever and especially not with me." He swallowed hard. "I'll take you back to the hotel if you want."

Her wide eyes settled on his face. "I don't want to go back to the hotel, Clay. I want to be here with you."

One thumb gently caressed her lips. "You can stay down here, or I will. Whatever makes you comfortable, Meg. Whatever you want. Do you remember what I told you?"

"I—I'm not sure," she mumbled in confusion.

"I know the meaning of the word no in several languages but you only need to use English." A reassuring smile curved his hard mouth.

The one Meg gave him was far more tremulous but just as sincere. "Then I guess you know the meaning of the word yes, as well."

A soft ballad drifted up the winding staircase. Music, chosen by Meg before she left Clay alone in the living room and disappeared into the loft, filled his cottage. Waiting a decent length of time proved difficult but, Clay discovered, going to her was almost as hard.

Halfway up the steps, he stopped. His heart thumped like a jackhammer and his mouth contained enough cotton to knit two sweaters. So much time had passed since he'd been with a woman that he doubted his self-control. Besides, all he had to do was look at Meg and he got hard.

His fingers tightened on the railing. As much as he wanted Meg, he was afraid—afraid of hurting her, afraid of embarrassing her, afraid of scaring her.

"Clay?"

Her soft, sultry voice cut through his thoughts like a saber.

"Are you . . . coming to bed?"

"On my way," he replied. On shaking legs, he mounted the last few steps, then paused as his eyes adjusted to the darkness. With only the moonlight illuminating it, the loft was dim and heavily shadowed. In the single lustrous moonbeam peeping through the skylight, Meg sat propped against the brass headboard, her auburn waves tumbling across his pillow, just as he had imagined. Fierce, fiery desire struck him like a bolt of lightning, rooting him in place.

A smile played across her soft lips and her eyes gleamed like polished turquoise. She looked beautiful, he thought with reverence, beautiful and so desirable.

"Hi." Her voice was a shy whisper.

"Hi." His sounded suspiciously shaky.

Her gaze traveled over him; although he had shed his shirt, shoes and tie, his trousers remained in place. Unsure and uncomfortable, she shifted beneath the covers. "Aren't you . . ." Meg cleared her throat and glanced away.

"Of course, I am," he said, correctly guessing her thoughts. After stretching out beside Meg, but on top of the covers, he turned to her with open arms. She immediately entered the warm shelter of his arms. The blankets slid below her collarbone and his breath caught. Beneath the sheet she was naked. Blood roared in his ears while arousal pounded through him like a war drum. Wild, primitive demands rocked his body. With great effort, he kept his touch light and undemanding. He stroked her bare shoulders and whispered into her fragrant curls. "You're so lovely, Meg, so beautiful." She smelled of the now-familiar exotic flower he'd noticed what seemed like so long ago, but was only days. In such a short time, she had become part of him. Her scent and softness, her comfort and concern had reached deep inside him to a place no one else had ever touched, to a place no one else ever would.

With her fingertips, Meg explored the hard line of his collarbone, but her gaze remained on his face. "And you're very handsome," she whispered. One hand moved to his lightly bearded cheek. "Even with the stubble," she observed, voicing the thought she'd had in the restaurant.

Clay froze. "I—I should've shaved before dinner," he muttered, wondering how he could have been so negligent. Other men of her acquaintance, civilized gentlemen, would no doubt shave before a date. Chagrin rippled through him. "I don't usually shave every day."

Her fingers brushed the whiskers. "You must have shaved earlier. Your beard was getting heavy before."

"Yeah, well, I did shave when I got home yesterday, not today. I was working and I... well, I didn't think."

Seeing that his dismay was out of proportion, Meg hastened to reassure him. "I like it," she whispered. Her fingers trailed down his neck and across his shoulder.

Her delicate touch skittering over his heated flesh stoked the red hot coals of desire burning inside him. Going slow, he realized, was going to prove arduous. Already, passion incinerated sense. His hands slid from her slim shoulders, along her arms catching her marauding hands. "Meg..." His voice was so ragged that he barely recognized it.

Although Clay held her hands, she reached out with one forefinger to trace the scar on his shoulder. "You're not bandaged."

"It's healed, Meg." Since he'd left his sickbed, Clay hadn't taken his shirt off around Meg. He hadn't wanted to do anything that might make waiting more difficult. "I told you, I'm a fast healer." Physically, that was true, but emotionally, he wondered if he would ever recover from losing Meg. He pushed the painful thought away and began to massage her bare back.

She placed one palm over his heart. The speed and strength of its beating reassured her. "I'm glad."

Before he recognized her intention, she shifted to trace the gash with her tongue, then pressed her mouth to the erratic leap of the pulse in his neck.

His hand tightened spasmodically on her pliant flesh. "Sweet heaven, Meg, do you know what you're doing?"

"I think I do," she mumbled against his rapidly dampening flesh. One slim hand slid over his back before delving beneath the waistband of his trousers. "You've overdressed," she said with an audacity she hadn't known she possessed. The silk of his skin and the sensuous, purely male scent of his body joined to lower her inhibitions and incite her passion.

Clay's blood pressure soared at her plundering touch. "Sweetheart," he muttered as he extracted her grasping hand and placed it on his shoulder, "it's been a long time. I need to go slow and easy." More for her than for him, he knew, but didn't say so.

Meg shifted suddenly and her bare breast grazed his arm. A cascade of white-hot sparks burst over his flaming flesh, and a low moan broke from his lips. His screaming body nearly drowned out his rational mind.

Her gaze locked on his strained expression. In that moment, Meg knew that he was still worried about her. "It'll be okay," she whispered. "I won't fight you."

"I just want to make it good for you. I want it to be perfect." As he continued to gently stroke her back, Clay felt the last of her tension give and urged her to move so she straddled his narrow hips.

Although embarrassed color stained her cheeks, Meg moved at his direction, her gaze never straying from his face. As he complimented her with sweet words and praised her with gentle encouragement, she forgot the last of her inhibitions.

Clay wooed her with mouth and hands and body until she moved with trust and passion, both of which she found completely natural. Just as natural, but more familiar, was Clay's intimate touch. A touch that had Meg pulling him closer, a touch that had her spinning out of control even as she clung to him. Adrift in a sea known only to lovers, Meg felt waves of pleasure wash over her, waves initiated by Clay's skilled and tender guidance.

Between them there were no secrets, no shame, no pretense. When Meg once again became aware of herself as a separate entity, she lifted her head so she could better see his expression. In the semi-darkness, his eyes gleamed like aged doubloons but, to Meg, the richness of his unselfish gift was worth far more than gold.

"That was . . . wonderful," she whispered.

"I'm glad." A soft chuckle of male satisfaction rumbled through his chest before reverberating through her.

She let her head rest on his good shoulder. "You make me feel . . . I don't know, fantastic." Amazement underscored her admission.

He chuckled again as his arms pulled her closer. "Thanks."

"I ought to be thanking you." His selflessness and restraint still awed her, even as she anticipated more.

He gently traced her spine. "Next time will be even better," he muttered in a voice rough with yearning. Because he didn't want to frighten her, he kept his touch light and undemanding. Determination to proceed at a pace she set was what restrained him. He feathered a series of featherlight kisses down her slender neck and across her collarbone.

Meg knew what he meant, knew what he wanted and what she wanted, as well. As she felt him against her, hot and hard even through the barrier of his pants, need tightened inside her.

"I'm ready," she whispered.

Clay let his hands rest on her slender waist. "There's no hurry, Meg. This isn't a race," he assured though his pulse accelerated like a race car in high gear. "We have all night for a lot of nights." Yet, even as he spoke the reassuring words, doubt hit him like a blow to the gut. An eternity of nights with Meg wouldn't be enough, but Clay saw no alternative and no choice. His troubled thoughts were soon blown away on the breeze of Meg's promised passion.

Her arms snaked around his neck as her mouth descended on his with sensual intensity. When he admitted her tongue, she pressed inside eagerly, sampling the heated honey like a hungry child attacked an ice-cream cone on a hot July day. Licking and consuming, tasting and enjoying. At last, breathless, she lifted her head.

Clay's big hands cupped her hips as she moved against him. From between clenched teeth, her name hissed out in a plaintive plea. "Meg..."

"Yes, Clay." When she shifted slightly, his grasp tightened.

"Meg, I'm about to explode," he muttered in a guttural groan.

Her palms cupped his cheeks. "I need you, Clay. I want you."

Shuddering need racked him. "Remember what I said, Meg. If you want me to stop, any time..."

She pressed a forefinger to his kiss-dampened lips. "I won't," she assured him.

"But if you're uncomfortable." He swallowed hard. "You still trust me, don't you?" Anxiety clouded desire. He'd rather die than hurt or disappoint her.

Color seeped into her cheeks. "After what just happened... do you need to ask, Clay?"

His fingers drew intricate, mindless designs on her moist skin. "Because this time will be different, Meg. I'll be... inside you, deep inside you. Since you haven't had much experience, it may hurt at first. It may be scary for you." Fear of reminding her of a hideous memory, fear of reactivating her nightmares lanced through him.

"I told you, I won't start hitting you again," she said as her lashes fluttered down. Discussing intimacy made her uneasy and uncomfortable. She felt awkward and inept. "I won't hurt you."

"Sweetheart, I'm not worried about me," Clay said, speaking the real truth. "I'm scared to death I might hurt you."

When she saw the tender concern on Clay's handsome features, her anxiety was tossed to the winds. "You could never scare me, darling." She brushed a soft kiss over his open mouth. "And I know you'll try not to hurt me. Each time will be better, won't it?" A trace of leftover anxiety made her voice tremble.

"Better and better," he vowed. His hands slipped around to caress her rib cage before flickering over her breasts like twin feathers. When a shudder ripped through her, he stopped. "Tell me if there's anything you don't like, Meg, anything that makes you uncomfortable. I need to know."

She bit her lower lip and glanced away. "What about things I like?" she inquired in a tentative whisper.

"I'd like to know that, too. I like pleasing you, Meg. Tell me what you want, what you like."

"I like your kisses." Her voice was barely audible over her ragged breathing.

Clay, eager to please, did as she bade. Liquid fire roared through her veins as he scattered bold kisses over her exposed flesh. She grasped his broad shoulders when his mouth caught hers in a wild kiss that left her wishing for more. His tongue tasted, tested, teased until she was mindless with need, blind with desire.

Aware of Meg's growing pleasure, he stroked and caressed every inch that his mouth had already covered. His own arousal became nearly unbearable but he held off, still worried he might upset her by moving too quickly.

With measured motion, he paid homage to her. Nothing was as important as Meg, her comfort and her contentment. When she tore at his trousers, he went rigid. Her touch was like a match to dynamite. His fuse, shortened by building desire, was too short for his peace of mind. "Meg . . ."

"Don't wait any longer, Clay. I need you."

His hands captured hers as they closed over his tight buttocks. "You're sure, Meg?" If she denied him now, he'd explode anyway, he knew, but he would rather have humiliated himself than hurt her.

"Very sure."

With a shuddering sigh of relief, he rolled away to discard his trousers. Meg heard the crackle of foil, then he was back beside her.

"You said you weren't afraid, sweetheart, and you shouldn't be because I'd rather die myself than hurt you," he whispered before taking her mouth in a gentle, wooing kiss while his hands carefully aligned their bodies. Keeping his caresses light yet lusty, he again led her into readiness.

Her arms encompassed his broad back as her hands massaged the taut, sculpted muscles there. Meg relaxed and began to enjoy the texture of his muscular body beneath her palms. She again found the scars on his torso. The ridges and furrows were lovingly traced and gently soothed as if each one needed her ardent attention.

Clay knew the second the last particle of tension left her and released a pent-up breath.

With his hard muscles brushing her soft flesh, electrical charges jolted through Meg. He was so strong, so powerful, so undeniably male, yet she had no fear. Not of Clay. Not of his loving.

With care and consideration, restraint and reserve, his tongue filled her mouth while his hips rocked against hers in a prelude for what lay ahead. When he was absolutely certain of her want and willingness, both physical and emotional, he slipped slowly inside her, pausing to allow her time to adjust to him. Although primitive demands shook Clay, he held back and peered into her flushed face. "Are you okay, Meg?"

She heard the ragged yearning in his voice, felt it in his body and wondered how he maintained such ironclad control. Her body craved satisfaction, satisfaction only Clay could provide. She knew he was giving her time to adjust to this deepest intimacy, but the heat pooling in her belly made her want to scream in frustration. She shifted again, so he settled deeper. Twin moans split the night air.

"Love me, Clay, love me," she urged. She thought he mumbled something that sounded suspiciously like "I already do," but as he led her into the soft, hazy world of passion, reality fell away and Meg joined Clay, heart and soul, body and spirit.

Sunlight poured in through the skylight. Clay felt it on his face and rolled over to escape the intrusion of day. As he settled deeper into the soft bed, silken hair tickled his nose while the sweet scent of flowers filled his nostrils. Abruptly his eyes flew open.

As soon as he saw Meg, a sigh of contentment whispered through his lips. He hadn't felt so good in years. No, he amended, he hadn't ever felt this good. A silly grin tugged his mouth. It wasn't only good sex. No, he again amended, *fantastic* sex, and it was more, so much more. More than desire, more than passion, more than fantasy, more than he had ever dreamed possible.

Despite her relative innocence, Meg had stunned him with her response. At first, she had been somewhat tentative. Considering her only other liaison with a man, he hadn't been surprised. And even that minor hesitance hadn't lasted beyond the first moments. On the contrary, she proceeded while he held back, and from then on she had been like wildfire—red hot and raging out of control. Clay had gladly let the conflagration sear him, as well.

Thinking of the night just past brought his blood to a slow boil. With one shaking hand, he brushed her bare arm as deep, abiding love filled his heart. He pressed his eyes shut as the previously unacknowledged emotion surged forth, refusing to be denied any longer. At least, in the wake of their passion, Clay had to be honest with himself. He loved Meg Andrews and had for a long time, probably since the night in the cave. Yet, although he accepted his feelings,

Clay shied away from the idea of expressing them to Meg. After all, loving her didn't make him any more suitable, and admitting it would, undoubtedly, make their situation far more complicated.

Meg, sound asleep, turned toward him, her bare body brushing his. The purely male reaction of his body stunned Clay. After hours of lovemaking, he should have been completely satiated. That he wanted her again, so soon and so vigorously, amazed him. Accustomed to being distant and disciplined, he found his recent behavior rather shocking. Denying his wants and needs had become almost second nature, but with Meg, his restraint lay in tatters. He gazed at her flushed face with awe. In so little time, she had wrought drastic changes in his life. Even after she left, he'd never be the same, never feel the same. No matter how far apart they were, Meg would remain in his heart and soul and mind forever.

Her copper lashes fluttered, then opened. As her sleepy gaze fell on Clay, she smiled. "Good morning."

Her voice, soft and sexy, fell over him like a ream of pure silk. "Good morning," he mumbled as he shifted away in an effort to conceal his reaction to her nearness.

Meg sensed his withdrawal and scooted to sit against the pillows. Her fingers clutched the top of the sheet. "How are you feeling?" she asked, then inwardly chastised herself for making such a trite query. How should she act? she wondered as she searched his chiseled profile.

As his attention moved over her face, Clay noticed how fragile and fatigued she appeared. Her lips were swollen from his kisses, her cheeks and neck were scratched from his beard and her slight wince when she moved went through him like a dagger. He had been stupid and selfish, he thought with disgust. And he should have been the one asking how she felt.

He rolled away and yanked on the pants he had discarded by the bed. What must she think of him? Had he reminded her of that monster who had raped her? A knot of disgust formed in his gut.

His further withdrawal shattered the haze of slumber, and panic darted through Meg. Was he going to mumble some sort of nonsense about the two of them having no future before the sheets had even cooled? Was he going to remind her how different they were and ask her to leave? Her fingers tightened on the sheet.

"Clay, is something wrong?"

"It's nearly noon." His nerveless fingers trembled on the zipper and he cursed under his breath.

Meg stared at his broad back. Despite her misgivings, she couldn't help but notice how the soft cotton trousers clung faithfully to his lean hips, tight buttocks and muscular thighs, which only reminded her how close that beautiful body had been all night. A magical night, at least for Meg. In his arms, she had found unexpected joy. Evidently his experience hadn't been the same, she thought sadly.

"Clay," she began in a tentative whisper, "I'm sorry...but you knew...you knew I wasn't experienced. You must have realized I might, well, disappoint you."

He spun around in time to see her blink back tears. Contrition shadowed his gaze. "Oh, Meg, you can't honestly think I was disappointed."

She lifted her luminous eyes. "Then why are you so eager to get away from me?" Pain and confusion glowed in her gaze.

"Oh, sweetheart," he said as he collapsed beside her. When he opened his arms, she moved into his embrace. "I don't want to get away from you. I want to stay right here, stretch you out on this bed and bury myself so deep inside you that the rest of the world disappears, until there's just the two of us, until nothing else matters, not the past and not the future, just us here and now."

At his words, a hot blush stained her cheeks while warm contentment filled her heart. "When I'm with you, there isn't anything else, or anyone else. The past doesn't matter... In fact, it seemed like someone else's past, like it never happened to me at all. Last night, well, it was beautiful, Clay. I never imagined..."

"Neither did I."

Her head fell back so she could see his expression. "What do you mean?"

Crimson crept into his face. "I mean I never knew love-making could be like that," he confessed.

"But you're experienced."

Clay licked his lips. "I might have had many lovers, Meg, but I haven't been with a woman for a very long time and certainly with no one like you."

Feminine pride filled her. Aware of her powers, and of his vulnerability to them, she pressed a kiss to his corded neck while her hands slid down his bare torso to the open waistband of his trousers.

"Meg... that's enough," he warned in a strangled voice.

"I want you to stay in bed." Despite her newfound sexual assertiveness, shyness assailed her. "I want you," she finished in a whisper.

Yearning tore through him, but he remained as stiff as a chunk of lake ice. "What you need is rest."

"You said it's almost noon. I never sleep so late," she objected in a tone that made her sound like a petulant child.

A chuckle rumbled out of him. "But you never stay up most of the night making love, either."

The color lingering in her cheeks deepened. "It was the best night of my life," she told him.

"Mine, too." His hands reached down to keep hers from doing more damage. "Are you... how do you feel?"

"I feel fantastic," she assured him, knowing to say anything else was to provoke guilt, along with his hasty departure. And, despite the slight ache between her legs, she did feel fantastic. He had been so gentle and generous, yet powerful and passionate, as well.

"You'll be better after you rest."

She clung to him when he would have gotten up. "What about you? You never said how you feel. You're the one who got shot and you were up all night, too. Don't you need more rest?"

"Probably," he drawled, "but I won't get it lying beside you." Although he didn't say so, he hadn't gotten nearly as much sleep as Meg. For hours, he had lain wide awake, watching her and committing every detail to memory. Carefully extracting himself from her embrace, he got to his feet, then bent over to press a kiss to her brow, one that wouldn't start any more fires in either one of them.

Loss and panic darted through Meg. His withdrawal intensified the doubts dwelling in the dim recesses of her head. A troubled sigh left her as she realized how easily she might lose in her quest to pierce his emotional armor. Despite their intense intimacy, nothing had really changed. Neither his tender words nor his magical lovemaking represented commitment. Nothing he had said or done indicated a desire to prolong their relationship beyond her stay in his home. Soon, he would be lost in the murky world of the mercenary, retrieving other people's friends and loved ones from danger while placing himself in constant peril. Anguish squeezed her heart in its viselike grip. So did the urge to keep him close for as long as possible, safe for as long as possible.

"Couldn't you hold me, Clay? Just until I go back to sleep."

The sweet entreaty in her request stripped him of sense, something he'd lost along with his heart, it seemed. Although he knew he needed to pull back before he made promises he hadn't a chance of keeping, he acceded to her wishes. "Of course, sweetheart," he replied as he rejoined her. "I'll hold you for as long as you like."

Hearing his promise brought a fresh ache to Meg's heart. What if she asked him to hold her forever?

Chapter 13

When Meg awoke again, she was alone in the rumpled bed. A low, lilting whistle reached her from below and a smile lit her face. When Clay appeared at the top of the stairs moments later, it widened.

"Hi, sweetheart," he murmured as he perched on the edge of the bed. The sight of her there, amid the covers where he had spent too many lonely nights, did strange things to his respiration.

Meg stretched out her arms in silent invitation. Clay accepted without demur. He pressed one soft kiss into the delicate curve of her neck before drawing back slightly so he could see her face. The mauve shadows were gone, and her eyes sparkled with vitality and warmth. "How do you feel?"

"I'd feel better if I wasn't in bed alone." Her fingers sought the exposed skin above his T-shirt, gently stroking and searching.

Like bellows to ember, her exploration reignited his banked passion. His blood flowed like molten lava as she leaned forward to cover his mouth with a sizzling kiss that went beyond familiarity straight into lust. His fingers tangled in her silky waves as his senses reeled under her ardent attack. Rational thought receded behind a haze of desire.

At last, reluctantly, Clay pulled away. "No more, Meg. I can't take it." Longing flamed in his gaze and thickened his voice.

She pursed her lips in a parody of a pout. "You promised to stay with me as long I wanted."

Hearing her words made him realize he had to be careful not to make any more promises he couldn't keep. He settled back on the edge of the mattress and tried to regain his equilibrium. "You were sleeping soundly enough. Besides, I was just downstairs."

"I know. I heard you whistling. What were you doing?" she asked before she realized how nosy she sounded.

Clay stiffened slightly. "Household stuff," he replied.

"I can help with the chores," she offered.

He shook his head. "You're a guest."

Although she knew his words were meant to be polite, dismay flashed in her gaze before her copper lashes drifted down to conceal it. She was a guest, a guest in his home, a guest in his life, a transient, someone passing through.

Clay read her reaction as easily as three-foot print on a roadside billboard and frowned. Ever since leaving her side, he had toyed with telling her the entire truth. Although an internal battle continued to rage through his soul, he simply wasn't prepared to proceed. He still thought she'd find someone else if his selfish need didn't overcome his common sense. Being honest would likely intensify her romantic illusions and cloud her mind. As much as he wanted more than a few days and nights with her, Clay wanted her happiness and contentment even more. He wanted her to find the right man, a man who deserved her.

His hands tightened until his knuckles showed white. If he thought he was the best guy, he'd haul her out of bed and to the nearest preacher without a second's hesitation. But he knew better.

"Do you have many guests?" she asked in a valiant at
tempt at casual conversation.

"None," he replied with utter honesty. "No one else ha
ever stayed here. Hank's the only one who even stops by.
lead a pretty solitary life," he admitted as he glanced aroun
the sunlit loft. "And I'm not here all that often, or for ver
long."

As her gaze followed his, Meg sighed. "I'd think it'd b
hard to leave." She knew it would be for her. More tha
hard, excruciating.

His attention fixed on her face. "It is, now more tha
ever."

When Meg saw the utter hopelessness and bleak loneli
ness shadowing his gaze, she felt a flicker of fresh hope
"Do you really have to take this next job? Couldn't some
one else do it?"

"I'm afraid not," he whispered. Unable to keep from
touching her, he reached out to stroke the silk of her cheek

"Is it another rescue?" she asked in a breathless whis
per.

"Not exactly. I told you, I do other things, too."

"I remember," she murmured. "And I understand."

Clay wished to hell that he did. The rest of his life loome
ahead as barren as the past forty-two years had been. Th
difference was, now he knew what had been missing. No
he had an opportunity for the sort of happiness that elude
most of the human race.

His hand fell away and tightened into a fist. He still ha
nothing to offer Meg. He couldn't ask her to enter his worl
a world of shadow and subterfuge, a world where constar
separation and endless worry would eventually destroy the
love. And he couldn't see himself in her world, a world c
sanitary safety and security, a world where his love would b
a burden to bear, where having him for a husband was likel
to cause her isolation. As badly as he wanted to share his li
with Meg, he knew it wasn't enough. They both had to liv
in their real worlds, not the fairy tale they created togethe

Once Meg got home, she'd see that for herself, and he had to give her that chance, the chance to compare him to other men, better men.

"I guess there's not much chance your work will ever bring you to Ohio," she said. Already an agonizing ache squeezed her heart. After she left Puerto Rico, would she ever see him again? And, if she didn't, how would she survive?

"Not much." His heart battered his ribs with its frantic beating. Despite all the words of warning he'd repeated to himself countless times, his next question escaped through the barriers of sense and sanity and selflessness. "If... if it ever did, would you want me to come see you?"

"Of course," she replied quickly. Her gaze swept over his face. The restraints of shyness and anxiety flagged. "I love you, Clay. I know you think we're too different, that our lives are too different... I knew when I came here that I probably couldn't change your mind, but I never promised not to try," she reminded him. "The truth is, I can hardly stand the thought of never seeing you again, darling."

Both his hands balled into fists. His breathing became shallow and shortened, his heartbeat fierce and frantic. "Meg, I know you think you're in love with me, but when you get home, when you're among your friends, you'll see I'm right. You'll see I'm not the kind of guy you'd want to introduce to them." If she didn't see that now, she would eventually.

"I'm not Annette," Meg replied in a firm tone. "I'm not some silly little snob who doesn't know love from lust. I know I love you now and I'll love you fifty years from now. I can *survive* without you, Clay, but I'll never fall in love again. Even if we never see each other again, my heart will always be with you."

Silence echoed in the loft as he absorbed her words but he still couldn't believe she wouldn't change her mind, or that it wouldn't be better if she did. "I still think you'll see things differently when you get home so I don't think we ought to make promises we probably can't keep." He took her hands in his. "For the next few months or so, I'll be away. I won't be able to contact you then, and when I get back . . . well, there'll just be another mission and another after that." Resigned regret roughened his voice.

"It doesn't have to be that way," she protested.

A ragged sigh shuddered through him. "Meg, I told you I couldn't promise anything beyond the next two weeks and you said you understood. You said you could accept that." His gaze searched her face. "If you can't, well, maybe you'd rather leave now." His heart thundered in his chest. He didn't want her to leave yet. He wanted, needed, the next couple of weeks with her but the decision was hers. If she couldn't accept his terms, he wouldn't try to hold her.

Meg's lashes fluttered down to conceal the emotions churning through her. She wanted more, much more, than two weeks but she knew better than to say so. If she had any hope of claiming him from the dark, murky world of a mercenary, she couldn't give up so easily. He might not love her, but he cared about her and he wanted her.

"You're not getting rid of me that easily." Not since she knew he wanted her. Now he wasn't getting rid of her at all—not if she could help it.

He smiled. "Sweetheart, I don't want to get rid of you. You're the best thing that ever happened to me." His voice dropped a fraction. "I want you more than anything. But we both need to accept the truth."

"Then show me, Clay. Show me how much you want me and let me show you," she said, reaching for him.

Meg awoke to again find the loft deserted. A glance at the nightstand revealed the time—twenty after five—as well as a note from Clay saying he'd gone for groceries.

A wary grin lifted her lips as warmth spread through her. During the long hours of the afternoon, he had repeatedly demonstrated just how much he wanted her. Their love-making had been hotter and wilder than the previous night maybe because she had been more sure of both herself and him. If actions spoke louder than words, then Clay cared deeply about her.

After a refreshing shower, Meg slipped into the thick terry-cloth robe she found on the back of the bathroom door. Pulling it close around her damp flesh, she inhaled deeply and found her senses filled with Clay's purely masculine scent. Memories, like a river of hot lava, poured through her mind, then on to heat her body with fresh longing.

Loud rapping at the downstairs door interrupted her thoughts. Meg froze as anxiety filled her. Clay wasn't expecting anyone, so who could be below? A male voice reverberated through the door and up the stairs, one Meg found slightly familiar.

She darted down the steps and to the door, using the peephole to confirm the suspicion that Hank was their unexpected guest. She threw open the door and met the older man's suddenly shocked gaze.

"Hello," Meg said. When his attention traveled to her attire, she pulled the robe closer. "I suppose you want to see Clay."

Dumbfounded, Hank glanced back at her face. A puzzled frown crinkled his forehead, then recognition flickered in his eyes. "You the girl who came in my place looking for Clay?"

"Yes. I'm Meg Andrews."

"He find your brother?"

"Yes, thank you. He did. Everything is fine. My brother's probably being reunited with his children right now."

The frown deepened. "Your brother's not here?"

Color surged into Meg's face, but she held the man's regard. "No, he isn't. No one is, but you're welcome to come in and wait for Clay. He went shopping and should be back pretty soon."

"Can't stay," he mumbled. "Got to get back to work. Just tell him Carson's been calling every day for nearly a

week. I've stalled him as best I could but he wasn't happy
about Clay free-lancing and he wants to talk to him pronto.'

Anxiety swirled through Meg like a churning tornado
"Maybe I better write down the number." Who was Car
son and why was he angry with Clay?

"No need. Clay knows how to get in touch with him. Tel
him he better call pretty quick or Carson'll be sending
somebody down here. He's pretty upset."

Questions about this Carson trembled on the tip of Meg'
tongue, but she had no chance to voice them. Clay's Jeep
roared up in front of the cottage. Only seconds passed be
tween the time he killed the engine and appeared on th
porch beside Hank.

"Is something wrong?" The query was directed to th
older man. So was his attention.

Hank shrugged. "Depends on how you look at it. Car
son's been trying to get in touch with you, and he's not to
happy."

Clay grimaced. "He knows I went back to Costa de
Palma?"

"You know he keeps close track of his men." Hank's gaz
cut to Meg before returning to Clay's carefully controlle
features. "He's really on the warpath, Clay. You'd bes
come down to the cantina and call before he makes good o
his threat to send someone after you."

The unnatural color seeped from Meg's face as her anxi
ety quadrupled. The implication of Hank's statement sen
chills through her. Meg drew the thick terry more closel
around her shivering body. It failed to provide warmth, c
comfort.

Clay saw Meg's reaction and silently cursed both himsel
and Hank, although he couldn't blame his old friend fc
making certain assumptions and revealing too much. On
glance at Meg telegraphed how they'd spent the past hour:
The fact that she wore his robe only intensified the mes
sage. They were lovers. Any fool could see that. Despite th

foreboding squeezing his insides to mush, desire flowed through him.

With effort, he turned back to Hank. "I'll be down in a little while. If Carson calls before then, well, just tell him I got the message."

After Hank left, Clay ushered an ashen Meg into the cottage and urged her to sit down. When she perched on one of the twin sofas, he went to stand by the empty fireplace.

"It's not as bad as it sounds," he assured her. But he couldn't shake the dread hovering over him like a storm cloud.

Turmoil and tension left her chilled and shaken. "Who is this Carson? Why is he threatening you?"

Clay shoved his fingers through his sable hair. Although he knew the truth would add to her illusions about him Clay couldn't let her think Carson might send a hit man after him. "It's an idle threat, Meg. Carson isn't going to send someone to get me. He's just mad because I was supposed to be resting up for my next job, not going back to Costa del Palma."

"Why would he care what you do?" A sudden idea flashed in her mind like a bolt of lightning in the night sky. "Is your next job something to do with him? Did he hire you to rescue someone else, or something?"

"Mostly or something," Clay mumbled as he braced one elbow on the mantel and tried to marshal his thoughts. Somehow he had to tell her the truth without playing on her sympathies and enhancing her misconceptions. As much as Clay wanted her love, he knew he couldn't have it. The truth would only make him sound more appropriate for her.

Clay cleared his throat over the lump of pure, potent emotion clogging it. "I told you I do other things beside hostage retrieval," he murmured in an attempt to bridge the gulf between fiction and fact while reissuing the reminder that he wasn't a hero. "Some of them aren't so good or gallant. Some of what I do, what I've done, is pretty dirty," he hastened to point out again.

"Who is this Carson and what does he have to do with your work? Did he hire you or not?" Frustration sharpened her tone.

"He didn't hire me," Clay replied, "but he is my boss."

"Boss?" Meg echoed in a high, shrill tone. "How can you have a boss? I thought you worked for yourself." Suspicion narrowed her eyes to slits. "Just exactly what is your job, Clay?"

"A job title doesn't change a job, Meg. You already know what I do."

"Do I?" she asked with clear skepticism. Gazing at his familiar features, she had a sinking suspicion she didn't know him at all. "I thought your job title was something like soldier of fortune or hired gun when we met. Later, you let me think it was more like combination mercenary and man-at-arms." Her mouth flattened into a line of displeasure. "So, which is it, Clay? Or isn't it any of them?" Bits and fragments of their conversations spun through her head like leaves in a storm, but nothing made sense. Each word he spoke only added to her inner turmoil and confusion.

As a sigh of resignation left him, he ran one hand over his face. He now had no choice but to answer her questions directly. Her obvious annoyance and perplexity were now as much cause for concern as her innocence and illusions.

"I'm a federal agent, Meg. Carson is my supervisor."

For long, silent moments she stared at him as if he was an alien being, a man from Mars or beyond. Slowly, the fragments of past conversations stopped swirling through her and began to fall together. Suddenly she felt not only stupid and naive but betrayed, too. "You were never a mercenary," she said in accusation.

He shook his head. "It's a cover. One I've used for a long time. It gets me in a lot of places where I need to go."

Meg pressed her trembling lips together. "You lied to me," she said. "Over and over, you lied." His deceit tore at the very root of her newfound trust, baring the tender shoots of faith and exposing them to destruction and death.

Goaded by anguish and humiliation, she continued with barely a breath to sustain her. "I suppose in your line of work, lying is necessary, even recommended. I must say, you've very good at it."

Meg's irate reaction stunned him into silence. Prepared for relief, he hadn't expected rage. Under her scathing regard, he felt ripped and raw. "I'm sorry, Meg," he began in a hoarse whisper before she cut him off.

"Sorry doesn't do a damn bit of good," she shot back. "It doesn't make wrong right."

"I know that," he said. The cold expression freezing her features reminded him all too much of the woman he'd met in the cantina, a woman hiding behind a shield of indifference and arrogance to protect herself from hurt and harm. That such pain might be caused by him had his guts in knots. "Surely you can understand why I didn't tell you at first. I didn't know you, or the situation. I didn't know how things would work out. And later, well..." His voice trailed off as he tried to find the words to explain.

Gathering tatters of wounded pride and shattered trust about her, Meg lifted her chin. "There's no reason you didn't tell me later. None except you couldn't use the excuse of not fitting into my world to send me away." An unexpected pain ripped through her, and for a moment, her mouth trembled. "You never planned to see me again, did you? Everything you said to me was nonsense. There probably wasn't a drunken father, or a woman named Annette... It was all part of your role, a role you play so very well."

Her bitterness and contempt lashed him like a whip, laying bare his fears and need. "The only lie was in not telling you I was a federal agent. Everything else was true," he managed in a rough whisper.

"I don't believe you." When she spoke again, her voice and expression were remote and reserved. "After the first few days, there was no good reason not to tell me."

"Yes, there was," he persisted. "First of all, I may be a federal agent and not a mercenary but my job is still filled with violence and brutality and lies. I'm not like Dave Thornton, Meg. I don't sit behind a desk." He exhaled sharply. "And what I said about my childhood, it was all true and more. Yet, despite everything I told you, despite what you saw yourself, you made me into some sort of hero. If I'd told you I was an agent and not a soldier of fortune, it would've added to your romantic fantasies." As soon as Clay saw the flush of anger stain Meg's face, he knew he'd made a major misstep.

"Romantic fantasies? You make me sound like a silly schoolgirl or a frustrated spinster. You make me sound like I don't have a shred of sense." With every word, her voice rose until it was almost a shout.

Clay crossed to sit on the sofa opposite her although he yearned to wrap his arms around her and absorb her anger and anguish. At the moment, he figured keeping his distance was best. "Meg, I never said you were silly. I never said you were frustrated or didn't have any sense," he murmured, "but you did say I was a hero to you and I didn't want to encourage that notion."

Since she couldn't disagree with that, she took another tack. "That's a poor excuse for lying to me especially after I was completely honest with you. Especially after I told you my... deepest, most intimate secret and fear." Her voice grew so soft and hoarse that he had to strain to hear it.

"Meg, I told you, I only lied about my job title, not about anything else." As he repeated himself, he wondered if she was listening, or merely hearing and dismissing his reassurances. "I know I don't deserve you and that's most of why I didn't tell you what I do. I thought the truth would unduly influence how you feel, make you more susceptible..." He stopped before he said anything that might further incite her anger.

As he studied Meg's angry expression, he wondered how he could have been so stupid. Right up until he'd revealed his real job, he'd been worried about adding to her overblown image of him. Instead of increasing her regard, the truth had destroyed it. Anxious and alarmed by the possibility of losing Meg, Clay forgot his resolve and restraint. "You ought to have a husband who's never known violence, never caused death, never created destruction." He bowed his dark head. "I've seen and done things I could never, would never, tell you about...."

For a moment, Meg studied him. After opening her heart and mind and body to him, then catching him in a bold lie, Meg no longer trusted her own emotions, or him. Worse, she now knew how hopeless their situation really was. His lie proved that he didn't trust her at all. Battered by ambivalent feelings, she averted her face. She couldn't say what she had to if she faced him.

"No more lies?" she asked. Choked by defeat and disappointment, her words came out as a hoarse whisper.

"No more lies, Meg. Not ever." His deep voice was almost as strangled as hers.

Meg, her attention on the floor, felt only an aching emptiness, a vast desolation that killed her joy and her hope. She felt robbed of all optimism and Clay's refusal to trust her was the thief. Yet when she spoke her voice held no trace of emotion.

"Then I want you to promise to leave me alone." When she glanced back at him, her eyes were chunks of azure ice, her face a mask of porcelain. As he started to open his mouth, she held up one hand to stop him. "You encouraged me to trust you, believe in you. You berated me for letting you think Dave and I were involved, accused me of lying to you, yet you were living a lie the entire time."

She clasped her trembling hands together as she struggled for control. "You let me confide in you, tell you things I never told anyone else. I opened my heart and soul and—" She looked away. "You knew what happened to me, knew I didn't trust men..." Her jaw tightened. "A dozen times or more, you could have told me the truth." Her voice dropped several notes as she forced her attention back to him. "After Ted's rescue or last night, or this morning, or even this afternoon. You had any number of chances but you never told me the truth."

Although she was in danger of losing her control, Meg steeled herself to continue. No matter how ripped and raw she felt inside, no matter how great her anguish, she wouldn't break down in front of him. She had to salvage some vestige of pride, some shred of dignity. No one, not even Clay Terhune, could break her spirit. She stiffened her spine and squared her shoulders. "I could have lived with you being a mercenary because I never thought you without ethics or values, despite what you said. Now I know different. You lied to me, because you don't trust me. Because you don't trust anyone. Maybe dishonesty and suspicion are virtues in your work but I can't accept them. A relationship without trust isn't a relationship at all." She shook her head as sad acceptance filled her eyes. "You're too good at lying and pretending, or maybe I'm just too gullible."

"Meg . . ."

Her voice slashed through his. "Don't make more excuses, Clay. Maybe you felt justified in keeping the truth from me but it doesn't change the fact that you don't trust me." She released a pent-up sigh. "Maybe you can't trust me. Maybe you can't trust anyone. Maybe that's what living a lie does to you. I don't know." Her shoulders slumped. "I don't know anything except that you were right. The best thing I can do is go home and try to forget you." Bitterness filled her tone and expression. He had tried to warn her that they had no future, but she hadn't listened. She hadn't wanted to.

As Meg got to her feet and crossed to the staircase, Clay reeled with shock and sorrow. He'd been braced to let her go eventually, but not now. Not like this. How, he wondered, had everything gone so wrong?

Only hours earlier, he'd been euphoric. Now his spirits plummeted as he realized Meg was about to walk out of his life for good and he had no way to stop her. As he watched her retreat, anger joined anguish. If she really loved him, how could she say such things? How could she leave so abruptly? Why couldn't she try to understand his reluctance to reveal the truth? While he couldn't really blame her for being hurt and upset, why wasn't she a bit relieved?

When Meg hesitated on the bottom step, Clay started to get to his feet, then stopped. Letting her go was the best thing for both of them. It was what would happen in a couple of weeks anyhow. Knowing they'd only have stolen moments between missions, stolen moments when they met between their worlds, on the edge of darkness and light, was what had kept him from being honest in the first place. It was what kept him from arguing now.

As she scampered up the steps without a backward glance, a bleak realization took root in his mind. He'd been right all along. What Meg felt for him was infatuation, not love.

He sank back on the sofa and buried his head in his hands.

Chapter 14

During the long three months since leaving Puerto Rico, Meg had only spoken Clay's name once, yet now, he was here. Here. Nervous anticipation tickled her spine. Just one glance, she told herself, one glance to see that he was truly all right, then she would go back to her cottage and he need never know she had spied on him. Still, she stood in the entry of her brother's house as if she were a redwood rooted high in the mountains.

On that one occasion, that she had uttered his name, Meg had been surprised out of her indifference by a phone call from Carlotta. The older woman expressed concern about Meg's well-being, as well as her brother's, while Meg, aching for some tie to Clay, babbled like a brook about her family and job until Carlotta stopped her with a single question. Had Meg heard from Clay? Meg's negative reply had led Carlotta to admit she had had only one brief call from him, one that left her worried enough to contact Hank for Meg's telephone number. It was then Meg learned that the cantina owner was a former federal agent himself, a colleague of Clay's. Because Meg couldn't admit the truth to the kindly lady, she ended the conversation by thanking her for her concern and telling her not to worry about Clay.

Meg sighed. Too bad she hadn't taken that advice herself. Long months after leaving him, Meg reacted to news of Clay's impending visit with shock and anger and, unfortunately, anxiety. Even after Ted explained that the trip was business, part of an investigation into the growing unrest in Costa del Palma, her uneasiness hadn't abated. Even to herself it was hard to admit that, despite everything, she had fretted over his welfare as much as Carlotta. Knowing he had returned safely from wherever he had been eased her mind, if not her heart.

More and more, she wondered why Clay would come to Ohio—even for business. Another agent could easily handle this assignment, so why, really, was he here? For just a moment, she let herself hope.

Her efforts to dislodge Clay from her heart and mind had proved futile, as had her resolve not to come near her brother's house while Clay was a guest.

On trembling legs, Meg advanced until she could peek into the spacious living area. The figure on the sofa perched on the very edge as if prepared for immediate flight. Tension radiated from every line of his lean body as Meg drank in the sight of him and anger peeled away.

In a well-cut navy suit, Clay could easily be mistaken for a young executive, a neighbor who stopped in on the way home from the office. Although he had repeatedly told Meg he'd never fit into her world, he looked just like every guy on the block.

As she craned her neck for a better view, Meg saw the purple smudging his tiger eyes and new lines of fatigue around his sensual mouth. All his tan had vanished, as had all facial hair. Not even a trace of late-afternoon stubble darkened his square jaw.

With his pale countenance and bland attire, he was nearly unrecognizable as the man who had rescued her brother and stolen her heart. Meg had seen him dirty and disheveled, weary and worn, but nothing had prepared her for this tense, stiff stranger. Had his last assignment been so difficult? Had he been hurt? Had Carlotta been right to worry? Anxiety squeezed Meg's insides, and her hand flew to her throat.

The sudden motion, in his peripheral vision, drew Clay's stunned gaze. The little color in his face vanished.

Although Meg wanted to run and hide, she took a tentative step forward. She grasped the plate she held tighter.

For a fleeting moment, what might have been joy shone in Clay's tired eyes, then a curtain fell to effectively cloak any trace of emotion. He looked as cold and hard as the man she had met in Hank's bar.

"Hello, Meg." His voice wasn't as steady as he would have liked, and he had to press his hands together to keep them from trembling. He hadn't been sure, after her parting demand, what her reaction to his visit would be. He'd told Ted, out of pure cowardice, that his boss had sent him. Since it was essentially true, Clay planned to stick to that story until he knew for sure how Meg now felt.

"Hello," Meg murmured as she shifted from one foot to the other, dragging her gaze away from him as she did. She couldn't afford to let him see her ragged emotion or sense her ambivalence. She couldn't afford to show any weakness.

Clay sighed heavily as Meg averted her face. Her cool tone and dismissive attitude didn't surprise him, but they hurt, more than was sensible or sane. Aching anguish radiated through him.

His last mission had been as perilous as any he'd ever undertaken. Emotionally, physically, professionally and personally, Clay felt drained and empty. But he had finally reached a decision. He had to see Meg again.

Upon return to the States, he'd learned a crisis was developing in Costa del Palma and his boss thought Clay ought to handle the investigation. Since he was already in trouble with Carson, Clay couldn't ask for any slack, couldn't ask for a few days off to see Meg. So when Carson told Clay to send an agent to Ohio to interview Ted and Maria, he quickly volunteered to go himself. Not that Carson had approved. He hadn't. It had taken a great deal of arguing on Clay's part, and finally a threat to quit, before his boss agreed. Then Clay found himself in the capital only long enough to be debriefed, then briefed again on the new case. After a quick trip to the barber, a stop at his apartment for clothing, he'd been on his way back to the airport.

The overnight flight and change of planes hadn't helped his fatigue. Bleary-eyed and dull-witted, he was in no condition to woo Meg. He released a pent-up breath and tried to think of something intelligent to say, something that would keep her in the room awhile longer, long enough to assess the situation and weigh his chances.

When Clay said nothing more, Meg hastened to explain her presence. "I, uh, I just came over to return a dish," she mumbled, crossing to a side table and placing the plate there. She was suddenly very glad she'd thought of a good excuse to venture over to her brother and sister-in-law's house. Even though she hadn't figured on being caught snooping, she had been aware of that possibility. She glanced around the living area and adjoining dining room. "Aren't Ted and Maria home?" She hadn't expected Clay to see her, but she had expected her brother and sister-in-law to be around.

"They're upstairs with the boys, giving them baths and changing their clothes." When Meg finally settled in a chair opposite him, his gaze devoured her like a starving man did a crust of bread. The bland creature who had entered Hank's cantina months before was completely gone. In her place was the woman who had captivated and captured him, the one who had snared his heart and soul. The one who had shared his bed.

Clay exhaled sharply in an effort to dislodge the erotic images crowding his head. As he did, the memory of her vow to forget him, echoed in his mind. With her looks and personality, Meg could have her pick of men, and since she had overcome her fears, she no doubt did.

The knowledge scalded his soul. His hands tightened into fists as he thought of another man touching her, tasting her.... His palms itched for her texture, his mouth watered for her taste. His body thirsted for the satisfaction only Meg could give.

If anything, she had grown more lovely, more desirable. Her hair shone, her complexion glowed, and as his gaze moved inexorably on, her body again tempted him. A pair of shorts and a tank top left little to his imagination, not that he needed to see her to be caught in her web. Memory was just as effective a trap.

Her image taunted him every time he closed his eyes. Her scent and sound and softness were all branded on his brain. Nothing, not tedious work or physical danger or profound fatigue, alleviated the love and longing in his heart. He had driven both mind and body to their limits in the vain hope of finding surcease in sleep, but his efforts proved futile. Meg came to him in his dreams, loving and passionate, and in his nightmares, dismissive and cold. As he had told her, she would always be with him.

Lost in her own raging emotions, Meg didn't see the depth of his discomfort. Being near him almost made her forget her demand and his promise. Almost but not quite. She folded her hands in her lap.

He glanced beyond her and out at the sun-drenched lawn. As he did, Clay fought to marshal his thoughts. Although tempted to blurt out the realization he'd reached after countless days and nights alone and aching for Meg, Clay resisted. He had to be patient.

While he stared out the windows, Meg took the opportunity to study him more carefully. Even with pallor and obvious fatigue, he was devastating, more devastating than she remembered. Without his customary stubble and shaggy hair, he was every inch the lady's man she had imagined. He filled her senses, as well as her heart.

Her fingers itched to stroke his clean-shaven cheeks, to smooth away the lines of fatigue, to burrow through the close-cropped hair. The bone-deep weariness emanating from him worried her as much as the news that things were much worse in Costa del Palma. So did the vague sense that Clay was again in grave danger, or soon would be.

She cleared her throat. "Ted said you think he and Maria may know something that might help you."

His golden gaze traveled back to her. "My boss thinks so."

Meg stiffened at the mention of Clay's supervisor. "You mean Carson?" she asked in a hoarse whisper.

Clay saw her reaction and cursed himself for his continuing stupidity. "Yeah, Carson. He sent me here to talk to them." Which was essentially the truth, he told himself.

"Then I guess he isn't still mad at you," Meg said.

Clay shrugged. "Whether he's mad or not doesn't make much difference," he replied, wondering if Meg would care if she knew the tongue-lashing he'd received when he'd gone to Washington from San Juan.

He pushed the useless thought away. Playing on her sympathy was something he planned to avoid. "The situation down there is very tense. A couple of the drug lords are subject to extradition if they leave Costa del Palma. Some members of the resistance are helping us track their movements, which has led to increased violence and more threats."

"What about Juan and the others?" she asked with real concern.

"The village has been untouched." Clay's voice was as hard and flat as slate.

Meg wrung her hands. "But the men . . . Juan . . ."

His gaze darted away. "Juan's okay, but some of the others . . . It is a war they're fighting, a war to free their country from the drug lords in control of the government.

People die in wartime." His voice grew so hoarse that it was barely audible.

"Why doesn't our government do something?"

"We are doing something, Meg. That's why I'm here."

A flush rose in her cheeks as she realized that she'd forgotten, among other things, that Clay was a federal agent. "Why can't they be arrested like other criminals?"

"Because they're part of the legitimate government in Costa del Palma. As long as they stay there, they're safe."

Something in his tone reminded her of what he'd said about the resistance watching the drug lords. "But they do leave."

He nodded. "Yes, they do."

"And you're hoping to catch them at one of those times," she said as her stomach sank like a bag of wet cement. Hostage retrieval, he had said, wasn't his only function.

"Yes, we are, but we're also trying to keep a lid on things in Costa del Palma. Even if we arrest and indict a couple of these guys, they have cohorts in the country, in the government. We have to avoid a bloodbath, protect the innocent people and help them restore a democratic government."

"That won't be easy," Meg observed.

"No, it won't," he agreed.

Meg glanced away. "It's good Ted and Maria are here," she said, wishing she could hold Clay safe in Ohio as well but knowing she had forfeited that possibility months earlier.

Seeing Meg's dismay but not realizing its source, he hurried to reassure her. "Yes, it is and they are perfectly safe, you know. You all are. All I want is some information. None of you is in any danger." Only he was in danger. In danger of losing Meg yet again.

Meg, restless and fretful, jumped out of the chair and went to stand by the windows overlooking the sloping lawn. She didn't want Clay to see the concern in her eyes, concern for him.

Being apart hadn't changed a thing, she suddenly realized. She still wanted him, still needed him, still loved him although she had enough sense not to let him know. After all, he had lied to her, then let her walk away. Remembering his silence as he drove her to the airport, Meg ached with anguish. His failure to stop her departure, as much as his deceit, kept her from wavering. So did the belief that he hadn't told her the truth because he wanted to use the cover of a mercenary as a shield against commitment.

Because she could never regain her lost trust in him, Meg didn't plan to let Clay witness her weakness.

As she stood lost in thought Clay watched her. Sunshine streamed in around her, touching her long waves with bursts of gold and copper and creating a fuzzy blur, like a halo, around her head. Deep desire ripped through him. It took every ounce of self-control he possessed to keep from going to her, to keep from begging her to come to him. Patience, he reminded himself.

While Clay observed her, Meg fought her own inner battle. For months, she had tried to deny he meant anything to her, had tried to convince herself that he'd been right—that her feelings were merely infatuation. She had nearly succeeded, but seeing him again made pretense impossible. She hadn't changed, nor had her feelings, but Clay had.

The man on the sofa seemed a stranger, in appearance and in attitude. Other than the first flicker of happiness, he acted unaffected by her arrival. The way he looked at her from slitted eyes made Meg restless, as did his warning that he'd been sent by his boss. Knowing he hadn't wanted to come created another layer of pain, another layer of restraint.

"Meg, I'm glad you're here." Ted's voice cut through her morose thoughts.

When she turned to face her brother, Meg smiled a smile she hoped wasn't as phony as it felt. "Hi."

Ted flopped down in an overstuffed chair and thrust his long, jeans clad legs out in front of him. If he sensed any underlying tension, he didn't show it. "Sit down."

Meg perched on the arm of the chair she had recently vacated. "I can't stay," she mumbled.

Ted ignored her comment. "Too bad you didn't come a little sooner. We could've used some help with the boys. I don't know how they manage to get so grubby." He shook his head, but his lips curved into an indulgent grin. "Maria's reading them a story while I start dinner. But I needed a little break first. I don't know how you managed them alone, sis. They're a handful."

"It wasn't easy," Meg admitted, her smile becoming genuine, "but it was fun." As her gaze moved to Clay, disappointment seared her. She really did love children, had always wanted some of her own. After the rape, her inability to trust a man had made that dream seem impossible. Now, thanks to Clay, she was no longer terrified of intimacy, but her emancipation was a double-edged sword. Being comfortable with her sexuality didn't mean she cared to share it with any man. On the contrary, there was only one man she wanted, and though he sat only a few feet away, the barriers between them were insurmountable.

"Well," her brother was saying, "I'm glad you're still close. We're going to need your help when the new baby comes."

Clay stared at his host's pleased expression. "Baby?"

Ted glanced at the other man. "We're expecting an addition to the family in about six months."

"Congratulations," Clay muttered over the lump of envy threatening to suffocate him. He was powerless against the longing twisting through him. From hooded eyes, he observed Meg who was now studying her clasped hands.

How Clay wished he could look forward to sharing his love for her with a child. He gritted his teeth. Although he felt he was cut and bleeding, he managed to mutter, "That's great."

Ted's expression turned contemplative as he glanced from Clay to his sister.

If Meg had looked at Clay, she would have seen a wealth of unbridled emotion in his eyes but she didn't. She kept staring at her clasped hands and wishing he hadn't been so adamant about taking precautions to protect her.

Ted cleared his throat. "We're very happy," he murmured before turning back to his sister. "Look, I'll go up and see if Maria needs any help with the boys. Sometimes it takes both of us to get them down to dinner. I'll be back in a few minutes," he said as he quickly exited the room.

A nervous Meg watched her brother leave. Afraid to look at Clay, she kept her attention fixed on the empty doorway as she struggled to think of something to say. Ambivalent emotions tore her in opposite directions. Because she still loved Clay, despite everything, she longed for his company but, because she knew he didn't feel the same, she wanted to leave before he realized she was still vulnerable to him.

Clay's emotional state was as volatile as Meg's. The words he had rehearsed on the flight from Washington flew out of his head as he studied her profile. Because he sensed she was set to flee at the slightest provocation, he found himself muttering, "I'm sorry about breaking my promise, coming here when I said I wouldn't try to see you again." Clay's voice grew hoarse. "I meant to keep my word." But good intentions meant little when confronted by his passion and need for Meg.

Something in his tone made her turn a baffled gaze on him. "You said you were sent here, Clay."

The misery in her tone and expression, along with the confusion, loosened his self-imposed restraint. She deserved to hear the truth. "No, not really," he admitted. "My boss wanted me to send an agent to interview Ted and Maria, but I insisted on coming myself, despite his vehement objections."

Shock slacked her finely-etched features. "Why, Clay"
Why did you insist on coming?" Hope again thudded in he:
battered heart but anxiety muffled it.

Committed to complete honesty, Clay sucked in a reas
suring breath before responding. "Because, where you'r
concerned, I've got very little sense and almost no con
trol." His gaze swept over her face, a face that had haunte
his dreams for what seemed an eternity. "The past fev
months have been pure hell, Meg. The truth is, I'd made u
my mind to come here, to try and see you even before I go
back to Washington." His gaze skidded away. "Even
though I'd made a solemn promise to you, I couldn't hav
kept it any longer. I'd have come here on my own if I hadn'
had any other excuse."

Meg bowed her head. Fresh joy and bitter memories col
lided inside her. "You let me walk away, Clay. You took m
to the airport and dropped me off like I was a business as
sociate, one you wanted to get rid of as quickly as possibl
and not see again. You hardly said a word to me on the way
to the airport," she murmured as the bitter memory of tha
seemingly interminable drive resurfaced with stinging ven
geance. He'd acted like a stranger, the stranger she'd met i
Hank's cantina. A stranger who didn't trust anyone.

The anguish in her voice opened a vein of remorse an
regret. "I bit my tongue a hundred times on the way to th
airport to keep from begging you to stay, Meg, but I'
promised to leave you alone because I thought that was wha
you wanted. I thought that was what was best."

Her gaze shifted back to meet his. "And all these month
when you knew where I was but never called..."

"I couldn't call, sweetheart, though heaven knows
wanted to. I kept trying to do what you said you wanted, bu
if I'd been where I could've phoned without being ob
served or monitored, I would've called just to hear you
voice." A grin tugged at one corner of his hard mouth
"Being without you, thinking of the future alone...I al
most went crazy." His mouth flattened. "Letting you wal

away was the hardest thing I've ever done in my entire life, the most difficult and the most painful."

"It was hard for me, too," she said. "Even though I was hurt and angry..."

He reached for her hand. "You had every reason to be, Meg. It took me a long time, and a lot of painful and sleepless nights to understand why you reacted the way you did. I know now you must have seen my lies as the worst sort of betrayal, the most profound kind of deceit. Maybe almost as bad as being raped," he finished in a whisper.

Her hand trembled in his. "I trusted you, Clay, trusted you completely and it seemed like... well, I did feel violated and used. Especially when I realized how little you trusted me." Her voice quavered badly.

"I know that must be how it seemed. I didn't really understand why you were so angry and upset but I understand now." He got to his feet and crossed to where she sat. As he perched on the nearby hassock, he took her hands in his, then lifted one to his lips. "I'm only sorry it took me so long to realize how stupid I was." He swallowed hard. "I was worried about facing you, worried you wouldn't give me a chance to explain. Worried I'd lost whatever chance I'd had. Coming here was almost as hard as living the last few months without you and thinking I might have to spend my life in that same hell," he admitted.

His revelation warmed her heart and soul. "The past few months have been hard for me, too. I was still furious when I got home, but that wore off and I realized I had no way to contact you, no way to find out how or where you were which made me mad all over again." She bit her lower lip. "I hung on to the bitterness to keep from giving in to the desolation, I guess. I haven't been easy to be around, even though I tried very hard to put the past behind me... I couldn't." She put one hand to his smooth cheek. "I thought I could survive without you. Survive is all. Nothing more. No happiness. No hope." Her voice lowered a fraction. "Like you said, hell on earth."

The fear that he'd lost his only chance for happiness evaporated. As he pressed a kiss in her open palm, Clay trembled with love and longing. "No more hell, sweetheart. Only heaven." He held both her hands as his expression again grew solemn. "I know I was wrong not to tell you about my cover as soon, well, as soon as I started to care for you."

Meg's heart stumbled, stopped and started again. He hadn't yet admitted he loved her but she knew he must and hearing him admit he cared made her smile in relief. His presence, and his admission, meant some sort of shared future but they still needed to settle the past.

"I shouldn't have been so impatient. I should have been more understanding. I should have listened to you instead of stalking off." Regret shadowed her eyes. "I knew about your childhood and Vietnam and Annette. I should have realized how many people had betrayed you, how hard it might be for you to trust anyone, even me."

His grasp tightened slightly. "It wasn't you I didn't trust, Meg, it was myself."

Meg studied him for a moment. "I know I must have reminded you of Annette at first. Hank and Carlotta both said you didn't trust women."

A rueful grin touched his mouth. "I've known Hank and Carlotta for a long time," he said.

"They've been very worried about you, Clay."

Bewilderment shadowed his expression. "What makes you say that?"

Meg hesitated only briefly before responding. "Carlotta called me a couple of months ago. She got my telephone number through Hank somehow. She said you never went back to see her like you'd promised, that you called when she was out and said you couldn't make it."

"I plan to go see her as soon as I can," Clay said. "I really couldn't get back when I wanted to. I had to go to D.C. almost immediately."

"I understand, and so did Carlotta, but she was worried, and she thought I might have heard from you." Their conversation replayed in Meg's mind. "We talked for quite a while."

Clay stiffened slightly. When he looked at Meg, he saw the light of knowledge gleam in her eyes. "She told you how we met," he muttered, hoping, probably in vain, Carlotta hadn't painted him as some sort of paragon.

"She said you and Hank were working with her husband against a group of South American terrorists."

Clay nodded. "Hank and I were partners back then. He'd sort of taken me under his wing. We got along well, and he was patient, taught me a lot."

"I knew you weren't really a loner," Meg observed with a smug grin. "I knew you had some close friends."

Clay's gaze bored into Meg's like a golden laser. "Hank and Carlotta are friends, but I've never been really close to anyone until you." His deep voice grew throaty with emotion. "I've never told anyone about my childhood or Annette. I've never felt comfortable or content with anyone else. Meeting you was like finding a part of myself, a missing part I'd never known existed."

"It was like that for me, too." Her thumbs played against his strong, but gentle, hands.

Encouraged by her touch and tenderness, Clay smiled. His poorly rebuilt defenses and tattered restraint crumbled. "Almost from the first, I felt that I'd always known you."

Meg offered a soft smile. "You didn't always act that way."

He clung to her slender hands as if they were a lifeline. "Like I said, I didn't trust my feelings. After...after the mistake I made with Annette, I was afraid." He drew in a steadying breath before revealing the inner turmoil he'd endured all those months ago. "You see, I was the one who got infatuation confused with love. I was the one who got emotionally involved under volatile circumstances. While Annette walked away unscathed, I lost all trust in my own judgment. Even after I realized I never loved her, I avoided relationships because I didn't know what real love was. Not having any experience with it made me doubt it existed . . ." His voice trailed off. "I'm not sure I know how to explain it," he muttered in frustration.

A glimmer of understanding shone from Meg's eyes. "I think I do," she whispered. "You didn't want me to be hurt the way you were. You didn't want me to get caught up in an emotionally charged atmosphere, then be disappointed later." Everything he'd said and done suddenly made sense. If only she had really listened before, Meg thought with a trace of sadness.

He brushed light strokes over the backs of her hands. "I'd rather die than hurt you, Meg. Despite how I felt, I wanted to give you a fair chance to find someone more suitable, to find a guy who would fit into your world, someone you'd be proud to introduce to your friends. I didn't want to sway you by glorifying my job or making myself out to be a hero, as tempting as the notion was," he admitted with a rueful expression. "You had enough illusions without me adding to them. The truth is, no matter what you call it, my work is filled with violence and treachery. Ninety percent of my adult life, I've pretended to be something, someone, I'm not." He released her hands. "When you said I'm an accomplished liar, you were right. It's part of my job, a big part."

She pressed one forefinger to his lips. "But it's not part of your personal life."

"No," he assured her. "It isn't."

His warm, moist breath sent prickling awareness through Meg. She ignored the urge to kiss him, knowing she had to reassure him first. "You've only done what you had to do in your work."

His dark lashes fluttered down and his voice dropped. "Some of what I've had to do has been damn ugly."

"Maybe so, but I know it's all been necessary. You'd never do anything that wasn't essential to an assignment, or to save some innocent person's life."

He shrugged. "I like to think so."

"Can you tell me about your work?" she asked. "How you got involved in it. I know you were in the army, but I don't know what you did when you got out."

Clay sighed. She was asking him to reveal a deeply buried part of himself. He didn't want to think about the past or how he'd drifted into his job. He didn't want to think about anything but the future, a future he hoped he'd spend with Meg. All the same, she deserved an answer. She deserved whatever she wanted.

"After Ted and Dave and I escaped from the POW camp, I was hospitalized for a while." When he saw her dismay, he smiled. "I had malaria and was sort of run-down," he explained, glossing over the details. "Anyhow, when I got out of the hospital, I figured on staying in the army. I didn't know how to do anything but be a soldier, and it offered security."

Something, Meg knew, the young Clay had never had at home, but she kept silent.

"Soon after that, one of my former commanding officers called me. He'd just retired from the military and was heading up a special task force on international terrorism. That was when terrorism was just getting to be a big problem." He seldom discussed his work, partly because of its sensitive nature but also because it might sound like bragging.

"I see," Meg murmured. "Sometimes you work with the FBI and stuff."

"Yes, we do a lot of intelligence gathering, so we network with different agencies. That's why I stay in contact with Dave. But mostly I've worked overseas. The task force is primarily concerned with international conspiracies, gunrunning, sometimes drug trafficking, but most especially retrieving American hostages held abroad or at least gaining information about their whereabouts and condition.''

Meg nodded, but anxiety curled like a cobra in her belly. The things he discussed with composure presented incredible danger. Although Meg was willing to accept Clay on any terms, she hated thinking about his risking his life on a daily basis.

"So you really are an expert in hostage retrieval," she said.

"Sort of. It's something I've been involved in a lot. Things don't always work out as well as with Ted. We're not always successful," he said.

Meg laid a reassuring hand over his. "But you do your best. That's what counts."

"I guess," he replied almost distractedly. The effect of lingering fatigue was beginning to take its toll. "My boss doesn't necessarily agree. He's the reason I didn't have time to go see Carlotta. I had to get back to the office in a hurry."

"Because he was mad," Meg recalled.

"Yeah," Clay agreed. "That's why he kept calling Hank . . ."

"Because he doesn't approve of free-lancing, even for a good reason."

"Because he doesn't like his agents doing anything without his approval."

Regret nipped at Meg. "I hope I didn't get you into too much trouble," she murmured.

He grinned then. "I've been in trouble with Carson before, Meg. He'll get over it." Feeling exhausted he inadvertently dropped his guard. "Anyhow, it was worth any amount of static. After all, I met you."

She returned his grin. "It was lucky for both of us, and Ted, too. We were really fortunate that you were available. I don't know what I would've done if I hadn't found you."

Recalling her determination, Clay chuckled. "You probably would've gone to that hellhole of a prison yourself."

"I didn't have that much nerve," she admitted. "If it hadn't been for you, I would have been completely lost in more ways than one. If you hadn't known what to do, how to contact Juan, Ted would still be in that awful place." Her mouth trembled. "I'm sure the fact that Juan had been imprisoned and escaped from there helped a lot."

Weary from jet lag and lack of sleep, Clay failed to censor his automatic reply. "Yeah, and it didn't hurt that I'd been there, too."

Because his eyelids were drooping, he didn't see the color ebb from her face or her eyes widen with alarm. Knowledge struck her like a hammer blow. "You were in prison in Costa del Palma. You didn't help Juan escape, you escaped with him." Her heart stumbled in her chest.

Suddenly aware of his error, Clay started with dismay. "Meg . . ."

She broke into his response. "Those drug lords arrested you, knowing you were a federal agent, didn't they?"

Consumed with guilt, Clay heard censure, not fear. "They knew what I was," he admitted in a ragged voice. The need to explain overcame him, but how could he expect her to listen to him again? he wondered with dread.

"Oh, Clay, how could you have taken such a horrible chance?" Terror tore through Meg. "If you had been caught . . ." Her voice, thick and unsteady, trailed off as a sick, sinking sensation made her heart plummet.

Some undercurrent in her tone made Clay search her expression. When he found not anger but apprehension, he asked, "You're not mad?"

"Mad?" she echoed. "No, but I should be. You took a terrible chance going back there, one I wouldn't have asked you to take if I'd known. You knew what would happen if those drug lords caught you again," she whispered.

"But they didn't. Nothing happened."

"Maybe not, but you shouldn't have gone. Hank was right when he said you needed a vacation. You'd just gotten out of that place, hadn't you?"

Clay sighed. There was no point in denying the obvious. "It had been a couple weeks since we escaped."

"How long were you imprisoned?" she asked in a tiny voice, dreading his reply.

"Not long, Meg," Clay said in an attempt to reassure her. "Only a few days."

Meg understood what he didn't say. "They didn't plan to execute you, did they?"

Because he couldn't tell her that he most likely would have been tortured to death, Clay sidestepped a direct answer. "I knew the risks when I joined the task force. Getting captured is one of them." So was being brutally interrogated.

Bile rose in her throat. "Ted said your shoulder has taken a lot of abuse," she murmured.

Clay frowned. Sometimes Meg was too intuitive for his comfort. "It was dislocated in Nam, and in the prison."

Although she had promised herself not to interfere with his career decisions, Meg spoke from her heart, not her head. "They can't send you back down there."

He reached out to squeeze her hand. "They're not, sweetheart."

Her shoulders slumped with relief and her face relaxed. "Then why are you here talking to Ted and Maria?"

"Because I'm sort of in charge of the investigation. My boss thinks it's a good idea to keep me behind a desk for a while." His gaze traced her lovely features. "Actually, I think that's where I'll end my career with the task force."

"Behind a desk?" Hope leaped into her eyes. Behind a desk was certainly safer than behind a gun, but fresh doubt assailed her. "You really think you'd be happy pushing papers for the next twenty years or so?" she asked with trepidation. She couldn't imagine this hardened warrior finding satisfaction playing government bureaucrat.

"No," he admitted, "but I think I'll be leaving the task force much sooner than that."

"Leaving?" Meg failed to keep the hope from her voice.

Clay grinned. "I've been thinking about quitting for a while."

"For how long?" she asked in a throaty murmur.

He gave her a wink before stifling a yawn. "Since that night in the cave, I suppose." A grin, diffused by the yawn, lifted his lips. "And again when you were in the hall and I saw the look on your face." A look he'd been afraid to believe.

"I didn't know I was so transparent," she retorted.

"You aren't, not at all. But that look, well, it gave me hope that lust might turn back into love." His fingers gently stroked the sensitive flesh of her inner wrist.

Tingling anticipation spiralled through Meg. "The love was there," she admitted. "It always has been. It always will be. All you have to do is look a little closer."

"I intend to look a lot closer, sweetheart." His fingers trailed up her bare arms.

Meg smiled, then got up to scribble a note to Ted and Maria. "Let's go to my cottage, Clay," she said in response to the question in his eyes. "We have a lot of time to make up for."

Meg was the first thing he saw when he woke. Slowly, her lashes fluttered open to reveal the sea-blue eyes that never failed to soothe him.

"Good morning," she whispered.

Her sweet breath fanned his lips, making him long for her kiss. His gaze went to her mouth as her tongue darted out to moisten her lips.

"Good morning," he responded before covering her open mouth with a bold, compelling kiss that sought, and found, an eager answer.

As she returned the thrust and parry of his tongue, she felt him react to the passion stirring between them and smiled.

Clay felt the satisfied smirk and tore his mouth away. When he lifted his head to gaze down at her, his expression softened with long-suppressed emotion. "I guess we still have some time to make up for," he whispered.

"I guess."

He lifted her hand to his mouth and pressed a kiss in the palm. "I wasn't sure you'd even see me, let alone allow me in your bed."

His words and touch proved to be a lethal combination, one that sent waves of longing through her but, seeing the dark smudges beneath his eyes reminded her that what he needed was rest. "Well you're here and you're going to be staying here for a while."

A cocky, purely male grin lifted his lips as his arched brows rose a fraction. "Can you define how long 'a while' might be?"

Her nose crinkled as she grinned. "That depends," she murmured.

"On what?"

Meg's grin widened. "Well, uh, things."

The invisible bond between them, one that misunderstanding, distance or time could never destroy, became a palpable force.

Clay's expression went from amused to solemn. "What if I want to stay forever, Meg?"

Her heart beat so hard, she was sure he must hear it. "Oh, Clay," she whispered.

He swallowed hard over the emotion clogging his throat. "I love you, Meg. More than anything. More than anyone. More than I ever dreamed possible." His fingers played over her bare arms. "I don't want us to be apart again, Meg, not ever." He swallowed again. "What do you think about me living here? After we're married, of course," he hastened to add.

Meg could barely contain her joy. Clay loved her. He wanted to marry her. He was not only willing to give up his job, he was offering to live in Ohio. The delight swelling her heart surfaced in her radiant smile. "I don't want us to be apart, either, but you don't have to move here. We can live wherever you want. As long as we're together. That's all that really matters.''

"I'll be happy wherever you are, Meg, and I know you'd be happiest close to Ted and Maria and their kids.''

With both hands, she cupped his jaw. "You'd really live here?'' she asked as her heart filled to bursting.

He gently laid his hands over hers. "Sure. I don't know exactly what I'll do but I've got some money put away, enough to get along until I decide what to do.'' He paused to clear his throat. "You still haven't given me your answer, Meg.''

"I didn't think I needed to state the obvious,'' she said before she leaned forward to brush his lips with hers.

Clay's fingers tangled in the silk of her hair. "Sweetheart, you make me want to start the honeymoon before the wedding.''

Meg chuckled as she sat up. "That doesn't sound like a bad idea, especially if you have to go back to Washington right away.''

"I doubt if Ted or Maria know anything that I couldn't phone or fax,'' he murmured, "so there's no reason I couldn't take a few days off.'' When he gazed up at her, he let all the love and longing he felt surface in his gaze. "I'd like to get married as soon as possible but I suppose you want a formal wedding and all the stuff that goes with it.''

Meg chuckled at his pained expression. "I don't care what kind of wedding it is, as long as you're the groom.''

"Then, maybe we could get married this week,'' he said hopefully.

"As long as you think you can stay, I don't see why we can't.''

"There are things I'll have to clear up in Washington but you could go with me.''

Meg smiled again. "That sounds good,'' she said, eager to stay with him.

He grinned back at her. "Then, what are we waiting for? Let's get the marriage license.''

Meg caught his arm as he started to slip from the bed. A puzzled expression on his handsome face, Clay glanced back at her. "What's the problem?"

"I don't want a big wedding but I thought we might have a small ceremony here in a few days."

"A few days?" Both disappointment and frustration roughened his voice. "Why wait a few days?"

"I only plan to get married once," she replied with a laugh, "and I'd like to have a special dress for the occasion. Besides, I thought you might like to invite Hank and Carlotta, and they need a few days to make travel plans."

The frustration dissolved into satisfaction. "You're right. We're only going to get married once and it would be nice to have some close friends with us." He settled back beside Meg and pulled her into the warmth of his embrace. "I'll do everything I can to make you happy."

"You make me happy by just being with me," she whispered. "You gave me back my self-confidence, Clay."

"No, sweetheart," he murmured. "You did that when you left the safety and security of your home to save your brother."

"Well, you freed me from my fears and anxieties," she whispered.

He gently stroked her back. "And you freed me, Meg. From the loneliness I couldn't admit, even to myself. You're the most important thing in my life and you always will be. You're the center of it, the light, the color, the promise." His warm breath stirred the hair at her temple as his lips moved over her brow. "Before I met you, I didn't live, I existed."

His touch kindled the barely banked fires within her, fires only Clay could start, only Clay could quench. "I just hope you don't miss your job, the adventure, the excitement. Not much ever happens around here," she mumbled.

He grinned then. "We'll change that," he promised before the humor left his expression and tone. "I don't expect things to be perfect, you know. I don't expect a fairy tale. Just because I've never been part of a real family doesn't' mean I think we'll be living like people in a Norman Rockwell painting. I know there are problems and pitfalls and I'm prepared to work through them." His fingers gently cupped her jaw. "Just be patient with me, okay?"

"Okay," she agreed. "We'll be patient with each other." But when her mouth found his, the deep kiss had little to do with patience.

When Meg lifted her head a fraction, Clay released a shuddering breath. "Right now I'm at the end of my patience, Meg, and I plan to give you a demonstration of just how impatient I can be."

"Promises, promises," Meg murmured with a laugh that was squelched when he claimed her mouth.

As he worked his magic, Meg relaxed, secure in the knowledge that they shared a deep and abiding love, one that would see them through whatever lay ahead. Their life together might not be a fairy tale but it would be filled with the magic potion of love and trust.

Epilogue

"Clay is very good with the children," Maria observed as she joined Meg on the wide deck.

Meg smiled fondly as she watched her husband giving piggy-back rides to his daughter and niece. "Yes, he is," she agreed. "He dotes on Maggie. She may only be two but she's had Daddy wrapped around her little finger since the day she was born."

Maria's mouth twitched. "It must be hard on Clay to be wrapped around two different little fingers."

Meg chuckled. "Clay is a wonderful husband and father." She glanced at her sister-in-law. "For a while I was worried he might be unhappy after he left the task force, but he loves photography. It's amazing how quickly he caught on. Even Ted says Clay has a natural talent for it." Her pride shone through in every word.

"Clay does have an excellent eye. And he has more patience for developing photographs than Ted."

"Their partnership has worked out really well," Meg concurred. "For all of us, since the studio keeps them at home most of the time."

Maria smiled. "That has been an additional benefit."

Meg's gaze travelled back to where her brother was taking her husband's place with the little girls. When Clay saw her, he waved. Before turning back to her sister-in-law, Meg returned the gesture. "I think I'll see if he wants some lemonade."

Before Meg made it half-way, Clay met her, sweeping her up in his arms and swinging her around before pressing his lips to hers in a quick kiss.

When he put her back on the ground, she laughed up at him. "You looked like you were having fun," she said as she slipped one arm around his lean waist. Even after four years of marriage, his touch kindled the always barely-banked fires of desire he had ignited in her so long ago and far away. Any doubts she'd had about him adjusting to domesticity had proven foolish.

"I always have fun with my family," he told her with a smile. One big hand massaged in her back as if he couldn't keep from caressing her, if only in the most casual way.

"And you're never sorry you gave up being a wild warrior?" Meg asked although she needed no proof of his happiness. It was in his eyes, eyes that widened with surprise, then crinkled with humor. Meg felt heat invade her face as she realized she'd given away something she'd kept to herself for more than four years.

"Wild warrior?" he asked as he peered down into her flaming face. "Is that how you thought of me? Or maybe that's how you still think of me," he suggested with a chuckle. "Maybe, when we're in bed together, it's not your photographer husband you're holding and loving but some wild warrior you found in the wilds of South America."

Meg grinned although the hot color remained in her cheeks. "Since they're the same person, it hardly matters."

His expression grew serious and subdued. "You're right about that, sweetheart. All along this other guy was inside me, the one who wanted to belong someplace, the one who wanted to belong to someone." His hand rested on her waist. "The one who was afraid to admit his loneliness. You're the one who saw that I wasn't really a loner, just alone."

"Just like I'm the only one who sees the wild side now," she whispered.

"Only because I've got a rather untamed wife," he teased as his hand slid up to ruffle her hair.

Her head fell back so she had a better view of his handsome face. "I only hope you're half as happy as I am," she murmured.

"Happy doesn't do what I feel justice, Meg."

"You really never miss the task force, do you?"

"Hell, no." His fingers slid through the silk of her hair before moving to stroke her slender neck. "How could I ever go back to living in the shadows when I can be with you in the sun?"

She grinned up at him. "Seems like I can recall a time when you weren't so good with words."

"I never could put my feelings into words. I still can't. There's so much inside me, Meg, so many feelings and emotions for you and Maggie." His gaze drifted to where their daughter played with her uncle and cousins. "For Ted and Maria and their kids, too. When we all sit down at holiday...I can't begin to describe the joy, the contentment, the pleasure that swells inside me. When I wake up in the morning with you beside me, when Maggie climbs into my lap and puts her little arms around my neck...you have no idea how much you mean to me, how much this family means to me." His golden gaze warmed with love and commitment and promise. "From that first night when I touched you, from then on, there was no retreating into the shadows. Even if you hadn't let me into your life, I coul never have been content with the old life, not when I knew what I'd missed, what I found with only you.''

''What we found with each other,'' she murmured as she rose on her toes to feather a series of light kisses over his mouth.

Clay was about to enter a more potent exploration of his wife's willing mouth when he felt a pair of chubby arms go around his leg. He relaxed his hold on Meg and glanced down to his daughter's turquoise eyes, wide and serious and so like her mother's, peering up at him.

''How 'bout 'nother ride, Daddy?''

Clay peeked at Meg who was already slipping from his embrace. She leaned down to brush an errant curl from Maggie's flushed forehead before turning back to Clay. ''Yes, Daddy, what about a ride?'' she asked in a whisper for his ears only.

As Clay swept their child onto his broad shoulders, he winked at his wife. ''You'll get your ride later, sweetheart.''

As she watched him amble away, Meg murmured, ''I plan to, darling, I definitely plan to.''

* * * * * *

If you've been looking for something a little bit different,
a little bit spooky, let Silhouette Books take you on
a journey to the dark side of love with

Every month, Silhouette will bring you two romantic,
spine-tingling Shadows novels, written by some of your
favorite authors, such as *New York Times* bestseller
Heather Graham Pozzessere, Anne Stuart, Helen R. Myers
and Rachel Lee—to name just a few.

In May, look for:
FLASHBACK by Terri Herrington
WAITING FOR THE WOLF MOON by Evelyn Vaughn

In June, look for:
BREAK THE NIGHT by Anne Stuart
IMMINENT THUNDER by Rachel Lee

Come into the world of Shadows and prepare
to tremble with fear—and passion....

SHAD2

OFFICIAL RULES • MILLION DOLLAR BIG WIN SWEEPSTAKES
NO PURCHASE OR OBLIGATION NECESSARY TO ENTER

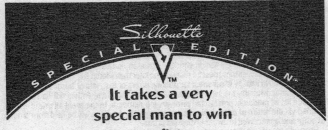

WHERE WERE YOU WHEN THE LIGHTS WENT OUT?

SILHOUETTE

SUMMER Sizzlers '93

This summer, Silhouette turns up the heat when a midsummer blackout leaves the entire Eastern seaboard in the dark. Who could ask for a more romantic atmosphere? And who can deliver it better than:

**LINDA HOWARD
CAROLE BUCK
SUZANNE CAREY**

Look for it this June at your favorite retail outlet.

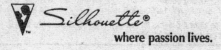

Silhouette®

where passion lives.

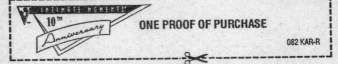